Text Classics

MENA CALTHORPE was born Ivy Bright Field in 1905 in Goulburn, New South Wales, and baptised Philomena. From childhood she was a keen writer. She attended a local Catholic school, Our Lady of Mercy College, and subsequently became a schoolteacher.

In her late twenties, during the Depression, she married Bill Calthorpe. The pair left the Southern Tablelands for Sydney, where at first they ran an unsuccessful shop in Paddington. They lived in the Sutherland Shire, in the city's south, for the rest of their lives.

A committed socialist, Mena Calthorpe was a member of the Communist Party for some years and a lifelong member of the Labor Party. Working in a range of office and manual jobs, she wrote in her spare time, and was active in the Australasian Book Society and the Australian Society of Authors.

In her widely praised debut, *The Dyehouse* (1961), Calthorpe— encouraged by her husband—drew upon her experiences of a textile factory and other workplaces to create a deftly observed account of working life in postwar Sydney. The novel was published in translation in Europe, and republished in Australia in 1982.

The Dyehouse was followed by *The Defectors* (1969), published by the Australasian Book Society, which dramatised unions' internal power struggles. Calthorpe's third and final novel, *The Plain of Ala*, a saga of Irish migration to Australia, appeared twenty years later, when she was in her mid-eighties.

Mena Calthorpe died in 1996.

FIONA MCFARLANE is the author of *The Night Guest* and *The High Places*.

ALSO BY MENA CALTHORPE

The Defectors
The Plain of Ala

The Dyehouse
Mena Calthorpe

Text Publishing Melbourne Australia

textclassics.com.au
textpublishing.com.au

The Text Publishing Company
Swann House
22 William Street
Melbourne Victoria 3000
Australia

First published by Ure Smith 1961
This edition published by The Text Publishing Company 2016

Cover design by WH Chong
Page design by Text
Typeset by Midland Typesetters

Printed in Australia by Griffin Press, an Accredited ISO AS/NZS 14001:2004
Environmental Management System printer

Primary print ISBN: 9781925355758
Ebook ISBN: 9781925410112
Creator: Calthorpe, Mena, 1905–1996, author.
Title: The dyehouse / by Mena Calthorpe ; introduced by Fiona McFarlane.
Series: Text classics.
Dewey Number: A823.3

CONTENTS

The Art of Work
by Fiona McFarlane

I FOUND my second-hand copy of *The Dyehouse* among the glorious chaos of Gould's Book Arcade in Sydney's Newtown. I had never heard of Mena Calthorpe, but after reading the first line I knew I'd buy it: 'Miss Merton came to the Dyehouse one windy afternoon when smoke from the railway-yards drifted darkly over Macdonaldtown.'

It wasn't just the authority of that sentence, the energy of arrival; it was also that Newtown, where I lived at the time, is right next to Macdonaldtown. Calthorpe assures the reader in a preliminary note that 'The "Macdonaldtown" of the story is...fictitious, and no accurate description of a real place is intended' (she called it Emmatown and Lewistown in various drafts): yes, yes, I thought, as I walked home through the gentrified streets of my Macdonaldtown, by the railway-yards and the rows of terraces with their 'gleaming brass name-plates'. *The Dyehouse* is set in a textile-dyeing factory in 1956.

There are no more factories in Macdonaldtown, there's no more smoke; still, Calthorpe's industrial inner Sydney remains recognisable. But hers is a city of girls in summer frocks emerging from filthy red-brick factories, of terrace slums, of men in overalls, of early mornings and long commutes, of trains and smokes and smoke-stacks. There are beauties to this Sydney, but it's a long way from the harbour.

The Dyehouse is a novel about the workers of the Southern Textiles Dye Works, and so it is a novel about work. According to Studs Terkel, the great American cataloguer of labour, this means that it is, 'by its very nature, about violence—to the spirit as well as the body'. And this is true— Mena Calthorpe was a socialist, and it's impossible to read *The Dyehouse* without noticing its political commitment. But the spirits and bodies of Calthorpe's characters are always specific and convincing. We meet Miss Merton first, looking for and finding a job in the Dyehouse office: a 'precise, maiden lady, well into middle age', with a neat skirt and sensible hat. How easy she might be to stereotype; and yet we get hints of an unusual sensibility: she hears victory or defiance in the sound of passing trains. We meet Patty Nicholls, office worker, dreaming with complicated innocence of marriage to the boss; and we meet the boss himself, the head of the Dyehouse, Renshaw: 'Miss Merton heard him coming before she saw him. In the rhythm of his step there was something exciting; Miss Merton thought of spurs, of chargers and banners. More than six feet tall, he swung across the warehouse floor and through the doors into the vestibule.'

The vivid mobility of these characters! And there are so many of them. *The Dyehouse* is an ensemble novel, its cast organised by each person's association with the Dyehouse, yet each character is animated by a distinct inner life. There's Oliver Henery, detached and mocking, who works half-naked, his head tied with red cord, in the steam and heat of the dye vats; weary Barney Monahan, blindsided by his ageing wife's pregnancy, and canny Goodwin, who knows a woman who can help; Mr Mayers, engineer and Welshman, whose 'soft and burred' voice conjures 'tall houses with apples ripening in the attics'. And there's Hughie Marshall, head dyer, in love with the precise poetry of the job out of which Renshaw is determined to push him, after years of faithful service:

> All around the Bunsen burners were little snippets
> of colour wrapped in white. Every so often Hughie
> pressed them with his fingers, unrolled them and
> examined them for bleeding. Sometimes after the lights
> were out in the warehouse Hughie stayed on, stirring
> his squares of cloth in the metal beakers, lifting them
> lovingly to the light with the glass rod; nodding in
> satisfaction or flinging them down in disgust.

Hughie's treatment at the hands of Renshaw is illustrative of the powerlessness of the working man. But Calthorpe is just as invested in the individual conflicts of her characters as she is in the general conflict of labour. *The Dyehouse* makes this clear, as do her papers in the State Library of New South Wales: on the back of one of the exercise books in which she wrote the first draft of her novel I found, among the Arithmetical Tables, the name Hughie written six times in a mournful list. And still, the general: a note to her editor on the inadequacy of the basic wage.

So *The Dyehouse* is both a work of art and an art of work. Reading it for the first time, I admired Calthorpe's dexterous sentences, her skill with rhythm and pace, the emotional clarity of her characters; and I was equally struck by her unapologetic desire to bear witness to injustice, to change hearts. It all made me want to know: what is this book? Where did it come from? And who is this writer?

*

Mena Calthorpe was born Ivy Bright Field in Goulburn, New South Wales, in 1905, to a Protestant mother and Catholic father—'neither fish nor flesh', she declared in a 1987 interview. Her baptismal name, Philomena, was shortened to the one she was known by: Mena. At Goulburn's Our Lady of Mercy College, fifteen-year-old Mena wrote a novel that so 'startled and annoyed' the nuns they confiscated it. The Fields were friends with T. J. Hebblewhite, editor of the *Goulburn Evening Penny Post* and mentor of the young Miles Franklin; Calthorpe never knew Hebblewhite, but her childhood was spent in the company of his daughter Timpy, in his library of controversial books, and in the lingering glory of Franklin's success.

Calthorpe's father, a droving contractor, only employed union men and kept records of their poetry: the ballads and laments of the nineteenth-century overlanders, which Calthorpe loved and could recite from memory into her eighties. These early connections between work and art illuminate some of the beauties of her writing in *The Dyehouse*, from Hughie's love of weighing dyes as water drips from the laboratory ceiling to the incantatory rhythms of office work:

Clack! Clack! Up came the carrier and ejected papers onto Mr Dennet's table. There they lay: the Fanfolds! the Ledger Copies!

The Debits!

Mr Dennet took up his pen and began entering in the Control Book. The Comptometers sprang to life. Two young women with painted nails fell upon the papers.

Tic-tac, tic-tac. Now over to the files.

OK, Miss Brennan, you sort them out. City, Country, Government. Now break them up. A to K, L to Z, and into the files with them. Miss Bowden filed quietly, but Miss Graham sent the file flying. It flew back and forth, and her body swayed with it.

Mena Field taught in country schools until her marriage to Bill Calthorpe in 1934—as well as the Depression—brought her to Sydney. We have few interviews with or autobiographical notes by Calthorpe, but in all of them she tends to describe herself with self-deprecating humour. She laughs at her and Bill's inadequacy at running a corner shop in Paddington; at her arrival with a friend for her first Communist Party meeting in their 'best hats…high heel shoes, gloves, handbags—the lot' (*The Dyehouse*'s most militant character, Joe Henderson, has a special contempt for bourgeois women involved in the class struggle); at leaving the Communist Party in the early 1950s because she could no longer afford the stamps required for their mass mailings; at starting the peace movement in Sydney's Sutherland Shire because 'the world had to be saved, and no one but me in this shire would be capable of doing it.'

Calthorpe joined the Labor Party and was a vocal member of the largest branch in New South Wales (her singular second novel, *The Defectors*, published in 1969, is an insight into branch and trade-union machinations). She was for some time secretary of the leftist Australasian Book Society (she unsuccessfully urged the ABS to publish another classic Australian novel of work, David Ireland's *The Unknown Industrial Prisoner*). She worked, at various times, as a fruit picker, cannery worker, advertising salesperson, and roadhouse manager. And in the office of an inner-city textile factory, in a position much like Miss Merton's. As a member of the Staff, Calthorpe was expected to protect the interests of the Company at all times; but, like Miss Merton, her sympathies lay with the workers. She began to take notes, thinking, 'Oh well, while I'm preparing to write my great Australian novel, I'll write this.'

The Dyehouse was first published in Australia in 1961 by Ure Smith. It received mostly favourable reviews in everything from the right-wing *Bulletin* to the left-wing *Tribune*, and was commended for the Miles Franklin Award (Patrick White won, for *Riders in the Chariot*). A. D. Hope, who like many critics considered political novels to be of 'documentary rather than literary interest', conceded in 1962 that *The Dyehouse* had risen 'slightly above the usual dreary levels of novels devoted to causes and movements'. The 1964 edition I bought at Gould's was published by Seven Seas Books, an East German house; *The Dyehouse* was also serialised in an East German newspaper and translated into Czech, as befits a novel devoted to the lives of workers. Australia produced a lot of this kind of writing in the mid-twentieth century. Much of it was written by women, most with connections to the Communist Party: Katharine Susannah Prichard, Dymphna Cusack, Jean Devanny, Betty Collins, Dorothy Hewett. Much of it, like *The Dyehouse*, has been forgotten.

Calthorpe and *The Dyehouse* do and do not belong in this company. Although she identified as a socialist until her death in 1996, Calthorpe had left the Communist Party by the time she wrote *The Dyehouse*. Strike action is only a faint glimmer in the novel, the possible future ambition of Southern Textiles' newly formed shop committee. One of the few negative responses to *The Dyehouse* came, in fact, from the communist newspaper *Common Cause*: 'It would seem to be a weakness that such a competent writer has left the struggle for the future.'

Nor does Calthorpe limit her main characters to the shop floor: we have Miss Merton and Patty Nicholls in the Dyehouse office; the officious, frightened men of Southern Textiles' middle management; the godlike Chairman of Directors, Harvison, who keeps working from hospital after surgery; and Renshaw, who in all his charismatic, grotty glory must be one of the great villains of Australian literature, not least because of the attention Calthorpe gives to his point of view and psychology. Here he is after a night with Patty Nicholls:

> Renshaw handed her his comb. He was anxious to be rid of her. He helped smooth her skirt and held the mirror while she dabbed her nose with powder and marked in her mouth with vermilion lipstick. She was pretty enough, he thought, and eager.

She was like the smooth, lush peaches in an orchard
he had visited as a child.

But sitting in the car, impatiently waiting for her
to go, he felt no emotion; nothing but a faint feeling
of aversion he knew would deepen from now on.

This is Renshaw in full flight: falsely solicitous, evaluating, removed. He preys on his female staff with tactical patience and uses similar skills to undermine Hughie Marshall. But Calthorpe understood that a villain must be complex, that unsympathetic characters must still be human. Renshaw isn't spared her empathy (he frets over the difficulty of dyeing the new fabric, nylon), nor promised safety from injustice. As Miss Merton warns, 'The trap's set for us all.'

For a novel that has been considered an example of social realism, *The Dyehouse* isn't strictly realist. It's formally experimental and, with its episodic structure and its restrained lyricism—like matronly Miss Merton remembering the voluptuous beauty of the Monaro, where the poplars yellow and the water goannas doze—it refuses realism's mere witness. It pays playful attention to sound: 'Clack! Clack!' say the office papers; 'O-bloody-K,' says Renshaw; 'Cock-a-doodle-doo,' say the trains. It finds the music in words like 'zinc' and 'cloth' and 'kerosene'.

Towards the end of novel, Harvison brings in 'efficiency men' to help cut costs. They report 'Hours of time spent on repetition...What purpose does it serve?...What for?' But *The Dyehouse* is a novel in love with repetition: it spends whole paragraphs on 'names and numbers'; it fragments sentences just to plant the word 'green' twice on one line. A novel about the dyeing of cloth can't help but flare into gorgeous colour:

'The cloth lay in heaps piled in the trucks. Green, peach, deep gold, salmon, apricot, peacock blue, purple, plum.' And to notice the colours of Sydney, no matter how far from the harbour: 'the dense green of the sward, the warm colour of the sandstone, the jewel of the late-flaring bud'.

Reading *The Dyehouse* has been, for me, a process of rediscovery—of a lost voice, the precise, insightful voice of Mena Calthorpe. Of a lost Sydney—or perhaps only a displaced one. Of a lost literary tradition—the Australian books, many of them by women, that imagined work and the worker in the unreliable light of communism. What a pleasure to see it published again, in a new light. May it remain unforgotten.

The Dyehouse

All characters and events in this story are wholly fictitious, and no reference is intended to any person living or dead. The 'Macdonaldtown' of the story is also fictitious, and no accurate description of a real place is intended.

AUTHOR'S NOTE

I wish to record my appreciation of the help and encouragement given me by John Taylor.

M.C.

To Bill

CHAPTER ONE

1956

Miss Merton came to the Dyehouse one windy afternoon when smoke from the railway-yards drifted darkly over Macdonaldtown. More smoke rose from chimney-stacks and mingled in the surging air, against which all doors had been tightly shut. To Miss Merton, walking slowly, Macdonaldtown seemed deserted.

She was a precise maiden lady, well into middle age. The skirt that swirled about her legs was neat and unpretentious. Her hair was smoothed, parted in the centre, and she wore a bun—not the kind of thing that one could call a chignon, but a plain, neat bun, firmly pinned at the nape of her neck. On the back of her head was fastened a small, sensible hat of fine black straw.

She held a paper in her hand and was looking for a job.

She passed the corner, where water unable to escape from the Dyehouse lay in a wide scummy pool, fighting for gutter space with discarded newspapers and fruit peels. Clasping her hands, for she was slightly nervous, she inspected the red door. Then she slipped off one glove and knocked.

The knock had a hollow sound, and she stepped back.

The sooty windows were barred and closed. No life stirred. Only an engine racing past on the nearby railway lines broke the silence. A blast, and then a prolonged cock-a-doodle-doo, cock-a-doodle-*doo*. To Miss Merton, hesitating at the Dyehouse door, it sounded like victory, or defiance. She stood listening until the sound was lost to her.

Then she knocked again. She turned the paper over and looked at the advertisement. Southern Textiles Dye Works.

There was movement behind the door. Someone fumbled with the lock. She heard the click as the bolt was drawn. The door opened and a young blonde stood smiling up at her.

In the space of the few seconds before she crossed the threshold Miss Merton noticed the sweep of the lashes, the delicacy of the nose and chin, the fine bony structure of the face.

'Come in,' said the blonde.

She held the door open. Miss Merton passed reluctantly from the windswept Parade into the shadowy vestibule of the Dyehouse.

'You come about the job?'

Miss Merton nodded.

The girl picked up a scribbler. She smiled at Miss Merton, pushed open the swinging glass doors and disappeared into the warehouse.

Miss Merton heard him coming before she saw him. In the rhythm of his step there was something exciting; Miss Merton thought of spurs, of chargers and banners. More than six feet tall, he swung across the warehouse floor and through the doors into the vestibule.

Miss Merton smoothed her gloves and put her hands together tentatively. He opened the door into his office.

It was a large room dominated by a huge table laden with rubbish. Bits of cloth, samples of dyes, cigarettes squashed into bottles, and in one corner a heap of soiled white cotton shirts that gave off a slight, acrid smell of perspiration. A pair of shoes and several socks lay dejectedly nearby. Miss Merton refused to allow her scandalized eyes to explore further. She concentrated on the rolls of cloth flung up onto a bureau, and endeavoured to overlook the shirt and trousers hanging over the back of the chair.

Mr Renshaw was looking at her, taking in her thin maiden-lady features, her neat bun.

Miss Merton lowered her eyes and looked calmly back across the pile of dusty papers and chewed ends of pencils.

He didn't speak, and Miss Merton in her precise little voice began her recital slowly. His face was bland. No movement of muscle. No interest.

But there was something disturbing about his expressionless face. The fair, straight hair, the shrill eyes, the droop of the mouth. He picked up a pen and began doodling. A circle. Then another and another. And suddenly the eyes, withdrawn, opened wide. The dead mask of the face was swept away. The smile was sudden and electrical.

'When could you start?' he asked.

CHAPTER TWO

'When can we start?' asked the Chairman of Directors.

He was a small, bright-eyed man with bristling eyebrows slightly flecked with grey. He leaned back patiently, looking at the General Manager.

The answer, when it came, would not be exciting. And Larcombe would wrap it up in excuses. Harvison stared at the ceiling, thinking of the opening words of a trade-paper article he had read a few days ago. 'Created by chemical magic, nylon, the miracle fibre, is revolutionizing our textile industry.'

Bloody revolution, Harvison thought. His lips tightened. Where's the firing squad?

Southern Textiles had fallen flat on its face over nylon.

Larcombe moved uneasily. From the corner of his eye he saw the pile of newspaper cuttings on Harvison's desk. Advertisements. Austin's beating the drum about the nylon again. Nylon slips by Austin. Nylon panties by Austin. Long-legged girls in Austin nylon pyjamas. Little dreamy-eyed girls in filmy Austin nightdresses. The Sydney shops were bulging with Austin nylon.

'There's been a holdup out at the Dyehouse,' Larcombe admitted at last. He picked up the nylon swatches and slid them through his fingers. 'We're still striking trouble. Renshaw's still not quite topside of the dyeing and there's trouble with the setter.'

'There was trouble last month, and the month before, and the month before that.'

'Yes,' Larcombe admitted warily.

'And all the time we're lagging Austin's are pushing more and more nylon onto the market.'

Harvison hit the desk with his fist.

'What I want,' he said suddenly, 'is action. I want some results from Macdonaldtown. I want to see the next lot of nylon Renshaw gets out of the vats. I want to see it before it hits the setter. And I want to see it afterwards.'

He picked up the report on the Dyehouse and handed it to Larcombe. He pressed the bell and his secretary entered the room.

'Get Mr Cuthbert,' he said.

Cuthbert was the Company Secretary, a sharp-featured, pleasantly mannered man with slightly red-rimmed eyes; an astute accountant with a philosophic faith that all human enterprise must flow at last into the accountant's net.

'The Dyehouse,' said the Chairman of Directors, looking at the Company Secretary.

Cuthbert produced his figures. He balanced production,

9

expenditure, wages. Then he handed over the sheets and waited. He opened the door and glanced out into the General Office.

The racket of machines smote pleasantly on his ear.

Clack! Clack! Up came the carrier and ejected papers onto Mr Dennet's table. There they lay: the Fanfolds! the Ledger Copies!

The Debits!

Mr Dennet took up his pen and began entering in the Control Book. The Comptometers sprang to life. Two young women with painted nails fell upon the papers.

Tic-tac, tic-tac. Now over to the files.

OK, Miss Brennan, you sort them out. City, Country, Government. Now break them up. A to K, L to Z, and into the files with them. Miss Bowden filed quietly, but Miss Graham sent the file flying. It flew back and forth, and her body swayed with it.

Out of the files. Find a Bulldog Clip.

Good! City Debits A to K ready.

Miss Thompson, you start the initial adding. Smart work, Miss Thompson. Tuck that initial listing under the Bulldog Clip, and now over to the Dissection machine.

Miss Thompson tried the machine, then cleared it.

OK, £3.15.7 into A, £2.12.6 into F, 9/6 into Tax, 3/6 into Miscellaneous. Damn, what is it? Packing charge.

Miss Thompson's fingers flew over the keys. Clang, clang, clang, clang.

'Don't clear the machine,' someone called. 'Leave it for the Progressives.'

10

Miss Thompson flung the initial adding on the desk and unwound the dissection.

Plus this, minus that. Make the adjustments at the bottom. Luck, they agree.

Fill in the Summary Sheet.

Rush the Debits to the Ledger Room for posting. Soon they would be out again, when Mr Dennet would make another mark in the Control Book which meant that every Debit was accounted for.

OK, over to Miss Gleeson. Scissors, pincers, screws, paste, glue, book backing, white ink.

The Debits were finished for the day.

Mr Cuthbert closed the door reluctantly.

The Chairman of Directors was leaning well back in his chair. He was having nothing of Mr Cuthbert's figures.

He kept knocking them with his knuckles, saying nothing, but shooting up his eyebrows.

'Six months,' he said suddenly, 'and nothing to show for it. People still puddling about with dyes. Every other firm in Sydney with garments on the shelves.'

'Renshaw says he's practically on top of it now. Says he's really got its back broken.'

'He'd want to be,' Harvison said savagely. 'This isn't a benevolent institution. We pay to get results. If Renshaw can't get them, perhaps someone else will.'

He looked from Cuthbert to Larcombe sitting carefully on the edge of his chair.

'All right,' he said. 'What about the setter?'

'We're getting uneven results,' Larcombe said. 'Uneven

heating. Mayers is still experimenting. Getting the burrs off. We've had an odd good roll.'

'*An odd good roll.* You've got a first-class electrician and an engineer out there, and you tell me you get an odd good roll. How long before we go into production?'

Larcombe took a deep breath and plunged.

'Could be a month—even six weeks.'

'Bah,' said Mr Harvison.

He drummed with his fingers and looked at Cuthbert.

'Things will need to tighten up,' he said. 'It could pay us to call in Jamieson's efficiency people.'

He sat for a moment staring into space. He thought of a machine he had seen once. A smooth, grey machine in a large engineering works. It had fascinated him. Precision of action, smooth integration of parts.

A company could be like that machine. A company *should* be like that machine. *This* company would be like that machine.

CHAPTER THREE

Renshaw had a conversation with Miss Merton on the day she began her new job.

He had not bothered to pick up his shirts; bits of paper still spilled out of the drawers of the desk; a cupboard door gaped open to disclose a miscellany of papers, shoe brushes, soap, old coathangers and accumulated junk. The floor had been swept.

Today his face was different. He seemed to be smiling a lot, and despite the mess in the office Miss Merton was conscious of the pleasant mingled smells of soap and hair oil.

She looked about for equipment. No filing cabinets, no typewriter, no adding machine. Books lay about everywhere. Every now and then a tall, goodlooking girl with flat feet would bawl through the door, 'What's to go on number six?'

'What we need,' said Renshaw, 'is someone to organize a checking system. To hammer all this information into some kind of order, and then shoot it over to Head Office.'

Miss Merton was aware that he was approving her maiden primness, her almost old-fashioned posture, her hands folded quietly on her lap.

'We need someone like you,' he said. 'Never had anyone to help with the women.'

He looked at her sharply.

'Of course,' he said, 'we'll have to get you on the Staff.'

CHAPTER FOUR

Hugh Marshall woke long before dawn. Raising himself on his elbow, he listened. The milk cart went clattering down the street and the early trains were beginning to run.

There was plenty of time yet. He switched off the alarm and lay waiting for the shaft of sunlight to hit the top of the window. This was the signal to begin the day.

At fifty, Hughie was considered a pretty successful man by the inhabitants of Ring Street. He owned the neat, freshly painted semi-detached cottage in which he lived, and as he went past, clad in his clean white overalls, the neighbours said, 'Hughie did pretty well for himself—Leading Hand on the dye vats, and his house in his pocket.'

Hughie was proud of his house. When he closed the door at night he left behind the steamy atmosphere of the vats, the ceaseless swish-swish of the water, the clatter of machinery, the shrill voices of the men calling through

15

the mist. In here, with the old-fashioned curtains veiling the window and his armchair drawn up to the fire, he could forget the Dyehouse, except on those rare occasions when the hooter was turned on and the melancholy note floated out over Macdonaldtown.

Ring Street was in the best part of Macdonaldtown. The houses, though old and mostly built onto the pavement, had preserved respectability. The women swept the pavements early in the morning. The steps were scrubbed, and potted shrubs and palms were on the verandahs. There were individual touches, too: gleaming brass name-plates, wrought-iron bric-à-brac of sailing ships or islands, cutouts of South American peasants sleeping in the sun.

Behind the drawn lace curtains were glimpses of hallrunners, carpets, gleaming linoleums and comfortable chairs.

Few of the inhabitants of Ring Street worked at the Dyehouse. The older men were mostly retired railwaymen, and their sons were directed into trades. The Dyehouse, which sustained many of the residents of Macdonaldtown, found little favour in Ring Street.

It was a dead-end place.

But they all agreed that Hughie had done well. Leading Hand on the vats and a Staff man. He might end up anywhere.

Only Hughie, lying beside Alice in the still dark of the morning, knew the real story of his position at the Dyehouse.

Renshaw had used him. Learned what he could from him and done classes that he himself could never hope to

16

do. He was still Leading Hand on the dye vats, but Renshaw ran the whole place now, shouting and cursing through the warehouse, hounding the men on the presses, sneaking up in the lab, talking new theories that confused him.

But, Christ! He had dyed more cloth than Renshaw had ever seen!

The light struck the window and he stirred. Alice sat up in bed and Hughie went to the kitchen to boil the kettle.

He felt no joy as he stepped into his overalls, nor any sense of joyous anticipation as he opened the door and stepped out into the morning air. The neighbours early abroad nodded as he passed.

He wondered, as he slipped his key into the lock of the Dyehouse door, why one man could make life a hell for so many.

John Thompson woke in his bedroom at Granville.

The alarm burred in the dark morning. It was only a little after five, but he had a long trip to the Dyehouse and there would be trouble if there was no steam up before 7.20.

He switched on the light and looked at Evelyn. She was still sleeping, her bronze hair flung out across her pillow, her eyes shadowed by her lashes. He could hear the children in the back bedroom.

He bent over her. After twenty years of marriage he still wondered at the miracle of Evelyn. Under his scrutiny she opened her eyes, smiling at his face in the circle of the bedroom light. He put his arm around her, lifting her and holding her with an ever-new sense of delight.

She was out of bed before him, the light on in the kitchen, the food sizzling in the pan. They had little time for conversation; quarter to six was a deadline, and she kept running, bringing his coat, his hat; and finally with the time at a quarter to six he leapt through the front door heading for the station.

Hughie opened the Dyehouse door, breaking the alarm circuit. He would have to ring Safety Signals and speak the code, the assurance that all was well. The warehouse was dark and silent. Standing there he had a sudden feeling of loneliness and defeat. At one time he had liked to come in, liked to open up; to feel the keys of office jingling in his pocket, to get onto Safety Signals and give the code.

He had felt adequate and happy.

In the still darkened warehouse the empty fixtures were shadowy and lost against the ceiling. Only the white cloth gleamed on the lower plane.

He walked restlessly, standing before the silent rollers of an examining machine. The light filtered in through the roughly frosted windows with their coating of dust and grime. He noticed the scissors, the tall cones of cotton, the needles already threaded, the open tin of sulphuric ether standing in the corner.

It was getting on. He went to the door and looked out into Richmond Parade. The smoke was blowing in from the railway yards. People were beginning to pass pretty frequently now, on their way to the factories further down the street. A dark green car turned the corner, and Hughie felt his heart contract. But it was not Renshaw's car. It was too early for Renshaw, anyway. He closed the door and retreated to the dim warehouse.

Over and over in the night he had said to himself that he must have it out with Renshaw. Stand up to him. Win back his self-respect and the confidence of the men.

But how?

And he knew, suddenly sick and weak, that when Renshaw came in he would say nothing, hoping that Renshaw would be friendly, but meekly accepting his sneers and the lash of his tongue if he should choose otherwise. He felt shame and misery as he stood in the warehouse, uncertainly switching on lights and waiting for the fireman to come in.

The hooter suddenly broke the silence. Seven o'clock. And simultaneously John Thompson pushed open the Dyehouse door and reached for his bundy card.

Hughie followed him into the boiler-house, glad of the company. He had a few minutes, maybe ten, to spare. John put the billy on the gas with one hand and dropped his trousers with the other. He struggled into his boiler-suit. And while he was fiddling with valves, opening the boiler door, he was watching Hughie curiously. He wondered about Hughie. All the men were watching him and wondering what he was going to do about Renshaw.

But presently he ceased to wonder. He watched the gauges. The world was suddenly only pumps and gauges. The two sulky Colonials, lately converted to oil, sprang to life as at the right moment John applied the torch.

The lifeblood of the Dyehouse was beginning to flow.

CHAPTER FIVE

Renshaw was worried.

The textile game was jumpy. Stocks in the greige had been heavily eaten into, and there was much less margin for error.

In the old days, with the warehouse bulging with stock, mistakes were easily covered up. Streaky cloth due to faulty knitting, grease lines, or simply bad dyeing could be thrown aside to be considered later as re-dyes.

The demand now was for cotton, swami and nylon, and they handled little of the cheap milanese that had once sustained the Dyehouse. There was a considerable amount of commissioned dyeing in quality cloth. Renshaw enjoyed this. He had an eye for colour, and enjoyed the developing of rich purples, of new plums, greens, crimsons and royal blues.

The swami was standard.

His colours, as good as, and often better than anything offered by his competitors, satisfied him and presented no challenge to his ingenuity.

The cottons were troublesome.

When things went really wrong on the cotton, Renshaw was up and down the duckboards, cursing the pressers in a constant flow of obscenity, tearing the cards from the files, turning them over to read numbers, working out tallies.

Renshaw had ten pressers. They were thin itinerant workers who drifted in, worked for a while in the steam and heat, and presently drifted away.

Some men worked for years in the one dyehouse, and in the very large establishments the main body of the labour was stable. But in the smaller dyeworks labour shifted, working from place to place, pulling out, getting sacked, turning up again. Some men had been off and on at Macdonaldtown half a dozen times in five years. It was Renshaw's boast that he could take a man off the streets and make a presser out of him in twenty-four hours.

Few men of independent character remained long with him. In this spot, isolated from the administration, Renshaw ruled with a cruel and arrogant hand.

To Hughie the nylon invasion presented special problems. There were too many dyeing jobs on the vats. In the old days there were always two or three vats standing idle. Now each vat was in operation every hour of the day. The skilled vat hands were drifting away. It was almost a full-time job supervising the vats alone.

But the skill and joy of the job lay in the mixing of the dyes, the weighing-up, the measuring of the chemicals.

In the laboratory, with the condensation dripping from the ceiling, the experimental vat clacking, the bunsen burner and the pipettes, Hughie was happy. In the damp little laboratory, away from the demanding vats, he experimented with patches of cloth, sometimes producing a new shade and eagerly testing it for colour fastness—to water, cold, warm, hot; to sunlight.

All around the bunsen burner were little snippets of colour wrapped in white. Every so often Hughie pressed them with his fingers, unrolled them and examined them for bleeding. Sometimes after the lights were out in the warehouse Hughie stayed on, stirring his squares of cloth in the metal beakers, lifting them lovingly to the light with the glass rod; nodding in satisfaction or flinging them down in disgust.

Hughie had learned his trade in the Dyehouse. He lacked Renshaw's education in theory, but there was little on the practical side that he did not know, and it would have paid Renshaw to help him keep abreast of new techniques. But Renshaw guarded his knowledge. Hughie made a good whipping-boy when things went wrong.

On the third floor, Mr Mayers, the engineer, was getting the burrs off the nylon setter. Preliminary runs had been disappointing. The lead was too short. A feeding table became necessary. Mayers joked with the patient women working in the fumes, guiding the cloth onto the teeth of the endless chain. Unlike Renshaw he rarely panicked, but with stolid Welsh patience tackled problems, isolating them and straightening them out.

There were weeks of hard work ahead for him before the nylon would be coming steadily off the setter.

When the setter was in operation the fumes stole down the stairway to the office where Miss Merton and Patty Nicholls, the blonde junior, were writing up the tickets, the dyebooks, the PG cards, and the general records. In the winter, the girls on the setter closed the doors to keep out the freezing draughts that rushed up from the loading well. Here the hoist hung over the well, surrounded by a low wire barricade. A notice stating that the undersigned were authorized to operate it was posted on the wall. The notice was only four months old but none of the people named were now employed at the Dyehouse. They had drifted on.

At first it had been fun on the setter. There was nothing to do. Some of the more intelligent watched the gauges and worked out the setting heats. The younger women talked. Boy and girl talk. Husband and wife talk. Nearly always intimate and mostly uninhibited.

Others sat silent, mechanically feeding the cloth, eyes lacklustre; sweating in the summer, freezing in the winter.

There had been a stir over the 569812 cloth that was ruined in the vats. It was a special weave and Larcombe had arranged to take it to Best-Yet Sportswear. The management had been wooing Best-Yet for some time, hoping to present them with an alternative to the cloth being used in their sports- and swim-wear. The knitting division had come up with a smooth, satin-finished elasticized fabric. Hughie had worked on the experimental swatches of deep maroon, royal blue and green.

When the dyers' instructions went to the lab, Hughie rang through to the office.

Miss Merton, entering the tickets, looked up. She lifted the receiver from the hook and continued entering up her figures.

Knitted weight. Returned weight. Yards. Strings. Net yardage. And in brackets, the weight lost between the knitted weight and the returned weight.

'Hullo,' she said.

She could hear the clacking of the experimental vat over the phone and then Hughie's voice.

'Laboratory here,' Hughie said. 'I've had the instructions for the 569812. The new cloth. Looks wrong.'

Miss Merton put down the phone and called through to Patty for the dyebook. One roll of cloth. She checked it carefully. She checked the weight against the production sheet. She checked the number.

'Weight seems all right,' she said at last.

'Instructions look wrong. Screwy. Proportions must be wrong. It says *ounces*. Renshaw in his office?'

'No,' said Miss Merton. 'I'll take a look round and let you know later.'

She put down the receiver and walked out to the greige warehouse. The truck was in, unloading rolls onto the dock. The tally had been wrong and Renshaw was supervising a recount. Miss Merton waited patiently. The driver leaned against his truck, confident of his count.

When the rolls had been restacked Miss Merton handed the dyebook to Renshaw.

'Hughie rang through from the lab, about that roll for Best-Yet. He says the instructions look wrong.'

'He does?' said Renshaw. 'Well—what a bloody waste of talent!'

His face hardened as he handed the book back to Miss Merton. He had not glanced at it.

'Hughie's job here is to do as he's told. He's got his instructions in black and white, written down. What's on the instruction is what we want. Blokes get paid good money here to think, and Hughie's not one of them.' He went quickly through to the mangles.

Miss Merton looked at the book. It wasn't often that Hughie was wrong about the dyeing.

She stood in the storeroom outside the laboratory door thinking of what she would say to Hughie.

Glauber salts were piled here in stacks. The dense-soda-ash stack had fallen over and some of the bags had burst open. There was hydrosulphite in drums, peracetic acid in tall-necked carboys, muriatic and sulphuric acids in squat two-gallon jars; softeners, bleachers, fixing agents. Their smells—sour, bitter, sickly-sweet—mingled here and spread outward to every corner of the Dyehouse.

Miss Merton opened the door.

Hughie was sliding the glass up from the delicate balances. Miss Merton watched him as he lifted the tiny weights from the box. Then he slid the glass carefully down.

All along the bench the weighing-up was ready for the vats. No. 6, No. 8, No. 12. Hughie was waiting for a confirmation on No. 10, the new elasticized cloth.

'Must of been a mistake,' Hughie said. 'Seems funny for a bloke to write ounces. Renshaw always writes pounds or grammes.'

'He does,' Miss Merton said, smiling. 'But he says this instruction is right. It's what he wants.'

Hughie weighed up carefully.

'Just the same,' he said, 'I'd take a hundred to one that it's wrong.'

When Hughie saw the cloth after the dyeing he knew that something was really amiss. He had followed Renshaw's instructions carefully, and with the cloth still in the vat he left Bluey in charge and went in search of Renshaw.

'I told you the instructions were wrong,' Hughie said.

He, as well as Renshaw, knew the importance of this roll. The cloth would not strip. The dyeing needed to be accurate.

In the damp laboratory Renshaw picked up the dyeing instructions. So much this, so much that. And suddenly '28 oz' leapt off the paper at him. 28 oz! How the hell had he ever written it? 28 oz! Why, any numskull would know it should be 28 grammes. He put the book down.

'You bloody ignorant son of a bitch,' he said. 'And you call yourself a dyer!'

'I knew it was wrong,' Hughie said. 'I rang through. I got your OK on it.'

'O-bloody-K! You should have pulled the roof off the place.'

Later, with the roll dried, pressed and in the office Renshaw prepared to face Larcombe.

The contract was important, and Larcombe would be difficult.

'I don't know,' Larcombe said. He was exasperated. He would have to make explanations to Harvison. Go into all the details of the thing, make excuses. Bad work at the Dyehouse always reflected unfavourably on himself. It was one thing to lose a contract because they didn't like the cloth, and another to lose it because of faulty workmanship.

'Couldn't you doctor it up?' he asked Renshaw, not too hopefully. 'Strip it? Looks like you put a teaspoon too much in.'

Bloody teaspoon, Renshaw thought. How the hell do they get to be General Manager?

Larcombe leant over the cloth. His face had the look of a frustrated child's.

In a matter of seconds, Renshaw came to a decision. He had been toying with the idea for a long time. He had been on the lookout for a likely-looking boy ever since his first clash with Hughie. Now, with the cloth drab and unlovely in Larcombe's hand, the idea clarified.

'I've been thinking of replacing Hughie,' he said suddenly.

He raised his eyes and looked squarely at Larcombe.

'We've been carrying him for a long time. You can't teach old dogs new tricks. I'm not blaming him. You know yourself that Peters was no more than a trial-and-error man. He trained Hughie up that way. But it won't wash today.'

'He's been with us a long time,' Larcombe said doubtfully. He was used to Renshaw firing and replacing men. 'He started with us straight from school. I reckon he'd be well over thirty years with the firm. I think I'd wait awhile. Think it over.'

'He's no dyer,' Renshaw said shortly. 'I plan to put him over the vats. I'm going to take young Jimmy Collins and train him up for the lab. I'll supervise the work myself. There'll be no more of this kind of thing.'

'What'll Hughie think about that?' Larcombe asked.

Renshaw's face was blank, his eyes averted.

'He can bloody well think what he likes. Most blokes would have fired him over this. He's still got his job. Same pay. No thinking to do. Anyway, I want him out of the lab. These trial-and-error days are over. We just can't afford mistakes. They're too costly.'

He patted the roll of elasticized cloth.

'We can't stand too much of this and continue to attract business.'

'I suppose so,' Larcombe said.

Now that the decision was made, it seemed wise enough. His mind flew back to the cloth. He would take the roll over. The cloth was good. He picked up the swatches, so lovingly dyed by Hughie. The deep maroon was a champion, the green rich and velvety, the blue royal and clear.

'I'll take the roll and swatches over.'

He picked up the roll and went swiftly to his waiting car.

Renshaw whistled in his office. It was easier than he had thought. As easy as that.

Tomorrow he would talk to Hughie. Nothing tough. Nothing offensive. He would arrange to send young Collins to Tech.

He had leapt a hurdle and felt pleased.

CHAPTER SIX

Often at lunchtime Mr Mayers would carry his billy of tea from the machine shop to Miss Merton's office.

Mr Mayers had one foot still in the Rhondda Valley. As they talked, Miss Merton glimpsed the home of his youth; the little Welsh town on the river, the tall houses with apples ripening in the attics and home-made wines in the cellars.

Listening to him, she felt the quickening of her own lost youth. His voice, soft and burred, beat out the tread of the miners' feet, pictured the closed mines and the poverty that lay like a pall over the village.

It reminded her of the Depression, of Stephen, and of that day in summer when Stephen had looked at her.

He had come down the road one day when the Monaro, shorn of frosts, smiled with wildflowers, and the pale fronds of the willows dappled the water. Miss Merton met him, walking, at the spot where the back road crossed the creek.

She was walking, too, and leading a pony by its bridle. There were many men on the road in those days, drifting from town to town, picking up a day's work now and then, checking in for the dole at the next town.

Stephen intended washing for gold.

It had been cool in the sitting-room of her old home. The chairs were deep and comfortable; the door opened onto a wide verandah and the shrubbery ended in a small apple orchard before the land fell away to the creek.

In the evenings Stephen tramped down from his hut at the crossing to talk with her father. The Government was paying a meagre subsidy to men fossicking for gold, and Stephen, washing on the river, eked out a living.

Miss Merton, sitting in the dim sitting-room of her memory, picked up her needle. She was making a Venetian supper-cloth. She scarcely raised her head as the men talked.

Everyone was talking politics now. Stephen, hunched in his chair, his long legs shot out before him, his head resting on his chest, talked politics too.

Stephen was rotting. He said he was rotting. Deprived of the right to work, all men would rot, Stephen said.

There was far too much dangerous talk, Miss Merton's father said. But Stephen laughed; a peculiar, bitter laugh.

'The wheel turns,' Stephen said. 'Our time will come.'

'Thesis,' Stephen said. 'Antithesis, synthesis.'

'Environment.'

What did Stephen mean? Miss Merton knew little of philosophy.

Environment? That meant the river, the dim sitting-room and the chairs, the bread baking in the brick oven in the kitchen, and the secure knowledge that God made every man in His image.

Miss Merton's father walked restlessly to the window. From here he could see the belt of pine-trees, the solid box posts and the white painted gate that marked Hagan's homestead. There was an air of permanency about Hagan's place, just as there was about his own. But less than two months ago Hagan had gone walking down the river, and close to the spot where willows screened the water had bent his head onto the muzzle of his gun, pulling the trigger with his foot.

The Banks, acting quickly, had taken Hagan's place over.

Miss Merton's father, resenting change, moved at the window. He thought of the labour that old man Hagan had put into the property. Wastage, he thought bitterly. He looked suddenly at Stephen slouched in his chair; at the dark, handsome face, the bitter twist of the mouth.

Here was wastage, too. And plenty of others like him were being wasted.

But—'He's a revolutionary,' Miss Merton's father informed her. 'Paid to go about stirring up trouble, no doubt. Change! Who wants to change the system?'

Who wants to change the dim sitting-room of the past? The apple orchard, the fowls strutting in the barnyard, the turkeys?

'Stephen,' Miss Merton called one evening. It was the last of the summer days. The poplars by the gate were yellowing, but the willows were green. In the shallows the water goannas dozed, nose to nose. Occasionally one flopped from the branch of a tree into the river. The water was clear, the sand visible on the bottom.

Stephen was sitting beside Miss Merton.

In the hills behind Hagan's a kangaroo drive was in progress. Now and then the full cries of the drivers were carried on the wind.

Stephen had not joined the hunters. The war had sickened him of killing. Even the sound of a rabbit crying in one of the traps along the river flayed his nerves. The kangaroos were not a menace in the district, Stephen said. It was almost like murder to shoot one.

She sat beside Stephen.

Her hair was down, hanging almost to her waist. Tomorrow was her birthday. Then she would coil it into the neat, firm bun that was to stay with her all the days of her life.

It was almost sunset, and with it came that sadness that seems part of sunset in the bush.

Stephen had stopped speaking. His tormented face was turned to the west.

Then suddenly he turned towards her, and she knew that he was really looking at her for the first time. He watched her steadily, and suddenly a smile like a fleeting ghost touched his lips. He put out his hand and caught her by the arm. Not gently. He held her thus, looking at her.

Stephen!

He was gone. Miss Merton sat listening to the noises in the trees, the last calling and twittering of the birds.

Then she began to run. Down the bush track skirting

the briars, over the hill to the bend that cradled Stephen's hut. It was dark now, but Miss Merton, flying on towards Stephen, cared little for it.

The door was open.

Stephen had lit a hurricane lamp and was putting tea into a black billy. A bed was in the corner, two chaff bags strung between forked legs. He put down the billy and for a moment he lifted her in his arms, running his rough chin over her silky hair.

Behind him lay the bitter road from the Great War, the closed doors of the factories, the insistent voices of authority, 'Move on'.

He put her down gently. He had nothing to offer her. The dark roads straggling from town to town; little tents huddled on friendly land.

He poured tea from the billy into the two pannikins.

Tea? She looked at Stephen and Stephen looked at her across the table. The hurricane lamp threw a glow over her long, soft hair.

She was trembling a little. She took the tea and raised it to her lips. In the silence she could hear the lapping of the water on the stones.

'I'll be moving on soon,' Stephen said. There was no emotion in his voice. Moving on? Away from the river? From her? What would life be without Stephen?

And suddenly he began talking again. Not of love, not of her. He was talking politics.

Useless to tell him how much she loved him.

She put her head down on the rim of the pannikin and wept.

CHAPTER SEVEN

It was late when the car turned the corner.

Most of Wentworth Parade was dark, but a light was still burning in Barrington Terrace. The light would be in the bedroom-cum-kitchen that Patty Nicholls shared with her invalid mother.

Now, well after midnight with the moon high, the drab outlines of the terrace were softened. A tree, hardy survivor of an avenue planted years since by the Council, thrust its shadowy arms almost to the lighted window.

The clatter and noise of the day were over and the familiar sounds from the railway-yards scarcely disturbed the night.

Renshaw lit a cigarette. He was feeling satiated and weary.

He wished Patty would go quickly. Yet he knew she would hang about, nuzzling into him like a puppy, waiting for the words of endearment that he felt too weary to formulate.

His hands strayed down over her throat and onto her young, firm breasts, but he was too tired to be really interested. Patty's face was upturned to his, her lips still tremulous and eager. He bent over her, kissing her now without passion, trying to disguise his impatience. His eye strayed to the hands of his watch.

'Nearly time to go, sweetheart,' he said.

She sat up, straightening her hair. Her mother would be waiting, sitting up in the corner of the untidy room, her sharp eyes ready to inspect her hair, her lipstick, her rumpled skirt.

Renshaw handed her his comb. He was anxious to be rid of her. He helped smooth her skirt and held the mirror while she dabbed her nose with powder and marked in her mouth with vermilion lipstick. She was pretty enough, he thought, and eager. She was like the smooth, lush peaches in an orchard he had visited as a child.

But sitting in the car, impatiently waiting for her to go, he felt no emotion; nothing but a faint feeling of aversion that he knew would deepen from now on.

With her hair combed down, ready to step from the car, she leant towards him. Her voice was soft and husky. There was rhythm and melody in it, but the accent was Barrington Terrace, and the beauty was lost on Renshaw.

In the light she looked little more than a child.

'You meant it—what you said?' she asked him.

He was used to this. Did he mean? Of course he meant. He stirred himself.

There was a technique that led to the pick-up, the romance, the moment of satisfaction. There was a technique for the brush-off too. It was gradual, but final.

'Did you mean it—what you said about us getting married?'

'Yeah,' he said.

There was silence. He wished she would go, stop standing there asking silly questions.

'I feel frightened,' she said. 'You don't think…?'

'I don't,' Renshaw said. 'There's not a chance in a thousand. Now be a good girl and hop up into bed.'

He looked again at his watch. Almost two o'clock.

The trouble with virgins, they always wanted reassuring. He wondered if the game was worth the candle. Fretful little bitches who hollered about marriage. No experience, no technique, and an hour's post-mortem after the act.

She stepped back, reassured, and Renshaw let in the clutch. He backed to the corner, then headed past the Parade. Patty listened to the hum of the engine until the sound was lost in the night.

Her heels were too high, and they gave her an odd look, like a doll teetering a little forward on its tiny feet. They also made a clicking, clattering sound on the pavement as she walked.

As she paused at the terrace door, a man passed. It was Oliver Henery, who worked on the mangles and helped load the vats.

'Good night,' Patty said.

Oliver stopped. His hair was straight and well brushed. He had a sardonic, amused grin on his face.

36

He doesn't like me, Patty thought. And that's because I'm Renshaw's girl.

'You mean "good morning", don't you?' Oliver said. He grinned a very sharp, knowing grin that was neverthe-less friendly.

'Time you were in bed,' he said, and walked on down the Parade. Patty saw him, now solid in the moonlight, now melting into the dark shadows of the houses, walking on towards the point where the two vertical lines of the street seemed to rush together.

Then, quietly, she slipped off her shoes and turned the key in the lock.

Mrs Webb, the landlady and custodian of the morals of the residents of Barrington Terrace, occupied the front room. She retired early, first cutting off all electricity at the main.

Patty closed the door behind her. In the darkness, the straight stairway rose out of the front room. She had almost reached it when she heard a movement. A body turned over in bed and she heard the scraping of a match. She shrank close against the wall. The match spluttered and slowly found the wick of the candle in the old-fashioned enamelled candlestick.

Mrs Webb held the candle up and peered into the room.

'Who's there?' she called.

Patty pressed close to the shadows.

Mrs Webb moved the light along one wall, then another, until it picked up Patty's shrinking form. She held the candle, outlining the girl's slight figure, her drooping head and outstretched arms.

37

Then she got slowly out of bed, draping a blanket round her shoulders, and advanced towards her.

Neither spoke.

Mrs Webb looked in turn at the shoes, at Patty's crumpled skirt, at the alarm clock ticking on the rickety table.

Then, drawing back her lips, she said one word. 'Slut.'

Now the spell was broken. Patty dashed for the stairs, running with no thought but escape up to the third floor. There pale light glimmered under the door, announcing her mother's vigil.

In her flight she had lost a new metal bracelet that had cost Renshaw seven and elevenpence. She searched for a while in the thick darkness, but it was nowhere to be found, and she sat, suddenly weak with emotion and the happenings of this extraordinary night, crying a little from excitement and fatigue.

When she pushed the door open her mother saw the shoes clasped in her hands, the new, gaudy baubles in her ears and round her throat, the tear-washed face and the bedraggled skirt.

All around, as far as she could reach with her still strong arms, the room was tidy. The ink-stained red cloth on the table was smoothed and neat, the thin globe of the kerosene lamp gleamed and the flame burned clean from the trimmed wick. Beyond the reach of her arms there were papers, clothes waiting to be washed, and Patty's still unmade bed.

She tried not to look at Patty.

There was tea in the thermos flask, hot and sweet, and Patty drank it gladly.

Then the lamp was turned low.

Raising herself on her hands, Mrs Nicholls slid into bed.

For a while there was the sound of Patty turning the mattress, straightening the sheets. Then, with the light out, the sound of Patty washing. Mrs Nicholls carried the thought into her uneasy sleep, until it became part of the drifting calls from the railway-yards, the occasional taxi, the clattering milk carts, and at last the shrill early morning whistle of the Dyehouse.

CHAPTER EIGHT

It was almost dark when Barney Monahan opened the gate and pushed into the garden. All around was scrubby bush-land, grey and depressing.

On the uplands a little beyond the house was a group of bloodwoods. Later, in the autumn, the trees would burst into a mass of feathery white gum blossoms, fragrant and honey-sweet.

Tonight they stood, dark sentinels, their long green leaves pointing downwards, the bark serried and marked by blood-red sap. Soon the possums with their grey furred coats would appear, carrying their young on their backs or in their pouches. They would merge with the shadows to become part of the grey night.

When Barney was building a shed the possums had built in the ceiling.

'You want to get rid of them,' neighbours said.

But he let them stay. Esther liked them, and fed them bread soaked in tea and sugar.

The house was remote from the Dyehouse. Barney had bought the land—rough, isolated and scrubby, on the edge of a sweeping reserve near where the train came round the loop from Sutherland. It was cheap, but it took every penny of his carefully hoarded money to pay for it. There was nothing left over for luxuries, and he and Esther had started in a tent bought second-hand in Oxford Street.

That was a long time ago.

Tenaciously, after his day's work at the Dyehouse, he had worked on the block with Esther, clearing the rough undergrowth but keeping the trees. Then the slow job of pegging out, digging, splitting stone for the foundation in order to save money; the period of scraping, economizing, going without. And gradually the small timber-framed cottage was raised. Into six squares they had fitted two bedrooms, a bathroom, a laundry, a kitchen-cum-living room. And there was his shed made from odds and ends of material and plain junk. It housed the tools, the tent carefully packed and tied to the ceiling, and the stretchers.

This was his home, the best he could afford, and he had struggled hard to get it.

Into this structure—peeling, and beginning now to need a fresh coat of paint—had gone his strength, his leisure and his youth.

At first, when he was younger, the journey home from the Dyehouse had been a joy. There were fewer people living so far out, and seats were always available. It had been good to sit with the windows up and drink in the clean air, to watch the houses swallowed up and the paddocks and trees emerge.

Now the journey was something to reckon with. A man was lucky to find a seat even on the early morning trains and more often than not he stood hanging onto the back of a seat, lifting his feet, resting them, bracing himself for the journey.

And then the day. Sweating in the Dyehouse. Pulling the cloth through the winches, packing down the hydro, loading the vats.

Then the rush for the train home; racing through the light summer evenings, or the dark, sullen landscape of winter. The walk from the station. Five, ten, twenty minutes. The last excruciating minutes! And then there was the menacing little house, demanding more paint; pipes to be fixed, cupboards not quite finished, electricity not yet connected.

Barney fiddled in the garden, unwilling to open the door, trying not to think of Esther. But finally, finding no comfort in the dreary grey of the evening, he pushed the door open and struck a match. The lamp's blackened chimney was a sharp reminder of Esther's absence.

He lit the lamp and looked critically round the room. It was small, mean and oppressive. The remains of his breakfast were still on the kitchen table. The bread was stale and hard, the eggshells white and flat. There were dishes piled on the sink. Cups smeared and tea-stained, an enamel plate, a teapot without a lid. The gingham cover had slipped from the homemade settee; there was a rip in its flouncing.

He went over, trying vaguely to straighten it up, to put the cushions into place.

He went through to the bedroom. The room was untidy, the bed unmade. The closed room smelled of stale tobacco. He put down the lamp and bent over to pick up a soiled sheet, but let it fall again on the floor. He threw the pillows onto the bed.

He sat down, running his fingers through his hair. He could see his reflection in the mirror; an ageing man with sallow face, hair still thick, but grey.

He went through to Kathy's bedroom. Here the bed was made, the quilt hanging evenly to the floor. The cheap, thin curtains were gay. On the toy-box that he had made from a discarded packing-case were ranged Kathy's toys. He bent over and picked up the cheap little black doll with one leg off. He had bought it eighteen years ago, when Kathy had been one year old. There was the giraffe that he and Esther had made for her fifth birthday. A fine tall giraffe, eighteen inches high, made from waste and graphed from a pattern Esther had found in an old journal.

How he had loved Kathy! Sitting now in the empty house he sought to recapture the joy of those earlier days. He picked up a book and turned the leaf. 'To Kathy on her twelfth birthday.' There was an album. He thumbed through it. Kathy sixteen, seventeen, eighteen. Kathy married, away from the struggle. Decently married to a man with a trade.

But there was Esther!

He brought his mind sharply and suddenly back to Esther.

The kitchen. The lamp flaring, the heat rising from the stove. And Esther, gaunt, hollow-eyed, grey and haggard, telling him.

God in heaven it was good! It was a bloody circus!

The makeshift kitchen; the flaring light; the dehydrated woman; the weary, ageing man! And the womb. The tenacious womb.

'It couldn't be,' he said.

He wanted to shout it. As though the very sound of his voice could make this thing not be.

How could it? Look at her! Her skinny arms, her stringy grey hair, her thin face with the cheeks fallen in because there were no teeth behind them.

How could it be? What spark could leap from the weary comforts of their love? What spartan seed nestle in that ageing womb?

'You're sure?' he said.

The stillness answered him. Her drooping figure, her arms hanging wearily from their sockets.

She turned so that the light fell harshly across her face.

No need for her to speak. Her hollow, tired eyes confirmed the answer.

She was sure. How many nights had she lain, looking into the soft dark, thinking? Being sure, before troubling him.

'But how could it be?'

The kitchen was suddenly a trap. He was struggling like a rat. The steel of the railway tracks, the revolving cloth on the brusher, the swishing of the water in the vats, the shabby little cottage, all clamoured and thundered in his brain.

'Perhaps,' he said evenly, 'you will miscarry.'

Barney put down the album. He lingered, unwilling to leave the clean freshness of Kathy's room. He went into the kitchen. There was no kindling for the fire. He went out into the dreary night and gathered a handful of gumleaves and candle bark. The axe was standing in front of the shed. He split the logs slowly and methodically. The action brought relief, and despite his aching arms he continued to work, splitting the logs and piling them in the woodshed.

CHAPTER NINE

There had been little sleep for Barney that night. Worn out, Esther slept fitfully. But with the lamp out and the cotton sheets drawn over his body, he lay looking up into the dark. He saw the embedded embryo, fighting to retain its slender hold on life. His mind leapt to the future. Doctors, hospitals, the inadequate Social Service. And in the background the grey, steamy Dyehouse.

But morning brought no solution. He had slept late, but it was still dark when Esther called him. He sat silently through breakfast, rubbing his hand over the stubbly growth on his chin. He was too late to shave and too tired to care about it. He put his razor in his bag. He would clean up at morning-tea time.

It was scarcely daybreak when he called goodbye to Esther and set off down the rough road that led to the railway tracks. Far off he could hear the train. It was coming round on the loop. He began to walk a little faster, and then to trot.

His breath came in great gasps and the backs of his legs ached. He should be easing up, slowing down. He was no longer young: the thought hit him suddenly. And all the time he had been going on, making the pace, being better than the youngsters, while time was creeping up.

The train was well round the bend and he began to run again. His head throbbed. But he must run. Like a rabbit—run, run in the dark morning. Forget the way the air was pumping and sobbing in his lungs. Forget the ache in his tired legs. Run. Trot, trot, run. Run grey-faced and unshaven over the broken ground. He was almost there. His feet were on the steps. Thirty and more of them, and then the platform, and already slowing to a stop, the train lights yellow in the coming dawn.

Goodwin had a reputation in the Dyehouse. He was 'in the know'. He knew a woman.

'Fifteen pounds down,' Goodwin said, 'and fifteen pounds when the job's done.'

He and Barney were talking together at morning-tea break.

'Thirty pounds?' Barney laughed. 'It's pretty steep.'

'Oh, well—you take it or leave it. It's not my pigeon. I can't say I had any finger in the pie.'

'What's it worth to you?' Barney asked.

Goodwin shrugged.

'I tell you I know this dame. I get Sweet Fanny Alley out of it. As it is I take a pretty big risk telling you. Yesterday

47

you were bellyaching like a cut cat over this, and now thirty's too steep.'

He pushed on past Barney.

'Wait on,' Barney called.

He had the money.

'We'll go down tomorrow after work,' Goodwin said.

But Esther would have to be told. Barney walked slowly down to the vats, thinking of what he would say to her.

CHAPTER TEN

In the afternoon of the next day, Esther set about tidying up the kitchen.

She worked mechanically, scraping the plates, piling them onto the sink, lifting the steaming kettle from the stove, listening to the hissing sound of the water as it hit the cold sink. She swept up the floor, went into the yard to fetch wood. She stacked the wood into the box until it was full. She rinsed her hands and straightened her hair. In the shadowy mirror her face was strained and her eyes were dark. There were purple shadows under them.

In the bedroom she stripped the bed, changing the sheets and pillowcases.

There was no need to begin preparing the evening meal yet. Barney would be late. She put the thought at the back of her mind.

With everything tidy, she walked towards the little

garden in front of the house. It was an effort to get down the verandah step, and she stood for a minute holding on to the post, listening to her heart. Her legs were heavy, and suddenly the sharp warning pains assailed her.

She sat down suddenly on the step feeling faint and dizzy.

The sun was still above the treetops on the ridges, but the gully was shadowy. Children were going past on the way home from school. Sitting with her head propped against the verandah post, she could hear them skipping and chattering, but they seemed a long way off.

They're only at the gate, she thought. I could call out to them.

At four o'clock Mrs Macaulay closed her cottage door. She had her basket, her string bag, and the list for her shopping. A middle-aged woman in sensible walking shoes and a dark floral frock, she came down the unmade bush track, looking inquisitively into gardens as she passed, waving greetings to people busy round their houses.

There's something funny going on at Monahan's—you mark my words, she told herself. Something pretty queer.

She stopped at the front gate. Esther was sitting on the verandah, her head against the post, her eyes closed.

'Good day to you,' Mrs Macaulay called.

Esther heard the call a long way off, through a mist. She tried to frame a reply.

'Well!' said Mrs Macaulay. She put down her basket and opened the gate. Esther could hear the footsteps. They were coming closer. With a tremendous effort she wrenched her eyes open and looked up at the kindly, inquisitive face.

Then her head drooped down. Mrs Macaulay was feeling her wrists, loosening her frock. She could hear surprised cluckings, like a flustered hen's. She could hear the wheels of a cart, Mrs Macaulay's shrill cry and a man's answering voice. Then everything was quiet and dark.

When she woke she was in bed. She looked at the ceiling. It was her own bedroom. There was a faint, clean smell of cologne; Mrs Macaulay had brought her own bottle over and had dabbed her temples and the front of her nightie.

A man in a grey suit was bending over her. Her eyes began to focus better. It was the doctor, the one from the stone cottage close to the station.

'That's better,' he said. He was drawing the sheets up round her shoulders.

She had the uncomfortable feeling of lying down-hill.

Oh, she thought, I'm packed up. My feet sticking up in the air.

She laughed weakly.

The doctor had turned away. He was writing something. Mrs Macaulay stood at the foot of the bed, a large white apron round her hips. She looked big and bright and competent.

'Well,' Dr Peters said. 'We'll have you right in no time.'

Mrs Macaulay retreated to the kitchen. She banked up the fire and set more kettles and pots of water on the stove.

'I wouldn't bother,' Esther said to him. She turned her head wearily. Then she closed her eyes, and drew her thin lips into a tight line.

Dr Peters came back to the bed. He stood for a long time looking at her. He remembered passing this cottage years ago, watching the man and woman labouring on its framework.

He noticed the neat, sparsely furnished bedroom.

'You don't want this baby?' he said gently.

She opened her eyes and looked suddenly into his face. There was no censure. It was a face of compassion and understanding.

She looked away, startled.

But she didn't answer him. Doctors, even the most kind and humane of them, knew nothing of her problem. Nothing of her fight and struggle, nothing of the long poverty of her life, nothing of the way Barney felt. They were the guardians of life. The problems didn't matter.

She felt suddenly weak as she remembered: Barney! Had they telephoned him? She struggled to rise in the bed, but Dr Peters pushed her gently back. Barney would be going to see the woman. She pictured the mean terrace, the dark and secret windows, the shabby door. A shudder ran through her and she closed her eyes.

Dr Peters bent over. He picked up her hand and looked at it. The nails were broken, the knuckles swollen and enlarged, the palm callused and hard.

'Your hand reminded me of someone,' he said gently. 'My mother had hands like these.'

Esther started to laugh. A weak laugh, which hurt her somewhere in the chest. Well it was funny, anyway. His neat suit, the stone cottage, the garden with the flowering shrubs, the white-clad girl opening the surgery door. And his mother had hands like these. It seemed a funny thing to say. She slipped back into the darkness.

In the evening Barney and Goodwin walked down the dim Parade.

Now that the thing was under way Barney hesitated.

'Risky, isn't it?' he asked Goodwin.

Goodwin grinned.

'She fixes up quite a few. Never heard of her having any trouble. That little sheila on the brushers was kicking up her legs again after four or five days.'

The house was two-storeyed and detached. There were trees growing in the front garden and flowers blooming in ordered beds.

'Looks all right,' Barney said. He had not expected this.

'I tell you she's all right,' Goodwin said. 'Good as a doctor. Cheap too, and still makes a pile.'

The door opened. The hall was wide, and seemed to run back into gleaming white walls. A tall woman in a grey linen frock stood before them. She was handsome, in her early forties. She looked well fed and well cared-for. An inner door opened. The office floor gleamed under the chromium-mounted fluorescent lights. The desk was massive and warm-coloured, like cedar. Barney sat down, feeling weak and dry, and looked at the woman. He took the notes from Goodwin and handed them to her. He felt hot.

The woman turned around, unlocked a drawer and took out the cash-box. She placed Barney's notes on top of the pile and snapped an elastic band around them. Then she locked the box and the drawer. She wore the keys on a heavy gold bracelet on her wrist.

They stood up to go. There was a funny noise. It sounded like someone whimpering. Then a long, agonized moan. A radio was suddenly turned up loud.

'What's that?' Barney said.

'Little girl,' the woman said. She was almost arch. 'Naughty little girl, but she's getting better.'

'You got a doctor here?' Barney asked. He was listening.

He got up quickly. The woman was speaking, but he was in the hall, through the door, out into the street, where even the smoke-laden air of Macdonaldtown seemed clean.

'You'll do your dough,' Goodwin said, catching up. 'There's no refunds. You know that, don't you? Don't you?' His voice was shrill with annoyance and surprise.

It was good on the train. Good as the stations rushed past. Good to be going home to Esther. The problems could be faced later.

He ran from the train, up the road past the houses with their yellow lights half-hidden in the gully. He could hear the possums scolding in the trees.

The lamp was lit, but the woman waiting beside it was not Esther.

When Esther woke again her mind was clear. She was no longer in the low double bed that she shared with Barney. She was in a long, narrow room. A hospital ward. The lights were on and outside it was dark. The nurses were taking off the quilts, folding them, getting the patients ready for the night.

Now that the pain was gone, she lay with the blanket drawn up round her, feeling drowsy and tired. The cottage seemed remote.

For years the sound of the train coming up the cutting from Jannali had governed her life. Time to put the kettle on, to stir the food simmering in the pot, to lay the cloth and set down the cutlery. It had been important for years, and now today it just didn't seem to matter.

The little nurse came in and took out the flowers. She shook down the thermometer and put it into Esther's mouth.

'All right?' Esther asked shyly.

The nurse smiled, putting the thermometer back in the sterilizer, but she didn't answer Esther's question.

'We'll have you on your feet soon,' she said. She bent over, pulled the pillows forward. Esther sank back and lay looking at her hands. The pain was no longer troubling her and she felt guilty. It was years since she had lain in bed like this. She had a mental picture of the kitchen. Well, things would go on just the same. Barney would get his breakfast, feed the chooks and be on his way to the station, just as when she was smoothing things out for him.

The night nurse looked into the ward. She was a bright, smiling-faced young woman. She went over to Mrs Finlay, who was very sick, and stood beside her for a few minutes. Then she pulled the switch and plunged the room into darkness. Esther settled down into her pillows. She made sure the bell was handy. But she lay for a long time looking into the darkness, listening to Mrs Finlay's laboured breathing, watching the flash of the light as the sister passed the door, listening to the hum and roar of the traffic as it sped along

55

the road that led to the southern suburbs. Pictures flashed through her mind. Barney meeting her years ago after the football. Walking home on a cool summer's evening. The open bushland, and the block they had chosen for the house. She wondered what had gone wrong with them. Yet she knew. Poverty had stifled them. She saw Barney lined and old for his years, waking long before dawn, herself bending over the stove, stirring the pots, hurrying the food.

They were caught in a treadmill, she thought. The others were caught too: Mrs Finlay, the pretty little bride from Miranda, the old lady in the end bed.

The light flashed through the door. Sister was bending over her.

'Not sleeping?' she asked.

Esther blinked her eyes and closed them against the light.

'Not very well,' she said.

The light disappeared momentarily.

'Take this.'

Esther reached up and took the tablets and the drink. She pulled the sleeves of her old-fashioned nightgown down to her wrists.

'You don't want to worry,' the sister said kindly. 'Things often turn out better than we think.'

The light disappeared. For a moment Esther saw the white dress, the legs strangely spindly, the painted door-jamb. Between waking and sleeping she thought again of Barney.

Mrs Macaulay would wait and pass the news on to him, before she began on the neighbours. She saw the inquisitive, astonished face, the hand on the knocker, the neighbour's inquiring glance. Well, they could talk now. She slipped into a quiet, restful sleep.

The next evening Barney was lined up with the visitors.

Esther saw him tiptoeing down the ward. He had shaved carefully, but he looked tired and grey. He had a bunch of yellow daisies in his hand.

He bent over, kissed her and sat holding her hand in his, hanging onto it and pressing it. He wanted urgently to tell her about the woman. About how he had changed his mind; how good he felt in the train going home to her. But instead he talked about work, how well he was managing at home.

'You'll be home soon,' he said gently. 'I talked to the doctor.'

The baby was safe.

And before he went Barney bent over, holding her hand under the blankets.

'I wanted to tell you, old girl,' he said. 'That deal with the woman—I called it off.'

He saw Esther's eyes fill with tears.

He bent over and kissed her gently.

'I wouldn't really have risked you,' he said.

Barney's behaviour had astonished Goodwin. To back out then! To take the cash out of kitty and walk out with Sweet Fanny Alley!

At work Barney was morose and uncommunicative.

'The dough's there—you can always use it,' Goodwin said.

And later, with Barney still disinclined for discussion, he said, 'You wouldn't call the coppers?'

'I don't call copper,' Barney said. 'And I got my problems. Plenty!' Esther, though out of hospital, was still far from well.

He was dragging the cloth through the winches, packing down the hydro.

'Can't understand him,' Goodwin said to Oliver Henery. 'Lays out his money, gets introduced to the real thing, then runs out and leaves his dough.'

'Oh, well,' Oliver said. 'There's one thing you can always bet on, dames will be always having kids.'

He looked across at Barney.

'Poor old bugger,' he said, 'you'd wonder any sheila'd be in it.'

'It's his missus,' Goodwin said. 'Lean old girl with grey hair. Must be close on fifty.'

'Many a good tune—' Oliver said, and laughed.

He didn't really like Goodwin, but he was handy to know in an emergency.

CHAPTER ELEVEN

Many people knocked at the Dyehouse door.

But the faces, as Miss Merton came to know them, were the faces of the defeated.

One by one the pageant passed, the faces white, disembodied blobs.

'You got a job for me?'

A mid-European woman, thickset and heavy in the legs. She had been walking for a fortnight, fighting through the maze of streets in the industrial areas. Her dark, anxious eyes had looked into half a hundred small, untidy offices.

'You got a job for me?'

Young man in a Harris tweed coat and an accent that jolted Miss Merton out of her apathy to examine him more closely.

What was he doing at the Dyehouse?

She noticed his hands, and listened to the cadence of

his voice. He sounded like theatre, like a world that existed outside the Dyehouse and the smell of hydrosulphite and sulphuric ether. Young man wringing his hands and just one step ahead of the police who were so soon to catch up with him.

Pale, apathetic men whose lives had been spent in the vapours of dyehouses, women with fallen wombs and strained stomach muscles. The load for women, officially, was thirty pounds. Officially.

'Any jobs at the Dyehouse today?'

They were working overtime now, and at full capacity. Jobs were getting hard to find. The migrants knocked at the Dyehouse door, searching in groups. Men able to speak English introduced smiling dark-eyed girls or weary, sullen older women.

Some of the men had been out of work for weeks, and their need made them desperate. But the Dyehouse was full. Some stood for a while peering into the warehouse, at the cloth in the fixtures, the trucks standing loaded in the aisles. Then they turned and walked out into the Parade.

CHAPTER TWELVE

There had been trouble over the sick-pay claims. Renshaw, moody and irritable over the fluctuating performance of the nylon-setter, had little time or patience to consider the personal affairs of the employees. In the main he left all such work to Miss Merton, usually glancing indifferently over statements and then signing them with a flourish. The thing had been building up for some time, and it finally exploded over the case of Barney Monahan.

Sick pay was always a contentious matter. There were fixed rules.

1. Employee must report sick within twenty-four hours.

2. Employee must fill in and sign statutory declaration, duly witnessed by a JP.

3. Employee must state reason for absence from employment.

4. Employee must ask that this absence might not

jeopardize his continuity of service (i.e., that he should not be penalized by losing proportion of his holiday pay, or lose long-service privileges).

5. He must claim payment for the day.

To the uninitiated the demands were formidable. The more experienced had the thing down to a fine art.

Move 1: Ring Miss Merton. In a husky voice announce sickness. 'Flu. You hope to be in tomorrow.

Move 2: Tomorrow. Lean through window to Miss Merton. Confirm previous day's illness. Wait until Miss Merton says, 'Oh, I'm sorry to hear that.' Bundy on.

Move 3: Mention to Renshaw that 'flu had laid you low the previous day. He gets snaky if he's overlooked.

Move 4 (if a woman): Report to head girl serious bout of 'flu previous day. Commence work.

Move 5: After breaking back of first job, chase about looking for the shop-steward. Get a statutory declaration form. Fill it in. Go in search of a JP—Mr Mayers is always happy to oblige.

Move 6: Take the statement to Miss Merton. Wait while she reads it. What's this? She says it's wrong.

'I notice there is no doctor's certificate,' says Miss Merton. 'You will have to make a statement about your holiday pay. You will have to ask that your absence should not interfere in any way with the proportion of your holiday pay due to you for this month.'

'Oh, garn,' you say.

Miss Merton picks up a pen. She writes in a bold hand, 'And I ask that such absence shall not jeopardize my continuity of service. I wish to claim sick-pay.' She hands it to you to initial.

Many New Australians were employed at the Dyehouse, and this added considerably to the work entailed on sick claims. Few of them could speak English, and usually they brought the form to Miss Merton, smiling and anxious for help.

'Larcombe says they're complaining about the sick-pay claims,' Renshaw said. 'Cuthbert wants every employee to personally fill in the statement on his claim.'

'Oh,' said Miss Merton. She was feeling tired and exasperated. It took up endless time trying to explain all the complications to people still struggling with the rudiments of the language.

'And Cuthbert says you've got to watch that "personal illness" angle. You've got to see that the statement is "my personal illness", and not "personal illness". Cuthbert says that personal illness could be the personal illness of wife or child. Sick-pay applies only to the personal illness of the employee.'

'I suppose he means Barney Monahan,' said Miss Merton.

'Oh, well,' said Renshaw, 'we've got to draw the line somewhere. Some of these blokes know a thing or two.'

'Yes.' Miss Merton pressed her lips together.

'Don't need to take it to heart,' said Renshaw. 'Just watch them for that "my personal illness" angle, and the rest is up to them.'

Miss Merton sat tapping her pen on her desk.

'It seems heartless,' she said. 'Wife sick. Everything

at odds. And this form waiting for "due to my personal illness". There's not much margin for the joys and tragedies in people's lives, is there?'

Renshaw bent over and patted her on the arm. He was sorry about Barney. But he was up against the blank wall of the Company.

'You're a bit of a sentimentalist,' he said.

She looked at him, suddenly angry.

'I don't know,' she said. 'We're all human beings. It's hard to see what else Barney could have done. According to this he could be just a malingerer.'

The bundy cards were on the table. She took them up and began writing in the reports.

She put the affair at the back of her mind.

She began writing up the absentees. The names and numbers of those who had reported sick. The names and numbers of those who had resumed work. The names and numbers of those finishing up, those drifting on, those sacked, together with suitable explanations.

Sometimes, under Renshaw's instruction, she wrote in 'mutual consent'. But Cuthbert found the phrase too elastic. 'Mutual agreement' was the term.

'I suppose,' said Renshaw when the phone rang, and Cuthbert voiced his criticism of the term, 'he could be right. Always sounded like adultery to me.'

Often, after the name and number of some individual more independent or aggressive than the rank and file, Renshaw instructed her to write: 'Never to be employed again by the Company'.

But that didn't mean much.

For Renshaw, moody, strange and unpredictable, could about-face with ease, and many men dismissed with this final stigma were now back at the Dyehouse. Words didn't always mean what they said—unless, of course, it was a Company directive.

CHAPTER THIRTEEN

Work began early each Friday.

On the vats the cloth was pushed through, so that it would reach the hydro and dryer in time to be dried out before the whistle blew. The vats were finished just after four, and the men began hosing down and cleaning up.

Hughie had the empty casks ranged near the dock. Renshaw had instructed him to take no deliveries unless the driver picked up the returnable empties.

In the lab, Marj Grigson was fiddling with last-minute jobs. She was cutting two-inch samples of cloth with pinking shears and pasting them into a sample book with Perkins' Paste. It was a tedious job and she was not very interested in doing it. But any time after four Renshaw was likely to come stamping into the lab and turn back the pages in order to look up the samples of the day's dyeing.

It was quiet as she worked. The experimental vat had

ceased to clang and in the main vat area the machinery had ceased turning.

In the storeroom Oliver Henery was straightening the dye tins. The shelves were dirty. He was brushing them down with a dilapidated banister brush. It was part of the Friday clean-up.

Oliver had been promoted to the vats. Not that it meant much. The loading was heavy and the wet-money poor.

'You don't want to look so sad,' Oliver called through the door to Hughie. 'You want to count your blessings.'

Hughie came and stood, leaning his shoulder against the door, watching Oliver moodily.

Oliver grinned. He was standing on an upturned cask, waving the brush about. His naked chest was smeared with ochre-coloured dye. His black hair was banded Indian-fashion with a couple of bright-coloured strings.

'Me, I don't care. For all I care this dump could burn down tomorrow.' He flicked the dust off the shelf and held up a rusty tin. The label was stained and discoloured. Hughie had been trying to straighten out the labels and get the dyes ready for the monthly stock count. The reckoning with Renshaw was never an easy one.

Oliver leapt to the floor with one graceful movement.

'You take too much from Renshaw, Hughie,' he said. 'Coming in here, throwing his weight around. Pushing you about. When he starts that sarcastic stuff again you want to clock him. Hit the bastard in the guts. You can't handle a bloke like Renshaw with kid gloves.'

He stretched. His stomach was flat and hard, and his damp shorts clung to his hips.

He looked at Hughie thoughtfully.

'You don't want to take everything that Renshaw likes to dish you out,' he said. He tossed the brush into the corner and picked up a piece of waste cloth for a towel.

Hughie grinned weakly.

'Why you bust your gut in this hell-hole, Hughie?'

Oliver looked around, then slowly back at Hughie.

'I been here a long time,' Hughie said. He was silent, thinking of his early days at the Dyehouse. Tommy Peters. Old Perry coming over in person to inspect the rolls. The night he and Peters had worked back and got onto that new yellow.

'I been here a long time,' he said doggedly. And then the final truth. 'I like the dyein'.'

He looked almost shyly at Oliver. 'I like making up these colours, working on a new range.'

Oliver flicked the cloth through the air. It made a splash of brilliant colour. He put it over his shoulder.

'Some blokes don't have to work,' Oliver said. 'Some bastards have money sunk in dye places just like this. Sit on their fat arses all day and make statements. They don't like the forty-hour week. These blokes don't know how it feels to work hard forty hours.'

He went through the chemical store to the showers.

The fireman had finished up. He was washed and dressed in clean grey trousers and a striped shirt. He was collecting the money for the diddley-dum. He kept rattling the box and laughing, marking the names off in the squares.

Through the glass doors Oliver could see Renshaw talking to Miss Merton, and across the way Patty Nicholls

68

sitting quietly, stacking up cards. She kept putting them together and then pulling them apart. She looked tense and nervous.

It was good under the shower. The water ran from the points of his dark hair.

All the men were talking easily today, planning for the weekend.

John Thompson was finished with the diddley-dum when Oliver clocked off. 'Got something lined up?' he called across the street to Tommy, who was polishing up his jalopy.

Tommy made voluptuous curves in the air with his hands. Oliver grinned and made an impolite gesture.

Girls passing from the factories looked at him with interest.

He smiled, raised his eyebrows and winked. He gave a lengthy wolf whistle. The girls giggled and stopped. They looked back over their shoulders.

He walked on down Richmond Parade whistling and thinking of the dog that he and Jackson had coming up.

CHAPTER FOURTEEN

Patty Nicholls had spent the weeks following Renshaw's visit to Wentworth Parade in an aura of happiness.

Routine jobs like checking the production, writing up the dyebooks, checking the PG cards against the shipping books, were suddenly invested with joy and interest. Swinging along on her high heels, her knee-high skirts fanning out over her roped petticoats, her fair hair gleaming and silken on her shoulders, she moved like a bright-coloured moth through the misty Dyehouse.

Miss Merton, looking at her over her reading glasses, sighed.

She was vaguely worried over Patty. More than once she had thought of speaking to Renshaw about it. But it was surely none of her business.

Renshaw himself was tired of the affair. But he was too skilled to bring it to an abrupt conclusion. He had taken

Patty out once or twice since the night he had driven her to Barrington Terrace, and although the relationship had been intimate he had not broached the question of marriage.

To Patty the matter seemed settled. Renshaw had said they would be married, and in the Dyehouse it was now accepted that she was Renshaw's girl.

She ran happily round the presses, picking up the tickets, twitching her skirts and smiling at the single men.

'Saw you over at the park,' Oliver Henery said.

He was pushing a load of wet cloth from the mangles to the dryer. He was stripped down to his shorts and wore a pair of rubber boots. He had a string of crimson swami tied round his head.

Patty looked at him thoughtfully.

Wisps of damp hair protruded from the rough bandeau on his head. His brows, arched and dark, gave his face a satanic look that was offset by a crooked, humorous smile.

'I must say,' he said, 'you seemed to be enjoying it.'

His smile was knowing without being malicious.

'Must see you some time.'

He leaned on the truck, smiling at her.

'I don't know what you mean,' Patty said.

But she turned quickly, stepping daintily over the pools of water, and headed back to the office. She could hear Oliver's jeering laugh as she crossed the warehouse.

It was a fortnight now since Renshaw had taken her out. In the office he was friendly, and in the lab where she had encountered him alone he had lifted her up and kissed her with some passion, but had returned immediately to his reading of the *Dyers' Journal* that her entry had interrupted.

71

But on Friday, after the pays were given out, Renshaw looked in at the office. He's going to take me out, Patty thought. He's going to ask me.

She sat at her desk tidying up her papers, putting books into shelves, stacking cards into neat heaps.

He was joking with Miss Merton. Telling her some funny story about two men and a car. It was a very decent story. He was laughing and looking pleasant. Patty stole a quick glance at him, but he was engrossed in his conversation.

There were ten minutes to go. Patty polished her nails on her skirt, waiting for him to finish talking.

They were going to alter the set-up in the office and put in a new machine.

Suddenly Renshaw looked up. He saw Patty sitting quietly at her desk.

His glance was cool and friendly.

'No need for you to wait, Patty,' he said. 'You cut along.'

She rose slowly, gathering up her bag.

He would stop her on the way out. He would say, I'll pick you up at 7.30, corner of the Parade. He would say, There's a good show on tonight at West's; or, What about that grassy spot near the oval? He would say, That ring— I've bought it for you, Patty.

But he only nodded as she went out through the vestibule to the front door.

Tommy Sanders was polishing up his dilapidated jalopy, and someone had painted a sign, 'The Love Nest', on its back. Girls were clattering past from Graham's factory. Girls in pink frocks, spotty frocks, gay frocks in flowered patterns; girls in high-heeled shoes, old run-over hand-me-downs, slippers or sandals.

They were all going somewhere. Maybe to West's. Maybe to the park. Someone was going out in Tommy's jalopy. Somewhere a girl was parting her hair, shaking out her frock, thinking of Tommy.

On this lovely evening everyone was going out with someone. Patty smiled wanly.

After the door closed she stood for a long time thinking. She had waited eagerly all day for Renshaw. Listening for his step in the warehouse, waiting for the door to open, hoping to hear his voice. Now she stood on the step outside the Dyehouse, trying not to cry, watching Tommy through blurred eyes as he worked on his jalopy.

The trains were coming through from the city. It was peak time. She could see the loaded carriages as the trains flashed past. She tried to think about them. About the strange people passing so swiftly, rushing past the Parade, scarcely taking it in. They were all wrapped up in their own problems. Thinking about the weekend fun. The girls they would take out, the boys they would meet, the games they would go to, the surf and the sand.

'Want a lift?' Tommy called across to her. He had finished with the jalopy. He was revving it up, trying it out.

She shook her head.

He backed, then turned. Patty watched as the car disappeared up the Parade.

Then she started to walk slowly. It was a fortnight.

Last weekend he said he was going to be busy. The new range was coming up. He'd be tied up over the weekend working on it. Patty hadn't minded last weekend. The work was urgent, and it seemed right.

But tonight.

She put the thought far away.

Oliver Henery was standing on the edge of the pavement when she turned the corner. He was singing, loud enough for her to hear. It was a bawdy number to which some promising Dyehouse balladist had added a few apt verses.

He fell in beside Patty, still humming to himself.

He didn't really like her. She looked cheap enough with all that blonde mess of hair on her shoulders and the powder streaky on her face. She looked as though she had been blubbering.

Blonde and dumb. Not even smart enough to recognize the skids when she was on them.

She had her top teeth caught over her lower lip, holding it tight, as though she were trying to stop the sobs from leaping out. She didn't look pretty. Her lipstick was smudged and it gave her mouth a grotesque, lopsided look. Oliver stopped singing. He stifled the wisecrack that was almost on his lips. He went as far as he was able to comfort her.

'You want to wake up, baby. Blokes are always after what they can get. You don't want to make it so easy. When you find yourself looking with an easy eye on some bloke, you want to make sure you've got your pants on. It's just plain stupid to come across to the boss.'

She let go her lip. She put her hands up, straightened her hair, and wiped her mouth with her handkerchief.

So Oliver knew about it. Perhaps they all knew about it.

They walked along in silence. The lights were coming on in the terraces. The youngsters were gathering up the boxes from the centre of the street where they had been playing cricket. A small mongrel dog crept out of a lane and began following them. Oliver bent down and patted it. It wagged its tail, opened its eyes. It put out its tongue, slobbering over his boots.

'Poor little bastard,' Oliver said. 'Bet it hasn't had a feed in months.'

The dog recognized the friendly tone and continued following them.

'You like dogs?' Oliver asked.

For the first time Patty laughed, and Oliver was surprised at how nice she looked.

'Don't know,' she said. 'I don't think we ever had enough over to keep a dog.'

In a house across the street a wireless was on loud. Someone was singing a sentimental ditty. A sailor passed with his arm around a girl. She had her hat off and her head was nestled close to his shoulder. Every so often they stopped. The sailor was kissing her to some purpose.

Oliver turned and walked back towards the terrace in which Patty lived. The dog was still following.

'You going to keep him?' Patty asked.

'Maybe.'

'You like dogs?'

'Some dogs.'

'You like this dog?'

'I like all homeless down-at-heel bastards. I like no-hopers, and blokes that always get it in the guts. I like this dog.'

Oliver began to whistle.

They were walking past the semi-detached cottages with the little garden strips. They were almost to the terraces with their overhanging balconies and doors with blistered woodwork and steps incongruously gleaming with black paving paint.

'How you come to work in this dump?' Oliver asked. He gestured with his thumb at the Dyehouse chimney-stack that dominated the landscape.

'I wanted a job,' Patty said. 'Jobs aren't that easy to come by.'

'Could a' done better,' Oliver said.

'I got a mother,' Patty said. 'Hasn't walked about in years. Haven't got that much time to be choosy.'

'Hard-luck story,' Oliver said. 'What did you reckon you were going to get out of Renshaw? You're too easy. The dames that make the grade with Renshaw keep their pants up.'

'You're cheeky, aren't you?' Patty said. 'You're bloody smart. You want to watch out. You'll fall over the gutter one of these days.'

Patty stood staring up at him. They were almost to the door. Oliver was swinging a string in circles. He was watching it.

'I suppose,' Patty said, 'that you haven't got a girl.'

Oliver shook his head. He was watching the string, but he started to smile.

'You're so right, sister.'

'That's pretty queer,' Patty said. 'Haven't you ever had a girl?'

Oliver stopped playing with the string. His face was a leer.

'I had my share,' he said, 'if that's what you mean. I've had a stomachful of them. You start taking out some little sheila, and the next thing you know she's got a mortgage on your future. Head down and arse up for the rest of your days.'

Patty was silent. She was thinking of Renshaw again.

'I don't mind a bit on the sideline,' Oliver said. 'But I'm not in the ball-and-chain stakes. I wouldn't knock anything back if it was offered to me.'

He put his hand out and squeezed Patty, but let her go quickly.

'I don't know why I waste my time with you,' Patty said.

'You weren't, for instance,' Oliver said, 'thinking of handing out a few favours tonight? But no, I can see the answer in your cold blue eye.'

He bent down and patted the puppy.

'You're a bit of a heel,' Patty said. 'A no-hoping good-for-nothing. Why, I wouldn't have you...'

'Don't run out of words,' Oliver said, 'they sound so nice. Don't you know when you're having your leg pulled?'

'Just the same,' Patty said, 'I wouldn't like to trust you.'

With the key in her hand she hesitated.

Now that Oliver had stopped speaking, the thought of Renshaw returned.

It would be Monday before she could hope to see him again. Friday night, the long Saturday, Sunday stretched before her. It was not that she distrusted him. Oliver didn't really know about her and Renshaw. He didn't know about their secret pact. But the weekend seemed interminable. Oliver had turned away when she called to him.

'Well?' he asked.

He was sick of her. He'd helped her out, stopped her blubbering, taken her home. He felt hungry and the dog was whimpering.

Patty hesitated. His friendliness seemed gone.

'I thought we might go out,' Patty said. 'Go out somewhere.'

'You thought we might go out?' Oliver said. 'Well listen, sister, you better think again. Haven't I told you? I've had a bellyful of dames, exactly as I said. Besides, I got to walk a dog for a bloke tonight.'

He came back and looked down at her.

'What's eating you, Patty? You're all tied in knots over Renshaw, and now you're trying to date me. What's wrong?'

'I don't know,' Patty said. She was crying again. She turned and put her face against the wall, her misery overflowing.

'Break it up,' Oliver said gruffly. 'I can't take you out, Patty. I got obligations. I don't want women nosing in.'

Patty turned around.

There was a light in the room behind them. Against the lighted window she could see Oliver's dark face, the black straight hair, the pointed brows, the wide mouth twisted into a perplexed scowl.

She wiped her nose and dabbed her eyes.

'You look a mess,' Oliver said. 'All that stuff smeared across your face and your nose red from crying. I can't take you out. You better try and pull yourself together.'

Suddenly he bent over. He pushed her nose with his forefinger. 'If you wash that black stuff out of your eyes, and about half that paint off your face, I might think about seeing you Sunday. Early in the morning.'

'Early Sunday?'

'Yeah,' Oliver said. He was grinning again. 'And you'd better bring your togs along. You can prepare yourself for a bit of strenuous exercise at that. You'll work so hard you'll forget you ever knew Renshaw.'

Patty laughed. It sounded suddenly gay and spontaneous.

'You wouldn't believe it,' Oliver said. 'Little girl looks pleased.'

Patty turned and put the key into the lock.

'Eight o'clock, Macdonaldtown station.'

He bent over and touched her under the tail. When she looked up he was halfway down the street. The dog was still at his heels. She could hear him whistling.

It was the obscene tune that he had been singing when she met him at the corner.

CHAPTER FIFTEEN

Sunday was leisurely at Macdonaldtown.

Most families slept late after the week's work and Saturday's exertion. In some of the houses people were bustling about, brushing their best clothes, getting ready for church. But mostly Macdonaldtown slept late.

Patty woke well before seven. The day looked fine and she pushed out onto the overhanging balcony to look up at the sky. Between the tops of the tall terraces she could see the blue. Even at this hour it was intense and sparkling.

She began cutting up slices of bread, not too thin, and spreading them with butter. It was cheaper to take something for lunch, and fun to eat picnic style.

It was getting on for eight when she kissed her mother and picked up her basket.

She went quietly down stairs. Mrs Webb was still in bed, the checked brown rug drawn up around her shoulders.

She raised herself on one elbow and looked suspiciously at Patty.

'You're stirring yourself early, aren't you?' she said.

'I'm going out,' Patty said happily. 'I'm going to spend the day at the beach.'

'Oh.' Mrs Webb looked at her from the comfort of her bed. 'I suppose in a sense you might say that a man's taking you out.'

'I suppose you might,' Patty said.

She walked across the room to the front door.

'Well, don't you be bringing any of those blackguards into my house. Now, I'm warning you.'

'Oh, no, Mrs Webb,' Patty said hastily. 'I never bring any men into the house.'

Mrs Webb fell back onto her pillow.

Patty opened the door and stepped into the street. Everything was clean and bright. The sun was well up and the tree outside the terrace looked green and fresh. She turned the corner and hurried up the Parade. People were passing on their way back from early Mass.

She glanced at the chimney-stack. No smoke issued from it. It looked dark against the clear morning sky. Boys were running down the street with bundles of papers under their arms. People back from church stood leisurely chatting.

Patty called across happily to a knot of people talking over a fence.

'Going out?'

Patty swung her basket and laughed. It sounded young and happy.

Suddenly the church bells began to peal. Pigeons, startled, shot up into the sky. Patty watched them as they circled. They had become a nuisance in the district and people were always complaining about them. But to Patty, hurrying along to the station, they seemed an omen of good luck. She would see Renshaw on Monday. The experiments on the colour swatches were over and, although the orders coming through were heavy, Patty knew the work from now on would be routine.

Everything was going to be all right. The very air seemed different today. The smoke haze had lifted from the railway-yards and the sky looked blue.

As she neared the station she stopped. She didn't want to be early, to be standing around waiting for Oliver to come. And then a sobering thought struck her. Supposing he didn't come?

She began to walk slowly, counting her steps between the electric-light poles. She followed the curve of the street.

There was a clock on the counter of the corner shop. She stopped. The blind was still up, showing a miscellaneous collection of sweets, fruit and wilted vegetables. There was a small glass case containing cottons, needles, silk and wool for darning. The grocery section was hidden by dark plywood shutters.

The clock was still going, ticking away the time in the empty shop. The hands said eight o'clock.

Patty turned cautiously and looked over to the railway station. Oliver was lounging against the corner post, reading the Sunday news.

'Hullo,' Patty said. She felt shy now and waited for him to speak.

He rolled up the paper, hit the post two or three times with it. He looked Patty over critically.

'You'll do,' he said. 'Or almost.'

He looked at her slyly. 'What makes you think you look better when you've got all that black stuff round your eyes?'

'You think it looks better without it?' Patty asked doubtfully.

'Don't ask me, sister,' Oliver said. 'All dames look alike to me. But I can give you the drum on this—I've never met one with two noses yet. But if it comforts you—yes, you do look nicer without it.'

They began walking up the steps.

'The tickets,' Patty said. 'I ought to get my own.'

She began pulling things out of her bag.

'So you ought to. I ought to make you pay for me, too. But just for once we'll say that it's paid.'

'Oh, but,' Patty protested. 'I asked you to take me. I ought to pay my share.'

'We're going to have a good day, if you'll stop squealing and carrying on so much. And you're going to work hard. Surf. Play on the sand. And no sentimental interludes or lying off on the quiet parts near the rocks.'

'Why,' Patty said, 'who'd want to lie off with you? You make me sick. You're pretty fond of yourself, aren't you?'

They stood looking at each other. Patty pressed her skirt down over her hips with her fingers. She could feel the smooth curve of her body under the skirt; the little bony

83

peak of her hip and the smooth line of her thigh. Oliver watched her quizzically.

They found a seat on the train close to the window and sat down. The train gathered speed.

Past Redfern, where they changed, the cottages with their little squares of gardens flashed past. The backs of the houses faced the railway lines. The sun beat on the sloping roofs of rust-marked corrugated iron, slates or grimy tile. Between the paling fences rose a medley of clotheslines. Choko vines screened verandahs and outhouses with their cool green. Pumpkins were ripening on the tops of skillion roofs, their green skins flecked with yellow and orange.

Patty sat watching the houses, the yards, the plots ablaze with colour, the empty unkempt spaces. The water in Cook's River ran slow and sluggish.

'Look,' Patty said. 'The little island!'

Seagulls were resting on the water, or walking about on the filling that was being dumped to alter the course of the river.

At the end of the carriage a portable gramophone was competing with a wireless. A young couple stood in the aisle, beating time to the music. Every so often the girl would whirl round, fanning out her skirt. The boy grabbed her, holding her by the wrists. He seemed to be hurting her. Then they sat down together, laughing. The girl turned the gramophone off and they sat with their heads together.

In the older suburbs, modern factories and ancient cottages were cheek-by-jowl. Then gradually the train began to climb. The factories slid back and neat suburban cottages took their place. Far away, Patty could see the sweep of Botany Bay.

'What's that?' she asked.

The shapes rose from the sand. They looked almost to be floating in the distance. Oliver followed the direction of her finger.

'The refinery.'

The train plunged into a cutting. The rocks were dark and damp, ferns trailed from crevices. Then they were out in the open with the pungent smell of gumleaves, sunlight sliding off their pointed tips.

'We're coming to the bridge,' Oliver said. 'We're almost to Como.'

He stood up to show her the oyster farms, but the tide was high and none were visible. Little boats were bobbing about on the water and men were walking about the boatsheds.

'Just over the bank,' Oliver said, 'there's a funny little pub.'

Patty craned her neck.

'And those tall trees,' Oliver said. 'They're those blue ones. Like they have at Grafton.'

They ran past the little picket fence. Then they were struggling up the cutting. New houses were showing through virgin bush. 'Barney Monahan lives through there,' Oliver said. He pointed to a distant belt of timber. Beyond, the bushland of National Park stretched to the horizon.

Patty leant back, thinking of Oliver. She slid a little until her shoulder touched his arm. He looked down at her, smiling. Then he put his arm around her. It was a brief, impersonal hug and he let her go almost immediately.

'Not far,' Oliver said.

The train pulled into Cronulla.

'I think we'll make over to the north side,' Oliver said.

He took her hand and began to run.

The breeze came fresh from the sea.

It's going to be lovely, Patty thought. I'm going to like it today.

Oliver stopped and looked at her. Then they were off again, with the soft breeze in their faces. And suddenly they turned the corner, and there was 'north', blue and sparkling in the sunlight.

'I'll have to change,' Patty said.

As she pulled on the black one-piece, several seasons old, she smiled to herself. Oliver would like this costume. She smoothed down her bust and hips. Then she slipped off her shoes, picked up her towel and basket, and was ready.

Oliver, lounging near a tree, saw her coming. She looked slim and shapely in the black costume. Her fair, honey-coloured skin glowed.

'Well?' Patty asked. She met Oliver's amused, challenging glance.

'You'll do. You look good. All but that messy hair. What're you going to do about it?'

Patty took a ribbon from her basket. She hesitated. She liked her hair loose and hanging about her shoulders. But she drew it back from her face, twisted it into a rough bun, and tied it up with a ribbon.

'I'll have my bathing cap over it,' she said apologetically to Oliver. She looked up, smiling into his eyes.

'A man ought to fix you up, sister,' he said.

He spread out his towel and sat down, hunching up his knees, and looking out to sea.

'You don't like me, do you?' Patty said.

It was a statement rather than a question.

'I don't like you when you act dumb. You've got some brains, and you weren't behind the door when looks were given out. Some blokes like them dumb. Me? I like them to think a bit.'

He got up and Patty followed him slowly.

He raced out to the water. The wave curled and he dived under it. He came up splashing and laughing. He grabbed Patty and the next wave went over them.

The water was warm, but the surf was flat.

'Warming up?' he asked.

He was smiling. She moved in under his arm.

It was getting late when they walked back along the beach to the dressing sheds. Patty took off her cap and stood shaking out her hair, drying it in the sun. Oliver was walking ahead, swinging his towel about.

It was the last of the surfing season, and autumn was just around the corner. Patty sighed. Despite the warm, still afternoon, the bright crowd and the sea, she felt sad.

He doesn't care whether I'm here or not, she thought.

'Wait on,' she called to him. 'Wait on, Oliver.'

She was standing under a pine, looking out to the sea.

He put down his towel impatiently, then picked it up and walked slowly back to her.

'There's a little boat out there,' she said uncertainly.

On the edge of the horizon he could see the boat, little more than a moving speck.

He sat down suddenly, and Patty sat beside him. She combed down her hair then flung it over her shoulder. She etched in her mouth with vermilion.

Oliver watched her. He was conscious of the sea, the warm summer breeze, the oversweet smell of her powder.

She edged over until she was lying close to him. The sunlight drifted down through the branches, making patterns on her legs and arms. Suddenly he bent over, spreading out her hair. Then he put his arm round her and dragged her over close to him. His eyes were half closed.

'What do you want, Patty?'

He pulled her close to him, holding her, looking deep into her eyes. Just for a moment Patty felt his arm tighten around her and she closed her eyes. She thought momentarily of Renshaw and his urgent, savage embraces, of the park and the dark shadow of the trees.

She put her hands onto Oliver's chest.

'I wanted us to be friends,' she said.

She sat up feeling confused. Oliver slid over in the grass.

Now that she was out of his arms, sitting a little apart, she felt shaken. Oliver lay stretched out. She could see the back of his head, the way his hair came down onto the nape of his neck, the smooth ripple of the muscle in his arm.

'Nice,' Oliver said. 'If there's anything I like in a dame, it's warm, friendly gestures.'

Patty said nothing. She felt angry. Mostly because she

had liked the way his arm had tightened around her, and the sudden warm impact of his body. She sat quietly looking at the back of his head, thinking.

He turned over suddenly.

'How are things with you and Renshaw?' he said.

Patty tossed her head.

'Things are just OK.'

'Reckon he's going to marry you?'

Patty moistened her lips. She could hear the pounding of the surf on the shore, the cries of the children, and the sudden thudding of her heart.

Oliver was sitting up, looking at her.

'D'yer think he's going to marry you?'

Now she began to laugh.

'You've got a nerve,' she said.

Oliver laughed. He got up easily. He looked friendly and happy.

'I don't know,' he said. 'A little more of that high-pressure stuff of yours, Patty, and we might have been sharing favours.'

It was dark when the train pulled into Macdonald-town. The lights were on in the terraces. Part of the way home Patty had slept, leaning heavily against Oliver's arm. She walked happily along the Parade. Oliver was walking casually. He was talking about the dogs, the horses, the trots. She was thinking of Renshaw. This was Sunday, and tomorrow she would see him, and everything would be right again.

They were home.

'It was nice of you to take me,' Patty said.

'Yes,' Oliver said. 'Remind me to show you how nice it can be, some time.'

He leaned close to her.

'Don't forget, Patty,' he said.

'You spoil everything,' Patty said. 'Why, today...' She paused, looking up into his eyes, remembering the warmth of his body, the sudden tightening of his arm.

She opened the door and slammed it quickly. She could hear Oliver's laugh, and then his footsteps, going down the Parade.

CHAPTER SIXTEEN

At first Hughie did not mention to anyone that he was out of the lab. He said that he was having young Collins sent to Tech, and to all appearances it was as though he had arranged the whole thing himself. Indeed, Renshaw was not altogether opposed to Hughie looking in at the lab occasionally, for he had broken his grip on the dye-mixing, which was the main objective.

But little by little the news leaked out. Someone got to know about the roll of cloth.

'Can't understand you,' Oliver Henery said. 'Why would you want to take the rap for that? God strewth, you've worked all your life in the place, and the only thing you really like is that dyein' job. I'd have a go at that bastard. He'd see reason or he'd be buying a new set of teeth.'

Hughie scarcely knew why he kept the matter to himself. He was playing for time, and most of all he was deciding what he would say to Alice about it. He knew that Renshaw had moved too swiftly for him to follow, and he cast about in his mind for a way in which he might resolve the situation.

Renshaw had gone out of his way to be friendly.

'You're getting on a bit, Hughie,' he said. 'And there's too much work here for one man. The truth is we've needed a chemist in the lab for a long time. These new textiles are touchy.'

He patted Hughie on the arm and went off whistling.

Of course the textiles were touchy, especially the synthetics. Hughie had worked long and stubbornly on the early experiments.

He wondered whether the new youngsters being trained up would ever feel the way he felt about the colours.

Standing by on the vats, watching the instrument panel, with the mists thick and grey, he thought of the thirty-odd years he had put in at Macdonaldtown. He had liked his job, and in that he was lucky. He had no dreams of advancement to higher positions. To him work was the cloth, the understanding that seemed to be in his fingertips when he started on the swatches.

This had given purpose and dignity to his labour, had compensated for the years of walking around the vats, for the lifetime spent in the shadows of the Dyehouse.

None of this he conveyed to Oliver. Oliver was not a dye man. He would not understand. He was an itinerant, a drifter. He moved about from factory to factory, seeking out the better-paid jobs when things were good. When jobs were hard to get a place like the Dyehouse tided him over until things brightened up in the heavier industries.

'But I notice you do your share,' Hughie said one day after one of Oliver's speeches.

'Sure I do. And you know why? A man's got to weave a bit of interest round anything he does or he'd go nuts. But I hope I never get it so bad that when the day comes for the boss to kick me in the guts I take it lying down. Anyway, there's always the Murrumbidgee and the swag.'

Hughie laughed. It was all right for Oliver. He had no ties. No wife. No child. No home to consider. Oliver hadn't built a life about the Dyehouse. There were lots of things for Hughie to consider. There was Alice. Not, of course, that Alice would fuss. He had always come first with her.

In his mind's eye he saw her smiling.

'Hughie?—why, yes. He's in charge of the lab now, you know.' Her pride in him was obvious and abundant.

It seemed monstrous that this little assurance, this little dignity that had helped him carve a niche in the small society in which he moved, should so ruthlessly be swept away.

'The trouble with you, Hughie,' Oliver said, 'is this. You've got too much faith in people doing the right thing. Especially bosses. You want to wake up to yourself. You don't want to be a fall man for Renshaw all your life.'

Hughie knew that Oliver was right. He had had the ball at his feet; but he had leaned over backwards helping Renshaw, and the ball had been taken from him. There was a time when his was the only know-how at Macdonaldtown. Surely, the first time Renshaw came into the lab poking about and asking questions, he should have acted as any other dyer would have done. He should have been polite, but told him nothing. When he began meddling he should have stood pat. But he had acted the part of a pleased little puppy, and now Renshaw had Collins in the lab, and he was standing by, watching the cloth turn in the dye vats.

Nor did this altogether spare him the lash of Renshaw's tongue. When things went wrong, it seemed that the blunders moved from the lab to the vats. Often the dye-mixing was wrong, and Hughie knew it. But none the less Renshaw maintained that the cloth was spoilt in the vats. He was too old to get out now, and besides the demand was for qualified men. He had grown up in the dyeing game, had started when there were two vats and old Tommy Peters had been in charge. Tommy had trained him. He had not been a theory man, and Hughie had followed in his footsteps. In the early days it had been a joy to work with Peters. He knew now that Peters had had the same love of colour, the same feel for it that he had. There were better jobs, easier jobs, healthier jobs. But this job, this changing of the grey, uninteresting cloth into rich jewel colours was his job. It was the work he loved.

When Tommy Peters died, not such an old man really, Hughie had moved up. The lab had been enlarged. A qualified engineer took over the care of the machinery and new vats were bought. There were twelve of them now, although No. 1 and No. 2 were not used as frequently as they used to be. Telephones were installed between the boiler-house and the laboratory. A simple call to the fireman would indicate that steam was needed on extra vats. The indicators were put up on the instrument panel in front of the vats. Not that Hughie altogether trusted them. He had opposed the idea of them going in. But he had to admit now that they worked out better than he had expected.

The engineer was a good man on his job and as time went on Hughie got to like and trust him. Mayers had a feeling for machinery, for making things. It was just the same thing that Hughie felt about the dyeing.

One afternoon Hughie came across young Ross Sims preparing cloth for a restrip. There were no restrips on roster for that afternoon.

'What're you up to?' Hughie asked. 'That rose swami's going on number four.'

'Well, Renshaw says this restrip's going on.'

Hughie stood looking at Ross. The youngster dropped his eyes. He didn't tell Hughie exactly what Renshaw had said.

It wasn't the first time Renshaw had countermanded an instruction. In fact, lately he had taken to giving instructions to young Sims or to Tom Gregory, by-passing him altogether.

If he failed to act now, he would probably end up loading the vats, with one of the youngsters in charge.

He stood up slowly. He was trembling.

It was no use talking to Sims or Gregory. They were not to blame. He walked slowly up from the vats, past the dryer to Renshaw's office. He stood with his heart pounding a little against his ribs, waiting for his breath to come easily.

He didn't think too clearly and he was no good at talking.

When he went in Renshaw was leaning back in his chair, studying a new formula. His eyes narrowed and his face hardened when he saw Hughie. Hughie looked at Renshaw. He knew he should be at him, telling him what he thought of him. Putting a case for himself that even Renshaw couldn't wriggle out of. Instead he stood smiling weakly.

'Well?' Renshaw said.

'It's that vat,' Hughie said. 'The rose swami for number four.'

'That's right,' Renshaw said.

Something cold inside Hughie said: Now. Say it now. Or just hit him while he's sitting there smiling.

But he didn't say it. He put his hand on the edge of the desk. He leant over.

'But I'm in charge of the dye vats,' Hughie said. 'You ought of told me.'

It was quiet in the office. Renshaw looked at Hughie and smiled. He looked at him for a long time.

'That seems reasonable, Hughie,' he said. 'I should have told you. The fact is, there's big changes on the way. Big shake-up. Big staff reshuffle. The whole fact is, Hughie, we're beginning to think in terms of giving the younger men a bit of a go. There's nothing final yet,' Renshaw said. 'I've been trying out young Sims.'

'But I'm only fifty,' Hughie said. 'I'm younger than Larcombe. And I'm used to the men.'

Renshaw shook his head. He looked sad, though there was a glint in his eyes. He liked to see Hughie squirm.

'I'll see Larcombe,' Hughie said. 'You couldn't do this to a man. I've given my life to this company.'

Renshaw laughed.

'I've always given you a go,' Hughie said.

It was the wrong line. With Renshaw you hit and hit hard. It was you or him. You didn't plead. It was no good reminding Renshaw of what you had done.

Nevertheless, Renshaw was not anxious for the matter to go to Larcombe. Not yet. He was playing around with Hughie, and when the time was ripe, after he had prepared the ground and soaped Larcombe up, he would act. In the meantime he would watch Hughie squirm.

In such a short time, how the tables had turned! Hughie had been in charge of the dyeing, and with just a bit more effort, a bit more inside, he might have been in the manager's job today. Now he was out, walking about the vats, pleading that his authority be upheld.

'Nothing to worry about,' Renshaw said. 'Not likely to come to anything at all. Anyway, I made a bit of a bloomer over Sims. I think I'll put him over the two old vats and number three. That'll give you the main jobs and it's plenty.'

He patted Hughie on the shoulder.

He stood up and walked around his desk. The two men stood facing each other. Hughie, the smaller, had the pale skin of the man whose days were spent in damp air, remote from the sunshine. His mouth was generous, bordering on the weak, his eyes dark and dreamy. Renshaw was tall and arrogant with strange, withdrawn eyes and a harsh, close mouth. The men looked at each other. And Hughie, at least, looked at himself.

Each man measured the other with his eyes, and looking at Renshaw Hughie saw that the day for bargaining was over. It was over a long time ago, but Hughie had been slow to notice things. Sims was coming up and he was a good lad. Soon there would be no one left who could remember the day that Renshaw had pushed open the door for the first time. The day he had come to take over from Ron James. The skids had been under James for a long time, before they were really put into motion. Looking at Renshaw, Hughie remembered this.

Renshaw had won that clash. Larcombe had driven over post-haste in a taxi, because his own car was at the garage and the situation was too tense to let it simmer any longer. The three men had talked for a long time in the closed office. People passing heard the raised voices and the angry rejoinders. Then Larcombe came out of the office. He shook hands with Ron James. He slapped him on the shoulder, and kept saying he wished him the best of luck. Renshaw had slipped quietly out.

The following day James was not in. A week passed, and when Hughie asked Renshaw about it he only laughed.

'Resigned,' Renshaw said. 'The pace was a killer.'

'Blokes are saying he was pushed out,' Hughie said. 'That he was sacked at the minute.'

'Blokes always know more than there is to know,' Renshaw said. 'This bloke had it easy. Things were due to change. He should have seen it.'

'He was pretty smart,' Hughie said. 'Good with colour.'

Renshaw turned his cold eyes onto Hughie.

'Did pretty well at chemistry and physics myself,' he said. 'There's not that much to this dyeing game.'

He got up and looked at Hughie.

'If there's one important lesson that's got to be learned it's this, Hughie. In the business world, no one's indispensable.'

'I know,' Hughie said. 'Blokes leave places, and you'd wonder how things could ever go on. But they seem to. A week ago you couldn't imagine Macdonaldtown without Ron James. Now I suppose things will still go on.'

'You're sorry to see him go?' Renshaw asked casually.

'Oh, well,' Hughie said. 'He was a good bloke to work with. And he was a friend of mine in a way.'

Renshaw turned and looked at him suddenly. It was rarely that Renshaw really looked at you. Hughie, looking into the cold, steely eyes, had shivered.

Now, standing in the office with the things he wanted to say unsaid, Hughie remembered the discussion about Ron James.

There was no need for the words he had planned to say. Renshaw had cut the ground from under his feet. The writing was on the wall. Changes were on the way. Soon Collins and Sims would take over the dyeing. He would potter about on the vats, still at the same money until one day Cuthbert would ring up and say, 'If Collins is in the lab, and Sims is over the vats, what's Hughie drawing his extra money for?'

Hughie saw it clearly.

And gradually his pay would go down. He'd start loading vats and taking a turn on the hydro and mangle, and in a little while he'd be back where he started, telling blokes about the days when he used to be in charge of the dyeing.

When Hughie returned to the vats, Sims had the restrip under way. He stood and watched him. Sims handled the cloth well and he was young and strong. He was standing by the vats, whistling. No doubt Renshaw had talked to him off the record, told him which way the wind was blowing. He had been primed up, and if he played his cards right he would take the reins out of Hughie's hands.

It was four o'clock.

There was no official afternoon-tea break, but Hughie picked up a billycan and went through to the machine shop.

Mr Mayers and Tommy were bending over a lathe. Hughie went over to them. Mayers wiped his face with his handkerchief. The cut was almost through.

'You look peaked,' Mayers said. 'You're taking it too seriously.'

Hughie put down his pannikin of hot tea. He looked at Mayers' honest face. In it was a combination of shrewdness and kindliness.

'You know anything, Bob?' Hughie asked. 'I got a funny feeling. You know the way things started with James? Little things at first, and then almost overnight he was out? I feel it's getting to be my turn.'

'Never heard any talk,' Mayers said. But Renshaw was close with him, too. He wouldn't be likely to discuss plans for replacing Hughie with him.

'I ought to get out,' Hughie said. 'Renshaw's working on me now. You knew he'd pushed me out of the lab?'

'You were a bloody fool,' Mayers said. 'You told him too much.'

'I think he's really going to make me eat dirt,' Hughie said. 'I think he's going to put Sims in charge.'

He picked up his tea and drank it down.

'Well,' Mayers said. 'I wouldn't take that. I'd see Larcombe. There's plenty of good jobs you could take on, Hughie.'

'I like it here,' Hughie said. 'Before Renshaw came I used to get a kick out of working on the dyes. I used to like to go home and tell Alice about how I worked out a new colour. And old Mr Thompson used to stop and ask me questions about the lab. Thirty-five years is a lifetime. A man can't just change.'

'No,' Mayers said.

He glanced at the layout in the machine shop. His desk, his drawing board, the cylinders of oxygen and acetylene, the lathes, the racks for the raw materials, the containers for the screws, nuts and bolts.

He picked up his log-book. It was neatly kept. The day's records had been freshly entered up. Yes, he supposed he liked this work. He knew exactly how Hughie felt.

'I'd find it hard to get in anywhere,' Hughie said. 'All the ads seem to want blokes that have come up through the technical schools.'

'I don't know. Most of these little dyehouses have unqualified men, and some of the big ones too. The game's really in its infancy as far as that's concerned, Hughie.'

'I don't know what to do,' Hughie said. 'I think I should go before I'm pushed out.'

'I'd wait,' Mayers said. 'Things have a habit of straightening out. I think I'd hang on a bit and see what happens.'

*

But things didn't improve for Hughie.

The best work went on No. 3; the special work and the show cloth. Sometimes Renshaw commandeered No. 4 and No. 5 and handed them over to Sims. Renshaw gave orders direct to Sims, just as he gave them to Hughie. Hughie no longer decided which work would be done, which vats used. Renshaw sent instructions straight to the laboratory. And on the 'Instruction to Dyers' sheets were instructions for the vats. The wools, the good elasticized cloth, were all under Sims' supervision. Hughie handled the cheap cloth, the routine cotton and the swami.

'I hope I never get so wrapped up in things as you, Hughie,' Oliver said. They were standing at the entrance to the vats.

'You never will,' Hughie said shortly.

He was worried and irritated. He had not been sleeping well, and had not yet discussed the problem with Alice. But any day now it must come up, and it was better to come from him than from a neighbour. Any day, anyone calling in for a talk with Alice might mention it casually.

Not once but often, at night, Hughie reviewed the situation. Between waking and sleeping, he thought of what he should do, how he should act, what he should say to Renshaw.

Alice, disturbed by his constant turning, by the perspiration pouring from his body, would sit up to ask, 'You feeling all right, Hughie?' He was feeling all right. The light would go out, and he was back in the soft darkness, turning over what he should do.

'I get no chance of seeing Larcombe,' Hughie said to Oliver. 'Renshaw makes sure of that. And anyway Larcombe doesn't like it. Not the right spirit.'

'Quaint,' Oliver said ironically. 'These abstract feelings take the bloody bun. Supersensitive. Never seem to flinch from seeing a man ploughing through this slush like a bloody animal. You'd wonder what makes them tick.'

'I think I'll have a final go at Renshaw,' Hughie said.

Oliver looked at him. His face was white and pinched, his eyes were dark and feverish from lack of sleep.

Poor bastard, Oliver thought. Poor bloody bastard.

'If the answer's the wrong one, clock him,' he said. 'Go for his belly and bring out his tongue.'

Hughie smiled fleetingly.

'Not the spirit, eh? Not quite the thing. How much of this spirit is there when it's applied to us?'

Renshaw's door was open. Hughie could hear voices, Renshaw's and Larcombe's. Pulling himself together, he pushed open the door, and before Renshaw could act he was inside. He felt light-headed and dizzy, as though he were suddenly far removed and was looking into the room from a distance.

He walked up to the desk. He leaned upon it because he felt weak and unsteady.

But his mind was clear. Clearer than he ever remembered it. He saw the fleeting alarm on Renshaw's face and the astonishment on Larcombe's. He noticed Larcombe's hat on the table, the way his hair kept kicking up at the side, the bald patch that he was endeavouring to hide, the sprinkling of grey hairs round his temples.

'What do you want?' Renshaw asked.

'I want to know about me,' Hughie said. 'I want to know where I stand, and I want to know now.'

He thrust out his chin and looked at Renshaw.

'But surely,' Larcombe said. 'Some other time, Hughie. We've got a big decision to make within the hour.'

Larcombe fiddled with a pencil. He sounded petulant and impatient. 'All lesser matters will have to wait, Hughie.'

Renshaw looked up and grinned. He looked relieved. And suddenly Hughie heard himself say, 'That's what you think. It's going to be decided here and now.'

Larcombe put down the pencil. He looked helpless. He turned to Renshaw.

'What's all this about?' he asked.

'Hughie hasn't settled down since I changed the set-up in the lab, and that's a fact.'

Larcombe looked at Hughie.

'Sometimes changes must be made,' he said, not unkindly. He was a weak man, but Renshaw wasn't able to fool him all the time.

'The firm expands. It grows up. New techniques become necessary. You've been a good servant to the Company, Hughie. We're not likely to forget it.'

'I been a long time in the lab,' Hughie said stubbornly. 'I don't mind Collins being trained up, but I think I should've been kept there too.'

Renshaw stood up quickly.

'We've been over all this before Hughie,' he said. 'Your record shows that we need a change. The Best-Yet wasn't the only cloth to be written off because of bad workmanship.'

'No,' Hughie said. He looked at Renshaw. He felt cold as though none of this conversation concerned him. 'I knew about the Best-Yet cloth and you know I did.'

'If you knew about it,' Larcombe said, 'why did you dye it? A lot of things depended on that roll being as near perfect as we could get it.'

'You gave the directions,' Hughie said to Renshaw. 'I only did as I was told.'

'I'm not going over it again,' Renshaw said. 'I don't want to go into the whys and wherefores of it. The plain fact is, I want a man with enough initiative to act when he knows an instruction is wrong.'

'You wanted me out of the lab,' Hughie said. 'You worked it. And now the vats. You've got Sims on the best work. I've given my life to this company. I need some consideration.'

'You want a rest,' Renshaw said. 'You've lost your grip of things. The work in the lab has picked up since you've been out, Hughie, and the cold fact is that Sims is making a better job of the nylon and the special cloth. The proof of the pudding's in the eating.'

'It's not that way,' Hughie said.

He leaned over suddenly and grabbed Renshaw by the tie.

'You worked it. Everything I did was always wrong. Even when you did the thing yourself it was my fault.'

Larcombe was on his feet. He looked alarmed.

'We want no violence, Hughie,' he said. 'Mr Renshaw has charge and he's in a position to judge these things.'

'You know you worked it,' Hughie shouted. 'You wanted to be the only one in the place with the know-how. Collins and Sims! It'll be a long time before they're trained up. And not too much of the real knowledge will be passed on to them. I know a thing or two, Renshaw—I'm not all that dumb. I sank my bloody all into this place. I let it suck me dry, and I asked little enough in return. Just to go on doing the things I love doing, the things I really know about.'

'All right, Hughie,' Larcombe said. 'Break it up. The decision's been made. We can't unmake a decision every time it upsets someone in the place.'

Renshaw was smiling. Hughie watched the smile. It spread until it almost reached his eyes. The last word had been said, and it was the skids. The writing was on the wall.

He straightened up suddenly. Renshaw was not expecting it. He was still smiling when Hughie hit him. He fell forward, grunting.

'Get up,' Hughie said. He pulled Renshaw by the collar, but he didn't stir. He was breathing heavily.

'You've knocked him out,' Larcombe said incredulously. 'He's out like a light.'

Hughie went quickly to the bookshelf. He gathered up his books. Larcombe was moving about uncertainly, undoing Renshaw's tie. Hughie got his books together. His mind was still clear; he took in every detail of the untidy office. He had known it for thirty-five years, and he would probably never see it again.

When he got to the door he looked back. Larcombe was still fussing over Renshaw. The Dyers' Instructions were piled on the table. The sample bottles of dyes were stacked in a neat heap. He would think of it thus.

All the way down the Parade the feeling of aloofness was with him. But when he turned the corner the thought of Alice came to him. It was too early to be home. He would go to the pub. He was not a drinking man, but tonight he felt the need of it. A good strong whisky and then another.

He could hear Stella the barmaid chatting in the ladies' parlour, and the laughter of the women. He took out a cigarette, tapped it on the packet and lit it.

'Finished early?' Tom Harris asked. Hughie picked up the whisky. He felt it trickling down his throat. He felt warm and confident.

'Yes,' he said.

Tomorrow he would talk about it to Tom. Tomorrow everyone on the Parade would be talking about it.

'Drink up,' he said to Tom.

It was getting late. Suddenly Hughie heard the hooter. The long, melancholy sound that had governed his life for so many years.

'Have to go,' he said to Tom. 'Wife waiting tea.'

He went out quickly. He was not anxious to meet any of the boys tonight. He must talk it over first with Alice. His steps flagged as he turned the corner of Ring Street.

CHAPTER SEVENTEEN

'He jobbed him,' Larcombe said in reply to Cuthbert's question. 'Right there in the office. Laid him out cold.'

'Might have had cause,' Cuthbert suggested.

Larcombe moved uneasily.

There could be cause, but he was not the man to want to investigate it. All he wanted was to get Renshaw back on his feet; to have him gathering up the Dyehouse reins, relieving him of pressure that he found almost insupportable.

'There's a man for every job,' Larcombe said, 'and Renshaw's the man for the Dyehouse. There's a few tough characters on deck out there.'

Cuthbert looked up from his papers. His glance was cold and probing.

'Would you call Hughie a tough character? He's never been in trouble in thirty-odd years. I tell you frankly, I don't like the taste of this.'

'He was truculent,' Larcombe said. 'Excited. Waving his arms about and shouting. He came in looking for fight.'

Cuthbert squinted along a line. He was adding figures and listening to Larcombe at the same time. He was a cold man. He loved and understood figures and what they stood for. He liked juggling with them. Estimating, calculating. People were figures. 69, Smith; 57, Jones; 84, Armstrong. He liked to use the numbers, to move them about like pieces on a chessboard. On a desk was a replica of the Macdonaldtown set-up. Cuthbert followed the movements of the numbers as they shifted from place to place. 69, Smith—four hours on the press, two on the mangle. 57, Jones—four hours on the mangle, two on the hydro. He moved the pieces on the chessboard.

He told himself that he was a just man. Hard, but just. No, not really hard. He thought of himself as firm, just, incorruptible. From this lofty altitude he interpreted the awards, and came to grips with the provisions covering employees' sickpay. He was not the man to favour friend or foe.

These were the rules; these the regulations; and these were the principles he lived by.

His universe was sparse, but ordered.

Hughie had been too long with the firm to be dismissed summarily. Even Miss Merton, writing up the Employees' Daily Attendance Record Sheet and the Staff Attendance Sheet, felt the need for guidance.

Renshaw had said angrily, 'Let it go. I'll speak to Cuthbert about it.'

But in the end it was Larcombe who approached

Cuthbert. The news was second-hand anyway. Cuthbert had heard it hours before via the grapevine.

Larcombe, sitting on the edge of Cuthbert's desk, felt uneasy and self-conscious. He felt that he should have handled the matter better, straightened it out before Hughie actually hit Renshaw. He felt that Cuthbert was judging him to be weak and a fool. But he continued to talk, making explanations and swinging his leg.

'There's a chair,' Cuthbert said shortly. It offended his sense of rightness that Larcombe should sit on the desk. Larcombe took the chair and sat down, suddenly quiet.

'What are you going to do?' he asked.

'Well,' Cuthbert said. 'He's a Staff man. There's his pay. There's extra money to be considered. How do you think he'll go for a new job?'

'No trouble,' Larcombe said. 'He's a pretty good man.'

'Thought he was through,' Cuthbert said. 'Washed up.'

'Oh!' Larcombe was tired of it. 'I can't have a chap that goes about clocking people, and anyway I might lose Renshaw.'

Cuthbert looked up.

'Don't like that fellow,' he said suddenly. 'Couldn't lay straight in bed.'

Larcombe watched him steadily. Cuthbert was not the man to like, or dislike, people.

'What do you mean?'

'Off the record,' he said, 'I've felt like taking a poke at him myself, many a time.'

He patted Larcombe on the shoulder, and steered him towards the door.

When Larcombe was gone he sat down. He glanced at the clock. He had wasted almost an hour with him. He began working steadily.

But he didn't settle down as he should have done. He had known Hughie for over twenty years himself. Not intimately; but then, how few men he knew intimately.

He was a quiet little man, this Hughie, puddling about with dyes and bottles, working contentedly for thirty-odd years in the damp laboratory. He remembered a winter's day when he had gone unexpectedly to Macdonaldtown. He had been appalled at the wet, cold atmosphere in which Hughie worked. He had thought, fleetingly, that something could be done to improve it. He would have something done. But the time passed and nothing came of it.

There was trouble in Shipping. Andrews came in. He had Advance Copies, Bill Copies, Costed Copies in his hand. He was talking about pillages, and waving Pink Goods Inwards about. He had Transfer Memos and Green Goods Outwards pinned together. Cuthbert put Hughie out of his mind. The mess had been building up in Shipping for some time.

He took up his pencil. Andrews was flapping about like a chook.

'No need for all this,' Cuthbert said. 'Give me the shipment numbers.'

He pencilled them neatly on his pad. He leant across to Miss Tombs. 'Get me Wilson and Turton on the line.'

Two ships had bonded and Shipping had slipped up on the Licence.

Andrews left the office. The telephone rang.

'You better come over,' Cuthbert said. He glanced at his watch. 'And get Turton down to the Customs House, quick-smart.'

CHAPTER EIGHTEEN

The room was bright, the cupboards newly painted, the china gay. The curtains were gingham in large red and white squares. There was a pottery bowl of paper roses and imitation fern leaves on top of the refrigerator.

Alice moved from the stove and closed the door, so that the smell of cooking food would not enter the little sitting-room. Hughie liked to sit in there after tea, reading the paper and gazing into the coal fire.

'Better get washed up,' Alice said.

Hughie walked out of the kitchen to the bathroom at the end of the verandah. Alice had laid out a clean shirt, underwear and socks. He put them on, still feeling the drink warm in him.

When he was dressed he came in and stood at the table with his hands on the back of the chair. His eyes were bright from the whisky and he felt warm. But when he spoke his voice was low.

Alice, ladling gravy over the meat, looked up.

'I've got something to tell you,' Hughie said.

Now the quietness left him, and something of the savagery that he had felt when he hit Renshaw revived.

'I got the sack, Alice. I punched Renshaw. Knocked him out.'

She placed the spoon carefully on the table and turned down the gas.

When she looked up Hughie was still hanging onto the chair, looking into space.

'You hit him, Hughie?' She took in a deep breath and expelled it slowly.

He sat down suddenly and Alice put her hands on his head, rubbing her fingers through his damp, thinning hair.

'Well, that could be something,' she said softly. 'Man hits boss, gets out, makes fortune. We've been in a rut a long time, Hughie.'

She moved to the stove.

'Come on,' she said, 'let's celebrate! Thirty-five years is too long to be in any job. Maybe it's the beginning of something.'

She rummaged in the refrigerator and brought out a bottle of beer. Pouring the beer into two long glasses, she held them up to the light and smiled.

'Mr Hughie Marshall, the eminent consultant to Must-Take Dyes, began his career as wood and water carrier at Macdonaldtown Dyehouse. Mr Marshall attributes his success to the fact that he unexpectedly severed his ties

114

with Macdonaldtown by laying out the manager with one deft blow. Interviewed by Mr Darcy Dyson the prominent boxer...'

The lines left Hughie's face, and he began to smile.

'I was worried for you, Alice,' he said.

But as the days went by, Hughie lapsed more and more into morose silence. For a while, neighbours dropped in to talk about the scene in Renshaw's office. But the subject was soon exhausted, and Hughie was forgotten.

'There are other jobs,' Alice said. 'Just look at those columns and columns of ads. People wanting men for all kinds of jobs. When our holiday's over, why don't you make a break for something new?'

'We'll see,' Hughie said. 'We'll see. We'll keep on watching the papers.'

Sometimes the very job would crop up, but carrying the stipulation 'aged between 25 and 35 years'. Highly qualified men to 40 years would be considered.

'I'd go after that job,' Alice said one day, as Hughie sat staring into space with the paper on his knees. 'You don't look nearly fifty, Hughie.'

She brushed his hair back with her fingers. It was sparse, but dark. Dressed in his best navy blue, with a red-and-white striped tie, he was presentable enough.

He took the paper and walked down Ring Street. He felt hopeful and confident. Perhaps he would show Renshaw after all.

'You fill in this form,' the girl said. She was pleasant and friendly. She placed a little heap of forms on a table.

He picked up a pen and began to write.

Name. (In block letters.)

Age? Hughie hesitated. There could be complications. Insurance. Superannuation. Finally he wrote in the correct figure.

Address.

Qualifications? Thirty-five years in the steam of Macdonaldtown. University of Macdonaldtown.

State particularly pass in physics, maths, chemistry. Physics? They didn't teach it at Macdonaldtown Public. No time for physics. Maths? Well, he could add and do decimals, and work in grammes, and manage fractions.

Chemistry?

He looked down at the blots and smudges he was making on the paper. The girl came over to him, smiling. A young man opened the door, picked up a form and began filling it in. He wrote quickly and with purpose. He had good passes in physics, maths and chemistry. Hughie stood looking at the incomplete form that he had in his hand.

An inner door opened and a middle-aged man called, 'Send in the next applicant, please.'

The girl looked at Hughie.

'Did you finish filling in your form? No matter, Mr Wiseman's ready to see you now.'

Hughie pulled out his wallet. It had the reference that Cuthbert had written out for him. 'Leaves of his own accord. It is with regret...' Ah, well, Staff people are never sacked. Not like the rank-and-filers. He leaves of his own accord. Hughie's throat tightened.

'Very interesting,' Mr Wiseman said. 'Practical man. Good experience too. Fact is, we're looking for a qualified man. Textiles aren't what they were. Synthetics invading the place. Pity you didn't qualify. Big future for the right man. Could do with a good vat hand. That be in your line at all?'

Hughie folded up the reference and put it back in his pocket.

'Sorry,' Mr Wiseman said. 'Wish we could accommodate you. You might handle the job at that, but I get my instructions as well.'

He shook hands with Hughie. Well, it was only the beginning.

'There's no need for you to worry,' Alice said when Hughie came in looking dejected. 'You've been out next to no time. Scarcely long enough for a holiday. And remember, you won't get a break for a full year once you start again.'

And once, feeling very adventurous, she said, 'Why don't you start something new? You could do a job as a process worker in an engineering place, or even sell things. That's clean and it seems easy.'

She was trying to whip him out of his apathy.

'I can't sell things,' Hughie said. 'And I can't do repetition work. I got a job. I'm a dyer. And that's what I'll be when I start work again.'

From time to time news trickled through from the Dyehouse. Renshaw was back. Larcombe had told him off. Larcombe had told him to watch his step. The cotton was faulty. Collins wasn't taking to the lab. Oliver Henery had sooled the Unions onto Renshaw over the loads that the girls were humping about. Renshaw was going to catch up with Oliver when the time was ripe. Barney Monahan's missus was having a baby.

117

Alice, tired of trying to jerk Hughie out of his dark mood, began searching round for ways of helping him. She found a copy of the telephone directory and turned to the pink pages.

She began listing all the textile companies and dyehouses. She met Mr Mayers secretly (Hughie would not have liked it) and worked out a list of the smaller dyehouses.

'The writing seems to be on the wall with the big places,' Mayers said. 'But these little places would jump at a bloke like Hughie. I sounded Weatherstone out. He's got a little place out Sans Souci way. He's thinking of putting in a few vats. He'd take him like a shot, but it could be a matter of six months.'

'It's not urgent,' Alice said. 'I suppose we're better off than most. We own the house—lock, stock and barrel. But Hughie worries me. He just sits there looking into space, pretending to read, but usually just sitting. I'm beginning to worry. He seems sort of sick.'

'Bit of a jolt,' Mayers said. 'Only job he's ever had. I'm against it myself, starting in on a job and never leaving it. They get you by the tit.'

The days slipped by for Hughie.

Each morning he was out with the paper under his arm, in quest of the job for a dyer.

'Still out?' Tom Waters' inquiring eye was raised above the fence railing. 'If you'd be interested, I hear that Dobbey wants a hand on his baker's cart. I might be able to put in a word.'

'No, thank you,' Hughie said. 'I'm keeping an appointment for a job as a dyer.'

'Ah, well—if I can help...'

'Thanks. Thanks a lot.'

'Nothing turned up in the dyeing line, Mr Marshall?' It was Mrs Marsden from the corner of the street. Her face was mean and spiteful. A stuck-up lot, that Hughie and his missus. It did them good to get it now and again.

'Nothing turned up yet, Mrs Marsden. Perhaps tomorrow.' In the Botanic Gardens he would sit and watch the trees, and think about the colour of the leaves. He could take that tawny yellow one, mix colour and match it. Or that russety-brown one, tumbling slowly to the ground. He would try that. He picked up the leaf. The colour was reflected back to him. It would not be so easy. He would try. The leaf fluttered to the ground. It was late autumn now; the rich summer flowers were spent, the spring bulbs had not pushed up through the ground, the poppies had not yet budded. A few autumn roses still clung to the bushes. The slender, leafless limbs of the deciduous trees cut across the sky. Bark brown. The leaves drifted down.

Hughie thought of the new range. The colour of the bark, of the yellow drifting leaves; the dense green of the sward, the warm colour of the sandstone, the jewel of the late-flaring bud. He would open the paper and make a pretence of reading it. Catastrophes. People making statements about this and that. People wanting clerks, cleaners, salesmen, canvassers. The dyers' jobs were few and far between.

He took out his reference and began reading it again. He leaves of his own accord. It is with regret...And for a moment it seemed that it was so. He seemed to have

119

forgotten about Renshaw. He put the reference back in his pocket. The leaves drifted down. His quick eye noted the stains, the flecks, the changing shades.

It was dark when he got to Ring Street.

'No luck, Mr Marshall?'

'None, Mrs Marsden.'

'Better luck next time.'

'That job's still open,' Tom Waters said. 'It might suit you as a fill-in. Isn't always easy to fall onto just what you want. Especially in your line. Kind of specialized.'

The inquiring eye was friendly.

'Just thought I'd mention it.' He was apologetic.

'I'll think it over,' Hughie said.

Alice was at the door. He took off his hat, hung it on the stand, and put the paper under the flounce of the settee.

'I wouldn't go every day,' Alice said. She was alarmed at the pallor of his face, the signs of strain around his eyes.

She put her arm round his shoulders. His body was tense and resistant.

'Sit quiet,' she said. Her voice was gentle with a quiet, crooning note. 'Sit quiet, my love.'

After the dishes were done they sat in the little room with the lace curtains and Hughie's brown leather chair drawn up to the fire. Hughie picked up a catalogue, and for a moment the colours caught his eye. Then he dropped it to the floor.

He sat curiously idle, with his hands hanging between his legs. Alice was making a cardigan in warm heavy-weight

120

winter wools. She had meant it for Hughie as a protection against the chills of the Dyehouse.

'Let's go away,' she said. 'We could easily afford a fortnight by the sea. And you need it, Hughie.'

'I need to be left alone. I don't want seasides and fussing. I want to be left alone to work things out for myself.'

'Sorry, Hughie.' She pressed her lips together. She was offended, but too worried to care much about it.

'Tom Waters offered me a job on a baker's cart.' He began to laugh.

'He means well,' Alice said. 'But he doesn't understand.'

'Should I take it, Alice?' His voice reflected his uncertainty.

'Not yet,' she said. 'There's plenty of jobs you can do if nothing turns up. I wish you'd relax and rest for a while, Hughie. You won't be fit to start on a job soon, if you don't let up a little.'

But there was no resting for him. Alice, waking in the night, felt his body tense and drenched with sweat.

'Be quiet, Hughie,' she would say, wiping the sweat from his forehead. 'Be quiet and rest.'

CHAPTER NINETEEN

'Good morning, Patty,' Miss Merton said. She was smiling, glancing over her glasses.

'Good morning.'

Miss Merton settled to her desk and for a moment there was the clacking of typewriter keys. Miss Merton typing reports. She was not typing quickly. Rather slowly and purposefully.

Patty picked up a duster and flicked about among her books. She had piles of dyebooks on the shelves. Some were old and the pages were mended with Durex tape. It was time most of them were dumped. If the card system was properly run, she could dump the whole lot in the garbage.

She flicked through the old cards. Rolls of cloth still in stock that should have been dyed and out years ago. She pulled out a fistful of old numbers. If she was managing this dump, she'd pull out every card that was more than three years old, and she'd want every roll found, assembled and assessed. All these numbers should be cleared out. She'd talked about it to Miss Merton one day.

'You can't run a business on these lines.'

Miss Merton had agreed. But the business seemed to be going along all right.

'They get a little upset when these suggestions come from us,' Miss Merton had said, 'especially Mr Renshaw.'

'I can't get rid of this rubbish,' Patty said now. 'All these old dyebooks. Some of this stock goes back to the Flood. While I've got these old numbers in the card system I can't throw out the books.'

She was swishing and flicking the duster aggressively.

'If I was Mr Cuthbert, I'd see that all stock up to a certain date was shifted, before new rolls could be picked out. Just look at this. And this and this.'

Miss Merton looked at the numbers. Patty turned up the production sheets.

'Six years old,' Patty said. 'The stuff must be rotten. They ought to tie it up in bundles and send it to Paddy's Market, and let me get the cards out and the dyebooks dumped.'

It was a perennial question.

Miss Merton smiled at Patty as she flew about, disturbing the dust and grumbling.

'They seem to like things as they are,' Miss Merton said. 'We have things flowing fairly smoothly, Patty. But those books are a nuisance, though.'

'I think I'll ask him,' Patty said. 'Only six rolls, and it

123

would clear up the cards and give me a bit more room on the bookshelves.'

Besides, it would give her the opportunity of speaking to him.

Goodwin was picking out rolls on the fourth floor. He was throwing them aside, pulling off the tickets and roughly calculating the weight of each roll. When he was ready he would take the tickets to Patty. She would record the numbers in the dyebook together with the respective weights, and then add up the totals. Renshaw would write in the dyers' instructions. Patty would take the instructions to the laboratory, and the tickets to Barney at the dyers' bench.

Goodwin worked swiftly and quietly. There was no one up here to talk to. Most of the new greige stock had been lifted up to the fourth floor at last stocktaking. Now it had to be picked out, loaded onto a trolley and lowered from the loading well to the ground floor.

When the trolley was loaded, he sat back. There was a sign that said 'No Smoking', but Goodwin pulled out his tobacco and rolled a cigarette. He lay back among the rolls for a brief smoko. Presently he heard footsteps. It could be Bluey, tired of waiting for the new vat, up to investigate. He peered cautiously round the corner of the stack. It was Renshaw. Goodwin put out the cigarette, crushing it in his fingers. He judged it best to lie low.

Renshaw settled himself on the edge of a table.

He was not far from Goodwin, and Goodwin crouched low, cursing himself for a fool. There was no need to hide himself. He was concerned with a legitimate job. But having embarked on this line it was too late to change course. Renshaw would want to know what he was doing, why he had hidden himself away. He'd take a set on him and follow him about, waiting for him to make a slip. He'd have no chance for a quiet smoko. He'd be hounded like other blokes he knew.

Goodwin heard the door open again, and the clatter of feet. He listened. A woman's footsteps. Perhaps someone to tell Renshaw he was wanted on the telephone. People were always ringing him up. Dye salesmen, and woolly-headed sheilas who seemed to see something fascinating in him. Goodwin hoped it was a sheila. It could put Renshaw in a good mood for days when a dame rang him up.

He raised himself cautiously and peered over the stacks. It was Gwennie Verrendah, the new sheila on the wrapping bench. A quiet little piece with soft brown eyes and smooth fawny hair. Religious, he'd been told.

God Almighty, Goodwin thought, what's she doing up here?

He looked impatiently at his watch. Any minute now Bluey was likely to come screaming up the stairs in search of the cloth for the new vat.

Renshaw was shifting rolls, stripping off tickets and handing them to the new sheila. Goodwin began to crawl along on his hands and knees. There was a door at the other end of the room. If he could edge towards that, with a bit of luck he could be through it. He could come racing back, up the other stairway, and boldly wheel the trolley to the lift-well.

But as he edged along, he kept wondering why Renshaw

had the girl up here. No need for him to be stripping off tickets, and there was plenty of work on the wrapping bench. As he neared the door he rose, lifting his eyes just above the level of the stacks. Renshaw had stopped working. He had handed the girl a bundle of tickets, but he was still holding them and looking down into her eyes. The girl was looking up at him. Her eyes were serious, perplexed. Then Renshaw took her hand in his. He looked at the tickets, then raised her hand slowly. He bent his head. Before he reached the door, Goodwin saw Renshaw's lips touch the girl's hand.

If that doesn't take the biscuit; kiss my arse, he thought. The hypocritical bastard! Waiting outside the Sunday School to get them. Someone ought to give him a toe in the place that it hurts most.

'Where you been?' Bluey asked. 'Does it take you half the day to pick out a vat and load up a trolley?'

'I've had a front seat on a bit of interesting scenery. A preview on our next act. I been cut off, Bluey. Renshaw's got a sheila up on the fourth. I was sittin' down having a quiet bit of a smoke, when in comes Renshaw and sits himself down on the bench.' Goodwin raised himself on his toes and wriggled his backside. 'And up toddles that never-been-kissed little dame from the wrapping. Renshaw starts pulling tickets off rolls, pressing them into her hands, and wrapping his slimy fingers round her wrist at the same time.'

'Well?' Bluey said.

Goodwin hit himself on the chest.

'Next thing Renshaw gives his dial a real wrench like Bogart when he realizes that he's got a bit of the real twenty-two carat. Sort of sad look. And then, so help me, if he doesn't bend over and kiss the sheila on the hand.'

Bluey grunted. Sims was waiting on the rolls for the new vat. He was interested, but too busy to wait any longer.

'Well, she'll want to have her hand on her sixpence if Renshaw ever gets her to the park. They tell me he never fails.'

Patty picked up the six cards. She shuffled them about in her hand. As she walked across the warehouse floor, she saw Goodwin going up the front flight of stairs. He was about to run up to the fourth floor, push open the stockroom door, and wheel the trolley to the lift-well.

'Seen Mr Renshaw about?' she asked.

Goodwin hesitated. He wondered if he should tell her. You're living on borrowed time, sister, he thought. I wonder if you really like that bloke. If you're sold on him. Might be better if you're not. Better for you.

Well, she was bound to get it in the guts sooner or later, and the sooner the better. He was conscious of the drama. Patty confident of her position. The door opening. The little dark-eyed girl in Renshaw's arms.

He let it rest there. What would Patty do? What, in fact, could Patty do?

'I think he's on the fourth.' Goodwin went leaping up the stairs taking two steps at a time.

Patty waited until Goodwin reached the fourth floor. The creaking of the winch told her that the trolley was on its way down. She gave Goodwin enough time to get down the back stairs before she began walking up.

127

It suited her that Renshaw was on the fourth floor. There would be no interruptions. Everything that she had wanted to say over the past weeks clamoured for expression. How lonely she had been! Even walking through the warehouse, twitching her skirts at the men or talking to the girls, she was lonely. But the memory of their past meetings rose up to reassure her. All the times he had begged her. When she had played hard to get, and hadn't meant it. And later, when she had let him have his way.

She would tell him today. Really talk to him. It must have added up. If things added up at all, it must have meant something to him, too.

Patty leaned over the barricading around the lift-well. Goodwin had got the trolley down. He was taking the hooks out of the ropes. The door leading from the loading dock to the lift-well was open. The sunlight streamed in and made a bright, warm patch on the cement. Patty looked at it for a moment. It reminded her fleetingly of the world outside the Dyehouse. Of the beaches, the sundrenched parks.

She opened the door quietly and looked down along the stockroom. The lights were on. After the sunlight down the lift-well, the room seemed dark. The lights were on, but the room looked shadowy. Even so early in the morning it was shadowy.

The tables were all laid out, all tabulated.

Table A. Table B. Table C.

And the stacks were all numbered.

Stack 1 Table A. Stack 2 Table A. Stack 3 Table A.

She was looking at the tables, and at the stacks. A stack had fallen over on Table 3.

She began walking along the room slowly. Each time she took a step it sounded hollow in the quiet warehouse.

Renshaw was there. She could see him. And although she moved towards him, she tried not to look. She noticed the whitewash peeling from the wall, the stain where the water had seeped in under the flashing. But suddenly she stopped. With an effort she raised her head and looked at him. The small, slim girl fled in alarm. She was crying as she ran past Patty to the open door.

Renshaw put the tickets carefully on top of the stack.

Well, it was bound to happen. It had been hanging fire for a long time. He should have hit her with it weeks ago. It never paid, this going soft and sentimental. When the time came, the knife was always the easiest. Love's young dream.

But he felt vaguely sorry for her. Perhaps it meant something to her. Well, time was a healer. It took care of it all.

'You were kissing that girl,' Patty said. 'You were pulling her about.' She looked as though she might cry, but her voice was quiet and composed.

Renshaw was conscious of a deep feeling of relief. No hysterics. No tantrums. She was going to be rational. Cold, haughty, offended. 'Come off it,' he said.

'You were mauling her about.'

Renshaw looked at her. He began at her feet, and his eyes travelled leisurely to her head. Then he smiled, a cold, repellent flexing of the lips.

'You'd better get down off that pedestal. Maybe get down a little closer to the earth. You and I are old friends, and we've been about.'

There was a subtle change in his expression.

'We're not old friends,' Patty said slowly. 'We were lovers. You said you'd marry me. You told me you were going to marry me.'

'Oh, well,' Renshaw said, 'even lovers, and husbands for that matter, have their little outside interests. You didn't expect...'

He began to laugh.

'You're a bigger fool than I thought you were, Patty.'

'You promised me,' Patty said. Her voice was suddenly unsteady. 'You couldn't lie, just like that.'

'You're building it up,' Renshaw said. 'If it hadn't been me it would have been someone else. You had a good time while it lasted. I took you out. Bought you things. It's not much use kicking now. There's a few warm-blooded bucks about Macdonaldtown, I can tell you.'

'I'll do something about it,' Patty said wildly. 'I'll get some advice. I'll see a solicitor.'

The smile was wiped suddenly from Renshaw's face.

He leant over and grabbed her by the arm. He screwed it up behind her back and pushed her over onto the table.

'You'll see a solicitor?' he said. 'When I've finished with you, you might be glad to see a doctor. I've met a few bitches...! You'll see a solicitor!'

Suddenly he dragged her to her feet and propelled her along the room until they were opposite the lift-well.

'It's a long way down there,' he said. 'The cement's pretty hard if you hit it, and accidents happen.'

He let her go. Patty stood looking down the lift-well.

When she looked at Renshaw the savage expression had left his face. He was bland, almost friendly. It seemed to Patty that it might never have happened.

'Yes, it's a long way down,' she said quietly. 'A long way down.' The clock opposite the lift-well said ten fifty-five. She looked at it stupidly. Ten fifty-five. How long did it take to pull down the world? Ten fifty-five. It was less than fifteen minutes since she had bounced confidently up the stairs and pushed open the stockroom door.

'How did you get on?' Miss Merton asked. 'Any luck?'

Patty shook her head. She had left the cards on the stockroom table. It didn't matter now. She would make cards out if any of the rolls came through. She took up the books and put them into the garbage. Then she began mechanically entering up her work.

At four o'clock she put down her pen, pushed the book to the back of the desk and straightened the cards. She had not been bothered further by Renshaw. He had disappeared to the laboratory. But the curious glances of the girls as they charged rolls in the warehouse told her that the story had grapevined around. Renshaw was finished with her. Well, she had been riding for a fall. Maybe some of the girls would be sympathetic. They would debate it and take sides over it. And plenty of them would say she was a bloody fool anyway. But mostly they would be sorry for her. They would say that she was only a kid, and it was a shame. And then they would forget about it. They would go on charging rolls, and tossing banter about, and forget all about her. It didn't really mean anything to anyone else. Only to her.

The little brown-eyed girl worked silently at the wrapping table. She had heard the talk about Patty and Renshaw, and she was conscious of the drama that was taking place around her. She saw them suddenly as she might see figures flashed upon a screen. They were going together. That meant the long glances, the quiet brushing together of the lips. Her knowledge of life was limited and circumscribed.

But it struck her as dramatic and shattering that Patty's world could have crumbled so easily; that Renshaw should have stood by her wrapping bench, watching her as she rolled the cloth in its heavy sheetings of brown paper; that he should have singled her out for his special attention. It was so simple that it reminded her of the Bible. And the man looked upon the woman. It reminded her, too, of the hundreds of stories she had seen on the films. Her mind spun around the drama and the swiftness with which Renshaw had moved. And all the time she had been working with her fawn's head bent over the rolls and her eyes cloudy with the dreams she was dreaming, Renshaw had been watching her. And when the time came he had sent for her. She thought of Patty suddenly with a pang of pity.

'I'd like to go home,' Patty said.

She was standing in Miss Merton's office looking white and strained. Miss Merton had heard the rumours. She was not altogether surprised. Patty had been tense and nervous for days, and Renshaw had pointedly avoided the office. It began like that, Miss Merton thought. And soon there would be nothing left but bitterness to show for the gay weeks and times they had spent together. She wondered briefly if this was the end. The sum total of loving, the wanting and taking. And if she and Stephen...She put the thought far away. There were other endings.

At the door Patty turned. She looked quickly at Miss Merton. At her thin, sterile body, at the grey wispy hair pulled back from her face. You couldn't win anyway, Patty thought. I wonder if she ever really loved anyone. If she ever loved a man. The thought brought her back to her own misery.

'You heard the news?' Patty asked. Miss Merton took a step forward and placed her arm round her shoulder. Patty, looking suddenly into her face, was surprised at the look of understanding. For a moment their eyes held.

'It's a hard thing when you're young, Patty.'

There was nothing else to say.

Patty opened the door. Miss Merton thought of platitudes. In time Patty would forget. The young always forgot, or nearly always. But she said nothing.

For Patty it was no better on the street. There was nowhere to go. The room at Barrington Terrace offered no solace or privacy. She began walking. At first slowly, turning over in her mind all that Renshaw had said. Then her pace quickened. She walked steadily down the street, out along the main road, to a spot where the streets and traffic converged into a narrow bottleneck.

She began following the tram tracks, scarcely aware of where she was, or why she was going. She had a gaudy women's paper in her hand. She had picked it up in her flight from the office.

Suddenly the tram tracks swung out, and she was at

the top of the hill. The streets plunged sharply into a valley. In some of the shops the lights were on already. She had walked a long way, wrapped in her misery. But it was no good. The tram tracks led on, but not for her.

She turned her face to Macdonaldtown.

CHAPTER TWENTY

The streets were shadowed as Patty passed the church, the air thick with the sound of children playing in the alleyways.

And suddenly she was on the steps. The door yielded to the pressure of her hand. She knelt in the half-dark looking at the small red light as it flickered before the altar. Here at least was peace and privacy. The tears overflowed. She bent her head upon her hands and began to cry.

She moved suddenly to the little side altar, where the calm waxen face of the Virgin looked out into the dim church.

'Holy Mary, Mother of God,' Patty said.

She got up, wiping her face with her handkerchief, and made her way into the street. The door closed gently behind her. Outside the church a man was loitering, exercising a dog in circles. It was Oliver. He had seen Patty's frantic dash up the church steps and he had waited quietly in the dim light for her to emerge.

He fell in beside her, holding the dog on a leash and suiting his pace to hers.

'Why don't you let me alone?' Patty said.

'Are you sure you want to be left alone? Right now I think you could do with a friend.'

'A friend?' Patty said.

She looked up, expecting to find the half-sexy leer that he usually assumed in her company.

But he was looking ahead, his face expressionless.

They began walking down towards the park. Oliver took off his coat and wrapped it around the dog. He heaped dry leaves together under the trees and bedded him down.

'Sit down, Patty?'

He indicated a seat in the glow thrown from the electric lights. He picked up Patty's magazine and turned a page.

'Pretty, isn't it?' he said laconically.

The girl leaned back in a gilt chair. The fire glowed on the pink velvet of her frock. The man was bending over her. He looked clean, smooth and well dressed. On the mantelpiece a heavy old clock gleamed in the firelight. The carpet was rich and expensive.

Patty looked at the picture too.

Suddenly Oliver threw the magazine onto the ground. He took her by the shoulders and turned her so that they both stood facing Wentworth Parade.

'Take a good look at that, Patty.'

Night had closed in. The Parade was a dark alley;

136

the tall terraces almost met overhead. The damp air was settling, heavy with its burden of dust and dirt.

'Look at it, Patty. It's ours. The sort of thing you might call our heritage. D'you reckon we can afford to get softened up with pictures of easy living, and stories of dukes marrying pantrymaids? We got to kick along in this. Somehow we got to get topside of it. And we got to know what to do about it.'

He put his arm on her shoulder and Patty looked up again, expecting to see the familiar jeering smile. But he was looking over her head into the dark, shadowy outlines of the Parade.

'We got to learn to be tough, you and I. How you think that dame in the pink velvet dress sitting in front of the fire got that way? You can bet she doesn't live in Barrington Terrace. You can bet she just turns on a tap, and the hot water flows into the bath. You can just bet she's never filled a kerosene tin with water and waited while it boiled, and then tipped it into a zinc tub. And you can bet she doesn't think much of people like you and me.'

'It is funny when you come to think of it,' Patty said suddenly. 'All the different things we get just because we're born.'

'Oh,' Oliver said, 'some blokes work for it. Get a bit. Make some lucky gamble. Some blokes are born with it. Some blokes get a break and marry a rich bitch. And people like us,' Oliver said bitterly, 'well—they just take out the bridle and ride us into the ground.'

'Do you want to change the world?' Patty said slowly.

Did he want to change the world? Well, what would

you think, mug? But you wouldn't want to be a fool, would you?

'Christ. Break it up, Patty. The world's a pretty big place.'

It was dark. The belt of gums planted to the east of the park was dense and shapeless. Under the lights the few shrubs made patterns on the freshly mown grass. The deciduous trees were bare, their dark arms arcs against the darker sky. There was no moon. Above, the night was studded with stars. They looked remote, calm and peaceful. Patty thought of the distant stars, the factories, the railway-yards, and Barrington Terrace. But her mind swung back to herself and her own problem. She wished suddenly that she could be free of Oliver, of her mother, of the mean little room that was her home. She leaned her head on the back of the seat and began to cry.

Oliver moved up close to her. He put his face gently against hers. They sat so until Patty ceased her crying.

'You got a problem about Renshaw?' he asked.

She looked up, bewildered and tongue-tied. Did she have a problem? She sensed the sudden hardening of his voice.

'You weren't all that big a fool, Patty?'

No, you weren't that big a fool. You should have foreseen this. Yes, you should have seen this coming. You were pretty quick at summing things up, weren't you? You could have passed the tip-off on to someone else. Were you too dumb to look after yourself? Were you all that big a fool? Just as Oliver said. All that big a fool?

There was no helping it. She began to cry again.

The dog rose, shook the leaves from his back and nosed up to the seat. A chill wind whipped up the Parade, lifting discarded papers and bowling tins along the gutter. Cars hurried along, stabbing the darkness with sharp beams of light.

Someone was singing in the pub. The yellow light streamed onto the pavement.

A goods train was pulling out. It came panting slowly past Macdonaldtown on its long run west. Patty sat up, listening, as the trucks ran in along the station and headed out to Strathfield. It could be going anywhere, she thought. Sometimes, she knew, men clambered aboard as the train slowed down, and were carried far from the jungle of the streets, to the open plains.

'It would be nice if you could just go away,' Patty said.

'What you want to run from?' Oliver said suddenly.

He bent over her.

'We can't run, Patty. Not us. You reckon we wouldn't like to run like other people? We got to stop put.'

She shivered. The wind was increasing in strength. The mass of trees was agitated. Clouds spread and drifted over the sky.

'So Renshaw made a decision,' Oliver said suddenly. 'And the answer's no confetti.'

He unleashed the dog.

'You better come clean,' he said. 'You going to have a baby?'

She shook her head.

'Then what's the trouble?'

'You know...if you haven't got much, and then one day

you give someone just about all you have, and they throw it back at you?'

'Yes.'

'Laughing. As though it was no value at all.'

She wasn't crying now. She was still and composed.

'We ain't got much,' Oliver said. 'But some of these bastards want to strip us down. Maybe after a while they get to feeling that we aren't built like them either. Where they've got lungs and heart and guts, and blood in their veins, maybe we've got wheels and gears and cogs. Maybe they don't mean to be that bad. We're just not human. Not in the way they are. They'd strip us down, all right. And mainly we let them.'

'How do you mean?'

'If Renshaw asked you to go out tomorrow, what would you say? If he came to you with some cock-and-bull story, what would you say to him? You'd go out with him. You'd be happy to go out with him. And I bet he'd have no trouble laying you on your back either.'

She thought over what he said.

'Maybe.'

'Right. Well, you better stop your whimpering. These blokes will strip you down as long as you take it. What do you reckon Renshaw's thinking about right now? I got ten bob to say he's got some new sheila in his car right at this very minute. You want to get a bit more inside, Patty. You're not the first dame that's been done over, not by a long shot. But you haven't lost your legs. You've still got your eyes. You can see. For God's sake, you've got a bit of guts left for yourself, haven't you? You've got to put first things first.

You're still alive. Your back's not broke, so you don't have to crawl. See what I mean, Patty? We got a lot to learn, and you've got from here to Hell to get over Renshaw.'

'Yes, I suppose so,' Patty said.

They began walking down the windy Parade. Patty's skirt whipped against her legs; the wind caught her hair and blew it back in a soft, fair stream.

'I've got plenty to learn,' she said to Oliver. 'I just suppose you're learning all your life.'

CHAPTER TWENTY ONE

Autumn merged into winter with sullen skies.

The tempo was increasing at the Dyehouse. Rolls were being pulled out and sorted. All hands were bent towards the final effort. June–July stocktake came. The auditors were in, spot-checking, picking out occasional rolls, counting the rolls in the fixtures, checking chemical and dye stocks, calculating the weight of containers.

Then suddenly it was over. A breathing space until December when it would all happen again.

The spring came early with an almost imperceptible softening of the air. The tree outside Barrington Terrace was a tracery of soft, delicate green. Potted plants began to appear on the lower window sills.

At the Dyehouse the work flowed. Fixture, vat, hydro, dryer, press, wrapping bench, warehouse. There had been a build-up of orders and Renshaw was trying to push the work through. Mayers was busy on a new machine. For him, the annual boiler inspection came up towards the end of September.

Patty avoided Renshaw. He had made no further effort to seek her out. What was to be said had been said, and so it rested. And there had been nothing more between Gwennie and himself. There was a ripe time for everything, and he could wait. But he often worked near the wrapping table, using it as a vantage point to bawl out orders to the pressers and the girls sorting the rolls for the warehouse and orders. Nor did he spare Gwennie when the pressure was on.

The rolls were coming off the presses. They were bulky and heavy. Renshaw watched Gwennie as she dropped the rolls onto the bench. She had the paper cut and ready. With one movement the main fold was round the cloth, the ends were pushed into shape. She slapped on the gummed paper and carried the roll to the waiting trolley. 'Twenty rolls for Newknit—and get a move on.'

The sweat gathered on her forehead and stood out in little beads. She wiped it with the back of her hand and caught up the gummed paper in the same movement. Renshaw sat on the bench and bawled to the pressers and the girls on the weighing-up tables.

At two o'clock the trucks were in. The pressure dropped. Gwennie wiped her forehead. She began cutting paper and Renshaw stood watching her. There was a right time for everything, and perhaps this was the right time for Gwennie. He bent over the table, fingering the stocks of gummed paper. But he was really watching her. She looked up and smiled shyly when she met his gaze. Then she thought of the morning in the stockroom, and the colour flooded suddenly into her face.

'Go out much, Gwennie?' he asked. He made it sound very matter-of-fact. A friendly inquiry.

She put down the scissors. She felt flushed and awkward. She'd never been out with a really strange man. Once or twice she had gone to a movie with her cousin, and one memorable day she had gone driving with a young man, as far afield as Tom Ugly's bridge.

'Not much.' She said it shyly.

'You miss a lot of fun.'

The elevator was not working. The men began carrying the bales of cloth down from the higher floors.

'Look here,' Renshaw said. 'I could take you out one weekend. Saturday or Sunday. I could take you to places you've never seen. Lots of girls come to work here, Gwennie. It's a long time since we've had a girl like you.'

She looked at him shyly. She was weary of standing beside the wrapping table, of lifting rolls that were almost beyond her strength, mechanically slapping on the gummed paper, pulling the tickets through, carrying the rolls to the trolley. But her morning alone with him in the stockroom had made her wary.

'Of course,' he said, 'if you don't want to come. Thought you'd enjoy it.'

He began walking away. He'd give her time. They all came good in time. He was almost to the presses when she called him.

'Mr Renshaw.'

He came back slowly. His face was friendly.

'Well? You'd like to come?'

She stood smiling awkwardly, the scissors in her hand. Her eyes were gentle and trusting.

'You'll have a lot of fun, Gwennie. I can promise you that. And you don't have to call me Mr Renshaw when we're alone.'

'I see Renshaw's dating that kid on the wrapping,' Goodwin said. 'He's had his eye on her ever since he cornered her on the fourth floor. That Gwennie.'

'Ugh.' Barney was tired. Esther had been unwell again. His days were long and his night's rest was often broken.

'I think I'll begin taking the odds,' Goodwin said.

'There's nothing too dirty for you to be in,' Barney said shortly. 'Bet you're in more shady deals than most fellows a bloke would hope to meet.'

'There's no shady deals,' Goodwin said. 'What do we work for, you and me? Do we come into this flaming morgue every morning because we like it? You can bet we don't. What do you work for? Money!'

'Money.'

'You put your head down and your behind up every day just to get it, you like it that much. Me too. That's because we've got no other way of getting it. But I tell you, Barney, I'm not going to stay bogged down in this hole all my life. Not by a long shot. I'm going to branch out.'

'What you intend doing?'

'I'm getting ready to set up a clip joint. S.P. betting, and a few goodlooking girls.'

145

CHAPTER TWENTY TWO

It was almost dark when the car topped the hill. The road ran down through the open parkland, thick with trees and scrub. Behind them was the dim little wayside dining room where they had eaten. Renshaw was in good form. At the arty little dining room, he had ordered strange food and a little wine. Gwennie had eaten shyly, holding her knife and fork rigidly correct and trying to act like a woman used to such afternoon outings.

Night came as they were driving along. Below them the road ran white, until it was lost in the dense darkness of the bush. Somewhere in the gully wattles were in bloom, and the sweetness of their perfume drifted up.

Renshaw stopped the car, then turned it. The gear slipped into reverse and they backed in under the canopy of drooping leaves. He switched off the ignition and reached for his cigarettes. The match spluttered in his fingers, revealing a glimpse of his fair hair and the angle of his face before it went out.

'Like it?'

He exhaled, and the long plume of smoke shot into the air. Gwennie was searching about in her mind for something to say. Something grown-up. Something sophisticated. Something that might impress him.

They sat for a long time looking out over the dark valley.

'Well, what did you think of it, Gwennie?'

'It was nice.' She fumbled shyly for words. 'Nicer than any place I've been to.'

'Don't get round much?'

He stubbed out the cigarette, and threw it from him. His arm stole along the back of the seat. Just above her head, so that she knew it was there. She leant forward a little, but he made no attempt to pursue her.

'Know this place?'

She was mute.

'Next Sunday I might take you on a trip and show you some of the country.'

He opened the door and got out.

'Might as well have a look around here,' he said.

They walked slowly down the road.

'It's funny,' Renshaw said. 'Meeting a girl like you makes a man feel different. Makes him think what a fool he's been.'

He put his arm around her waist. The night was warm; the scent from the wattles encompassed them. The gums were green and dark.

'Let's sit down,' Renshaw said urgently.

She swept the grass with its few silvery heads aside, and sat.

Renshaw leant towards her. She could smell the aromatic perfume of the cigarettes that he smoked.

Now don't start that touch-me-not bleating, Renshaw thought. You couldn't be all that dumb. Even if you lived in a capsule, you couldn't be all that sealed off. He reached out in the dark. He felt, rather than saw, her startled resistance. But her face was upturned when he kissed her.

For Gwennie, time stood still. Little pictures flicked over in her mind. This was happening to her. Not to some girl in a novelette. She was out on this hillside, with the city away to the east, and Renshaw had his arm round her. His lips slid suddenly down from hers to the base of her throat.

She cried out, struggling to sit up and clutching at his hands.

'Oh, don't,' she said suddenly. 'Don't do that.'

He made a soft, reassuring noise. Then his hands caught at the neck of her frock, and his fingers closed over her breast.

'You're going to like this,' he said thickly, 'and there's nothing to worry about.'

He was over her. She lay still, feeling suddenly dazed. She reached out frantically for a weapon. Something to hit with. She found the stone before she knew it.

'You bloody little bitch!'

Gwennie had scrambled free, and began running down the road.

Well, let her go. He could easily overtake her. He

liked them better with a bit of fight. Before the night was over the boot might be on the other foot. He got into the car. The engine roared to life.

Gwennie saw the light swing around, saw the vast emptiness of the bush, the yawning dark gullies, the solitary road running back into the city. She began to run again. Then the lights were upon her. For one minute she thought he would run her down. She pressed close to the trees as Renshaw stopped the car.

'What you think you're doing?' he said evenly.

He put his hand out, but she tore herself free and began running down the road that led to the city. When he caught her, he flung her to the ground. She lay still, not knowing what to do. To scream? To have someone coming out of the night to find her like this? To have to tell her father about it?

'You don't want to carry on,' Renshaw said. 'In a little while you'll feel better about it all. I told you I'd look after you. What're you frightened about? After a while you'll think it's great. Ever been with a man before?'

'No! No! Let me go!'

The words ended in a scream.

'I've had enough of you, sister,' Renshaw said. 'What do you think I brought you out here for, anyway? To fool about looking at the scenery? You were a pretty willing party. You think I'm going to let you go at this stage?'

Gwennie sat up and began to wail. It was not a loud crying but it could be heard a long way in the still night.

Suddenly Renshaw drew back his hand and slapped her across the mouth. And simultaneously two men came around the bend, tramping towards the city.

149

Gwennie listened to the sound of the feet as they drew nearer.

Renshaw crouched low. 'Keep quiet,' he said. His fist was close to her face.

But her wail rose, and the men stopped.

'Who's there?'

'Oh, some silly sheila changed her mind.'

'That so?'

'Take me with you!' Gwennie cried.

'Can't take you with us, lady. We're hiking down to the coast and then heading north.'

She scrambled onto the road. Around the bend the road dropped away. Unbelievably close, the little township huddled under the hill. She fell in beside the two strange men. Not far away there were trains running to and from the city. She began brushing back her hair, straightening the torn neckline of her frock.

She realized her days at the Dyehouse were numbered.

CHAPTER TWENTY THREE

But it was not Renshaw who made the decision about Gwennie. The Verrendahs, behind the doors of their over-clean sitting-room, discussed the situation.

'You said you knew this man?'

Her father's voice was cold. He had been, at first, secretly pleased that the manager of the Dyehouse had noticed Gwennie.

'I thought I knew him.'

She thought of the day on the fourth floor when he had cuddled her. She knew him for what he was then. But her eyes had not been really open.

'Has he shamed you?'

'No. No. Not that. I picked up a stone. I hit him.'

'Should we take you to a doctor?'

'No. No. Let me alone.'

'It should be stopped. I should see the police.'

He should see the police. Lots of people coming around and inquiring. The whole thing in the evening papers. Neighbours gossiping. Where there's smoke there's fire. Those religious ones, always pretty deep.

'You're sure you're all right? No more damage than that cut lip?'

'I'm sure.'

'Then perhaps we'd better say nothing. It might be better for you, Gwennie. We don't want any scandal.'

'We told you, Gwennie. About strange men.'

'I never want to see any men again,' Gwennie said.

'You've always got us.'

'Yes.'

'You know we love you, Gwennie.'

'I know that.'

'And know what's best for you.'

Her mother lit the bath-heater and ran the water into the bath. Mr Verrendah went into the kitchen.

'The best of men are a pretty poor lot,' Mrs Verrendah said. 'They're all dirty beasts at heart. You won't want to go back to that Dyehouse. Your father will call in and pick up your money. But you trust us, Gwennie. There's always a home with your Mum and Dad.'

'Yes,' Gwennie said.

She thought of the bushes, of the dark gullies and of Renshaw so close to her. She thought fleetingly of the boys and girls that she saw going off to the dances, holding hands. She shivered.

CHAPTER TWENTY FOUR

As his car pulled into the gutter before his house, Renshaw saw the tall figure loitering at the gate. He switched off the lights and sat back for a moment, feeling stunned. Verrendah was tall and square. In the dim light Renshaw took him for a plain-clothes detective.

She's blabbed, he thought in panic. She's been to the police.

There were witnesses. The two hikers. His mind swung round in circles. What good would their word be? Probably vagrants who'd done a stretch or two. Probably ducking the police at this very moment. He prepared to bluster.

'Get out, Renshaw. I want to see you. I'm Gwennie's father.'

Renshaw let his breath out gently. It was only Verrendah. He would handle him. He was cocky as he walked to the gate. It was only that bloody psalm-singing, come-to-Jesus bastard. Verrendah grabbed him by the lapels of his coat.

'What's wrong with you?' Renshaw asked.

'What would you think?' Verrendah said evenly.

'Gwennie.' Renshaw gave an ugly laugh. 'I did nothing to her.'

'You won't get away with this, Renshaw.'

'What you intend doing about it? Look, I took her out. I gave her a good day. I cuddled her up a bit and she hoofed it.'

'You struck her, you animal. You tried to force her.'

'Break it up. The kid's that full of notions she thinks any bloke that puts his hand on her is out to rape her. You want to let her circulate a bit. Get her out of Sunday School and let her see a bit of life. She'd get a man hung.'

'She won't be working under you again,' Verrendah said. 'You get her money made up and have it ready Monday.'

'Oh, well, if it's how you want it. I'll be sorry to see her go. Be sensible, Verrendah—you know what kids are like.'

He put out his hand, but Verrendah struck it aside.

'You haven't heard the last of this,' he said violently. 'I'll see that it's reported. I'll see that your wings are clipped. I'll go to the police first thing Monday morning. Decent people sending their kids to work there! You should be stopping this kind of thing, not encouraging it. But you haven't heard the last of it. I'll see that a spoke's put in your wheel. I'll get it stopped!'

CHAPTER TWENTY FIVE

Patty spent a long and unhappy weekend.

Her talk with Oliver Henery had cleared the air a little, but had not in any way resolved her conflict. She had been often in Renshaw's company in the weeks that followed, but never alone. Nor did she raise the question with him again. The matter was decided. The cards had fallen to Gwennie.

Working beside Miss Merton, she told herself bitterly that it didn't matter. In a few years' time they would all be dead. Everyone working in this building would be dead. For a while people would talk about them. Tell stories about them, sympathetically. Mostly sympathetically, and all in the past tense. About how good they were. But soon no one would talk about them. No one would remember them. They would be wiped out, like a slate being sponged clean. A new set of figures would appear. New people. It wouldn't matter then that she was suffering today.

But it did. What did it matter that she might be dead in five, ten, fifty years? Today was important to her. It was important to everyone who drew breath in the foul, damp air of Macdonaldtown.

Renshaw had not been actively unkind to her. When he got around to thinking of it, he felt that she had acted with dignity and restraint. Apart from her one flight from the office, there had been no acts or tantrums. And she had not gossiped. He wondered briefly what old Merton thought about it all. He wondered whether Patty had discussed it with her, and decided that she had not. Not the full gory details. Only the little-girl-in-love part. In a way he felt almost grateful to her. She had acted up well. And if anything went wrong, if the cards fell this way, and not that way, she was at hand.

Along with the thoughts of Renshaw in Patty's mind, was the new and surprising picture of Oliver Henery. A drifter, a wanderer from workshop to workshop. Yet you couldn't run away, he said. Wherever you run they get you. Wherever you go they catch up with you. The loud-mouthed, insincere Oliver Henery. The man who loved girls; who hated them; who cared for animals. And again the quiet Oliver Henery who had waited outside the church, who had talked to her in the park. The Oliver Henery who had walked her home, who had put a watch upon his tongue, who had made no attempt to kiss her at the door.

The Oliver Henery who had waited because he was a friend. The thought was a revelation. A man who could be a friend.

She looked up quickly, and there he was, standing at the foot of the stairs. He was stripped for work. A pair of khaki shorts hung upon his hips. He had a pair of rubber waterproof boots laced around his ankles. His chest was bare. He moved off into the warehouse. Patty watched him as he crossed the drying area. Beyond, the mist caught at him. She saw him vaguely for a second, then the steam blotted out his figure, as he moved deep down into the bowels of the Dyehouse.

Gwennie was not in on the Monday.

Patty noticed it as she went across to the bench where the girls were weighing up the rolls. There was no one on the wrapping table.

It could mean...?

That Gwennie had dealt with him. That she had seen through him; that she had somehow escaped.

It could mean that Gwennie had made trouble.

She stood at the bench, thoughts tumbling through her mind.

And if this was so, if Gwennie had run out, if Gwennie was never coming back, it could mean that Renshaw would be on the lookout for a girl again. It could mean...

She picked up the tickets and walked slowly back to the office.

It could mean that Renshaw would think of her again. She put the thought far away at the back of her mind.

But it persisted. And as time went on, and the whistle blew for morning tea, she began to smile. Something had happened, and Gwennie's reign was over.

It was almost ten o'clock when Renshaw came in.

He had pulled into the doctor's to get some advice about his injury. He was too busy to take the day off. He was not unduly concerned over his dark, swollen eye. He was not thin in the skin, and he could take all the ribbing that the men might be inclined to dish out.

But he had to find a girl for the wrapping bench. That was number-one priority. For certain, the rolls could not go out unwrapped. He called through the office.

'Patty.'

She came slowly into his office and stood with a pad in her hand, her pencil poised to take his instructions. She noticed his eye briefly, and the cut above the brow. So Gwennie had not submitted easily. She had fought back. Patty put aside her own guilty thoughts.

'Ring the labour exchange. We need a girl for the wrapping.'

It was said. She wrote it carefully on the pad. A girl for the wrapping bench.

'Junior?'

'Oh—useful girl. Better make it a senior, but no old crones. You'd better get Miss Merton to talk to them. And I don't want anyone straight from school, either.'

Patty wrote the instruction in silence. Once, the obvious question was on her lips, but she stifled it. In time the employees' attendance sheets would have to be made up, and then: 'Gwennie Verrendah. Reason for leaving: leaves of her own accord.'

It was enough that things were working out. There was no need to tempt fate.

She walked to the door.

On the threshold he called to her, 'That's a pretty skirt you're wearing, Patty.'

She looked up slowly, carefully.

He was already absorbed in his letters.

It was the first time he had noticed her since Gwennie began working at the Dyehouse.

CHAPTER TWENTY SIX

'Reckon I might clean up on this yet,' Goodwin said. 'I think the little sheila dumped him cold. There's no one on the wrapping bench today, and he says he ran into a door.'

'He's got a stinker.'

'Going to be hard to put up with for the next few days.'

Renshaw was irritable and uncertain. The Verrendahs sounded like people who might take some action. But as time went on and nothing came of it, things settled down into the same old groove.

Barney was having more time off than usual. Cuthbert complained to Miss Merton about it. He had been watching the sick-pay claims for some time.

'It's his wife.'

'What's wrong with her?'

Miss Merton delicately skirted the subject. 'I think there's a baby expected.'

'Well, get Mr Renshaw for me.'

'What are you doing out there?' Cuthbert asked Renshaw. 'Is Barney Monahan or his wife having this baby?'

'Oh, well, she's been pretty crook.'

'He still claiming sick-pay?'

'I don't know. I'll see into it. Haven't seen any declarations about.'

'We can't pay blokes for getting into bed too often.'

'Oh, well, I don't think he cops too much. Bit of bad luck. Wife's getting on. Not like a youngster, you know.'

'You defending him?'

'Hell, no. Only sorry for him.'

'Well, make sure about that sick-pay.'

There had been endless worry for Barney over Esther's pregnancy. She was under Dr Peters' close care. There were unexpected complications and the birth would not be an easy one. The doctor had prescribed medicines, exercises and rest. Barney was not really worried. Having babies was a common enough complaint. Barney had never met anyone who'd died of it.

But one day the doctor phoned him at work. He had sounded serious and Barney decided to give work away for the afternoon.

He sat in the waiting room furnished with comfortable, arty little chairs, reading paragraphs from old magazines and wondering fretfully what could be wrong.

When at last it came to his turn, he pushed the door open pugnaciously. He would talk up to these medicine men. He would ask them a thing or two. And he'd want a straight answer. None of this bone-pointing and backchat.

Peters was sitting behind the desk. He watched Barney clinically as he walked to the table. He was inclined to like the cocky, pugnacious little man. Must have been quite a fellow in his day. Footballer. But time had given him a hell of a hiding. Just one hell of a hiding.

He picked up Esther's card and smiled at Barney.

'What I can't understand,' Barney said, 'is why there's all this fuss. People we know have babies all the time. No trouble at all. And Esther's always been healthy.'

'You've got one girl, I see,' Dr Peters said, 'about nineteen.'

He was holding the card and looking at Barney.

'She's out of the State. Married. Living in Perth. I could bring her over, at a pinch.'

'It may not be necessary,' Dr Peters said. 'I think you will manage. I've talked to your wife about it. The main thing is that we'll need her in one of the city hospitals, and a little earlier than usual.'

'What the hell!' Barney said.

So she was sick. She was really sick.

'She going to get better, doctor?'

He felt a sudden sense of panic.

'I think it will go all right,' Dr Peters said. 'We'll do everything to see that things run a pretty even course.'

Barney's mouth was dry.

'We'll arrange to get her in early,' the doctor said. 'It could be pretty delicate, and they've got everything at hand.'

162

CHAPTER TWENTY SEVEN

After work, Oliver took a short cut through Ring Street on his way to The Crescent. Hughie was out, and he stopped a while to talk to Alice.

'I'm worried,' Alice said. 'Not so much about Hughie being out so long, although that's a problem, too. I'm worried about his condition. If I can't talk him into going to see a doctor, I'm afraid I'll have to take things into my own hands and get someone to call to the house.'

'Oh, well,' Oliver said. 'I wouldn't worry too much. Blokes get off-colour when they can't get into a job. Morose. They begin to feel there's something wrong with them. He ought to take something as a fill-in.'

'I think so. But it's no good. I've talked to him. It's all he ever wanted to be, and I don't suppose he'll change now.'

All the way to The Crescent Oliver thought about Hughie. He thought of him—clean, neat, courteous, tramping into city offices; into suburban textile offices. It should not be so difficult for Hughie to get into a job.

When he got to The Crescent, he went on until he reached the last house. It was a drab, unpainted place, built onto the street. Someone had broken the glass in one of the lower windows and a sheet of heavy cardboard had been fixed in its place. It was fastened with long nails and pieces of gummed paper. The heavy door, almost denuded of paint, sagged on its hinges.

Oliver knocked loudly.

Someone moved inside, and presently the door opened.

'Come in,' said Brother Martin.

Oliver threw his hat into the corner. Brother Martin and Joe Henderson were bending over the open fire. They had a billycan suspended from a hook hanging over the blaze, and they were stirring a savoury mess in a black pot.

The dog rose from the hearth and leapt joyously.

'Well,' Oliver said, 'this looks all right. Smells good, too.'

He spread the newspaper on the table, put down the cups, plates and cutlery.

'How're you cooking, Brother?' he asked.

Brother Martin looked up from the fire.

He wore a faded grey vest and grey trousers. His collar was fastened at the back. No one quite knew why. One day he came back from the office, carrying his briefcase, smiling a shy, introspective smile. He said he was Brother Martin. He began wearing his collar the wrong way round. He was harmless, and no one was concerned with his change of personality.

Joe Henderson worked when it was necessary, sometimes at the Dyehouse. At other times he sat about indulging in political discussion, earning a reputation for shrewdness and knowledge, in and around The Crescent.

The three had formed a partnership more than two years ago. Oliver and Joe paid the rent and bought the food. Brother Martin cooked it.

'Called in to see Hughie on the way home,' Oliver said.

'Still out?' Joe grunted. 'There's a bloke would have sold his mother. Couldn't do enough in a day. Did they place any value on that when the time came?'

Oliver ate silently. He was thinking. The spring was merging into summer. It was time for him to leave the Dyehouse behind, to strike out for a job in the heavy industries. By November the textile trade would flatten out, maybe go into a tailspin. They'd be laying men off, with little chance of them being picked up by other industries. After November, bosses thought a lot about the holiday pay; they were loath to put new men on. He would soon have to try the factories to the north, maybe take out a sickie or two.

Brother Martin left the table. He stirred up the fire and placed the pot of tea near Oliver.

'You feeling all right?' he asked.

'Fine,' Oliver said. 'Never better.'

'Got a bit on the liver,' Joe said. 'Gypped by that pert piece from the Dyehouse.'

'Speak no evil,' Brother Martin said.

'I was thinking about that Gwennie,' said Oliver. 'She wasn't in today. Mightn't mean much. Blokes are saying that Renshaw gave her the one-two-three over the weekend, and she's out.'

'She didn't need anyone to tell her about Renshaw,' Joe said. 'She knew his type. She knew she was going under Patty What's-her-name's neck. We can't shed tears of blood over these dames. If you look for it you get it. Best thing could happen to these women would be for them to get some education.'

'She was a pretty well-set-up little piece. Sixteen when she left school. Kept at Sunday School and church.'

'I said education. The role of women in society. Money—what it stands for. Constitutional barriers to...'

'Oh, for Christ's sake!'

'Anyway,' Joe said, 'I'll bet she lives in a world of make-believe. And I'd like, I'd just like to know what action they'd take against Renshaw. They'd be too frightened—too bloody frightened. People might talk. They're so respectable, they'd be raped and keep mum.'

'Careful, brother,' said Brother Martin. 'Keep watch on your tongue.'

Joe looked at him, leaned over, patted him on the arm and smiled.

'Money speaks all languages,' said Brother Martin suddenly. He smiled at Oliver and Joe.

'It should be our servant,' said Joe. 'It stands for things. We should be able to control it.'

'Some blokes can,' said Oliver. 'Some blokes look at a number. Say, twenty-seven. That's Jeremy Stein. Right. They pick up the number, Jeremy Stein mind you, drop it in the can. Sorry, can't carry any dead wood. Sure the warehouse's bulging with stock. Sure the dough will be rolling for a long time yet. And sure you made the rolls. Dyed them. Pressed them. But you know what? You put our payroll up about thirteen smackers a week. We'll see you when things pick up. Six weeks or so. After Christmas. What are you going to use for money over Christmas? Don't ask me, brother. Don't ask me. Been in a job all the year, haven't you? Taken home your thirteen smackers regular? Ought to have something put by.'

'Bastards,' said Joe. 'I get the gutsache just thinking about them.'

'They won't get me,' Oliver said. 'I'll take to the track first.'

Joe turned and looked at him.

'You could take to the track, and what would that prove? During the last big depression, blokes took to the track in thousands. Slept in dignity under bridges, in parks, in dog kennels, pigsties, cattle stalls. Don't get far by running.'

'No,' Oliver conceded.

He thought suddenly of Patty, and of the night they'd walked together to the park. It didn't matter where you ran. The place might be different, the people different, but the pattern was the same. You had the same thing to sell wherever you went. And in the long run you weren't much different from any other cattle offering for sale. And the boss knew it. Sure he knew it. What's that on his application form? Thirty-three years? Like bloody hell he is. Take a look at his teeth. This cock won't see forty again. The grey's sprouting pretty thick at the edges, there. Beginning to get that broken-winded look, too. We're going to pay out good money for this, real dough! That young rooster at the door might just fit the bill. Looks strong in the arm and thick in the skull. Sorry, mister, the job's just not tailored to your measure.

'We might learn something from that group that Danton's running,' Joe said facetiously. 'Upperclass bitches sit around and talk of social heritage. Got all the cures for the world's ills. Only don't disturb them. "The working man," that's us, "needs special guidance." Wonder how they'd go doing Leila's job on the brusher, or lumping those rolls up the ladders to the top fixtures?'

'I'm getting out of there,' Oliver said. 'Another four or five weeks and we'll be in to November.'

Brother Martin stoked up the fire. He filled the kettle and put it over the blaze to boil.

Oliver unwrapped a parcel, lifted out some meat, and put it down for the dog. Then they gathered up the dishes and began on the washing-up. It was the last chore of the evening and they were glad to have it over.

The light was out. They sat around the fire, gazing at the flames, suddenly silent. Brother Martin had his fingers together, repeating some prayer remembered from childhood.

'We're lost,' he said sadly to Oliver. He peeped almost fearfully into the shadows of the room. 'We're all lost.'

Oliver put his arm around his shoulder. He patted him reassuringly.

The dog had eaten the last of the meat. He stretched, nosed in between the men and curled up on the hearth.

Oliver switched on the light. The shadows fled. The fear left Brother Martin's face. He looked round the familiar room and smiled.

'Things will have to change,' Joe said. 'The common man's not likely to take too much more. Where's the justice of this automation?'

'Well, it's bound to come. Don't think the textiles will feel it for a while.'

'But the justice, man! Consider. All the accumulated labour and ideas. Men working and working. Then all at once it's there, the thing we've dreamed of, bright and rosy and shiny. What happens? Some shiny-arse walks up. Looks at it, takes out his bloody money. Money, mind you! Buys up the accumulated ideas and labour. Buys it for money. Shoves it into his office or factory. See a picture of him smiling in the morning paper, pulling the handle to prove that even a dumbbell can operate it. Anything about making things easier for the men he employs? Chopping down on hours? Raising wages? You can bet your sweet life there's nothing. "Mr Stripper says this machine will do the work of sixty men." They don't print the bit about the blokes getting the pay-off on Friday, or how the blokes feel, or how their wives feel. Mr Stripper feels like Jesus Christ. He rings up the Chamber of Manufacturers. He has a discussion. His face is set against any reduction of the working week.'

'We should be getting in early,' Oliver said. 'Before we feel the real impact. We should be working shorter hours now, cracking down on overtime. These places should be made to carry us for a while. All the Christmas stock dyed and ready. Blokes who worked their insides out, ten or twenty or so, got to go down for six weeks. Cost next to nothing to carry them. They made the stuff! It's in the fixtures. The trucks are carrying it out as fast as they can load it.'

'You ought to start something.'

'Not me,' Oliver said. 'I know the score there. Nearly all unskilled men and easily replaced. Before the axe drops I'll be off. Noticed some of the engineering firms up north advertising for men already.'

'Not running away?'

Oliver sat up and looked at Joe. He felt irritated and perplexed. There was nothing to be gained by stopping. Four weeks at the outside. Better to beat the rap. Might end up like Hughie.

'Not running away,' he said. His face was thoughtful. 'Looking after Number One.'

Joe looked at him for a long time. He shifted his position, putting his feet on the chimney-breast.

'I tell you, I'm no Sir Galahad. And what could I start? God Almighty, Joe, you want to think. You ever heard of the blind leading the blind? I tell you, I know the score. Everyone so frightened he's got the gutsache. Everyone working like hell. Thinking about his wife, and kids, and rent, and maybe the instalment on the kitchen cabinet or the TV set. Wondering what will happen if he can't pay. And working like hell all the time. Hoping that Renshaw will notice and maybe say, "Johnson, now—I can scarcely afford to let him go."'

'Well, no good getting involved,' Joe said. 'Every man for himself when the ship's sinking.' There was a careful

170

note of sarcasm in his voice. 'But it could straighten out,' he added. 'Funny game, the textiles. Jumpy.'

'Don't think much of its chances.'

Oliver went to the door and opened it. He looked up at the night sky. He could see the Dyehouse chimney. It brooded over the landscape like a gigantic god, its dark shadow stretched out over Macdonaldtown. All around it the cottages were huddled together. Soon the people would be sleeping. All around the Dyehouse the people would be sleeping. In Richmond Parade, in Ring Street, The Crescent.

He came back into the room. He caught a glimpse of Joe's bright, questioning eye. He sought for the word, the phrase that would confound him.

He knew all this claptrap. Better than Joe. Better than Joe could ever know it. Joe usually worked the heavy industries. It was different there. The attitude of the men was different.

'I tell you,' Oliver said, 'everything's right. Cuthbert's not the bloke to stick his head out.'

'Or his heart, either.'

'Well, you know how accountants are. You don't need me to tell you. He's got the law on his side, and never mind the rights of things. The law's with him. The most we could do would be to get a guarantee of preference for the men he's standing down. There's no law forces a firm to keep on men they can't use.'

'Well,' Joe said, 'you could holler. Make noises like you were hurt. Make noises like you were human beings.'

There was silence. Oliver looked across at Joe. It was hard to explain how he felt to a man like Joe. He wasn't

171

afraid. He'd drop Renshaw any day, and get out. Quicker than Joe, perhaps. But then Joe would start that medicine-man stuff. That putting of one fact alongside another. Tying them up. He'd get meetings on the job and spruikers out. He'd be in the middle of it and liking it. And if he hit the pavement, he wouldn't worry. Joe liked involvement, he really liked it.

'Oh, well,' Joe said. 'I suppose you know where you're going.'

He took out his paper and started reading. Brother Martin's lips were moving. He was repeating something under his breath. Oliver continued to stare into the fire. When he finally looked up he smiled. He had been thinking of Patty. Well, a man could be a fool. All kinds of a fool. But not as big a fool as all that. No, sir. He bent over and patted the dog. But his mind swung back to the Dyehouse. He began thinking about Hughie and Barney and young Sims. 'Want my brains brushing,' he said to himself. 'Must be getting addle-brained.'

CHAPTER TWENTY EIGHT

Something woke Hughie. Something like a deep gong struck somewhere and he sat up in bed, looking into the thick darkness that shrouded the bedroom, roused by its insistent call. With nerves strained and taut he looked into the blackness, listening. But there was nothing. The curtains stirred gently in the lazy breeze; Alice slept, breathing softly; the clock ticked quietly on the bedside table. The illuminated dial showed that it was three o'clock. Yet something had sounded. A deep, unmelodious clang. Even sleeping he had heard it, and he had struggled up.

He sat, fighting a sense of panic, holding onto the side of the bed. Still only the curtains moving at the window. He got out of bed cautiously, taking care not to disturb Alice. He went to the window, pushed the curtains aside and looked out onto the street where the sleeping houses lay one against the other. Overhead the sky was dark, pierced by pinspots of light. But there was nothing strange, nothing different.

The gong. The strange, harsh note that had invaded his sleeping! It was unfamiliar here, but still a known sound.

The gong on the back door of the Dyehouse! The unmusical clangour made by impatient carriers anxious to off-load their cargo and be on their way.

The Dyehouse gong.

Hughie shook his head. He had isolated the sound, and he breathed easier. That was it. He had dreamed it, the harsh, demanding call.

He had been dreaming. It was quite a step to the Dyehouse, and no carriers called at this hour. The sound of the gong would not carry so far, anyway. It was part of his dream.

He sat down on the edge of the bed, shivering.

He would compose himself for sleep. Lie down. Do the relaxing exercises exactly as he had been told.

But he went to the wardrobe and opened it quietly. The clothes were in neat heaps. Singlets, pyjamas, shirts. His hand groped and found the thick drill. Four sets of clean white overalls, washed, pressed and neatly piled. He took out a pair, smoothed the stack and closed the door.

He would go out for a while. Put on something warm and walk as far as the corner. Perhaps as far as the Dyehouse. He pulled the overalls on over his pyjamas. When he was finished he bent down and smoothed the thick, familiar material over his knees, his thighs, his waist.

Alice still slept in the dark morning.

His slippers were handy. He put his feet into them and

tiptoed again to the wardrobe. He took out the cardigan he had been wearing the day he hit Renshaw, his work cardigan. He had not worn it since.

He looked at the clock. It was three-fifteen.

He went quietly into the hall. Here he listened. Alice slept on, her breathing deep and even.

He opened the front door and stepped into the dark morning. It was quieter than he remembered it and he frowned, wondering when he was last up at three-fifteen. To the south lay the Dyehouse. He looked up. Against the deep, star-studded sky the chimney rose dark and immense. But he turned his back to it and walked down past The Crescent to the park. All was quiet. Under a heap of newspapers in a corner a vagrant lay sleeping. The seats, the light poles, the rotunda for the band, all looked strange, unfamiliar in the dark morning. He began walking down Wentworth Parade. Past the pub, now quiet; past the terraces wrapped in slumber. In one house a light gleamed on the lower floor. Hughie drew back into the dark to watch the picture framed in the light.

An early worker. Hughie could see his blue denim overalls, his thick wrists with the leather straps round them, the red of the woman's dressing gown, the food on the table. She was getting him ready for work. Fussing with sandwiches, putting food from a saucepan onto a plate. Working quietly, efficiently. The man picked up his bag; the woman reached up her arms and drew his head down towards her.

Hughie started walking again. He heard a door open, steps onto the street, then the door closing. The man came

175

with great strides, making for the station. He passed Hughie and called a muffled 'Good day' as he passed.

Good day, Hughie thought. Yes, it was morning. Soon the sky would be lightening, the stars paling. He passed Barrington Terrace, tracing the branches of the tree to the top window. He smiled fleetingly, thinking of Patty.

He turned the corner and he was in Richmond Parade. Just ahead loomed the dark bulk of the Dyehouse. A steam train passed slowly. Hughie could see the warm yellow glow, the steam spiralling; see the dark outlines of the men's figures; hear the warm friendliness of their voices.

But he would have to go back. Alice might wake any time. Find the bed empty; sit up, worrying; even raise an alarm.

Cats sleeping on the mat in the porch outside the corner shop stirred as he passed. They stretched, opened up their eyes, alert and watchful. And presently he was at the Dyehouse. He put out his hand and felt the solid bulk of the dark red-brick structure. It was the same. The same dark, shrouded, grimy windows. The broken lights on the fourth floor, the overhanging section above the office, the red door, the dirty white barricading. All just as he remembered it.

He put his hand into his cardigan pocket and pulled out his key-ring. He stood holding it in his hand, looking at the lock. It looked the same. It was the same. They hadn't changed it.

They hadn't called in his key. Why was that?

He slipped the key into the padlock. It turned easily and he slid the barricading back.

If the main lock was unchanged, if things were as they used to be...

The key turned in the lock. The door opened into the familiar vestibule. He went quickly to the signal control, picked it up and gave the code.

He glanced briefly around Renshaw's office. The same bottles of dye, the same cards, the same stale cigarette butts, the same rubbish trailing from the drawers. Nothing was changed.

He turned off the lights. He closed the front door and pulled the barricading to. He wandered aimlessly into the dark warehouse. In the boiler-room all was still. No light. No warmth. No John Thompson sitting on the packing case, smiling up at him. He walked like a ghost in a world of pipes and gauges.

But the smell was the same. He stopped in the warehouse and sniffed it up. Sulphuric ether. The tin was roughly opened, standing in a corner. Have an accident with that some day. Some day there'd be trouble and someone would get really hurt.

The stairs were inviting, reminding him of the greige stacked on the fourth floor, of the work waiting to be done, of the colours.

But he made for the vats. Still, silent, cold, the steel gleamed back at him. He went into the lab and turned on the light. The new range was on the table. The green. So that was to be the new green. And they were having trouble with it. The experimental swatch was thrown on the ground. It was out. Dead out. Flat, dull, uninteresting. He picked up the range pattern. Why, he could do that. Do it on his ear.

He picked up a pencil and began to write. All the particulars. He lit the gas, set the bunsen burner and began.

It was almost daylight. Hughie wrapped the cloth in white and placed it beside the range pattern. It was exact.

The dyer's instructions for the first vats were thrown on the desk. He rolled up the glass from the balances. No. 1. He weighed up carefully. No. 4. No. 6. No. 7. No. 9. He had them ready. All ready for the kick-off.

In the warehouse the trolleys stood stacked with rolls. 'Best-Yet'! Hughie ripped the paper. So they had got the contract after all. The first batch was on its way out. Not as good, not quite as good as the colour swatches he had dyed. He handled the cloth, smoothing its glossy satin surface. Not quite as good, but Best-Yet was taking it.

He went through to the presses. The cloth lay in heaps piled in the trucks. Green, peach, deep gold, salmon, apricot, peacock blue, purple, plum.

Sims was turning it out all right. The dyeing was good.

He thought of his earlier conversation with Renshaw. No one can be regarded as indispensable. No, that was true. Sims was carrying on. He was doing a good job. Hughie's trained eye knew where to look for the faults, and they were few.

He walked up the stairs. It was darker here. The windows were closed off. He kept walking up until he reached the fourth floor. The stockroom door was locked. He took out his key and opened it. He was singing softly to himself.

Now the room was in darkness. The rolls stacked on

the tables looked white and ghostly. He wandered aimlessly down the first aisle, touching the stacks, identifying the quality with his fingers. The greige stock was not coming in so quickly. Old Harvison was afraid of being caught. He was not allowing the greige to build up.

Hughie stood still. He remembered this room. When he was a kid, the very first day he started, he had helped Ron James stack rolls on the end table. It had been a hot summer's day and the cloth had stuck to their sweaty hands. They had sat down after a while, and old Boyle who was the boss then had come and caught them.

'Hard work lifting those rolls, you reckon? But never mind, Hughie, you're going to the lab with Tommy Peters tomorrow. And Ronnie, I'm going to start to train you up.'

But they hadn't gone straight to their new jobs. They had played about in the stockroom for a fortnight, throwing waste at each other, singing the latest songs, covertly smoking cigarettes. Taking about the future, looking at the future and wondering about it.

Well, James was out now. Pushed out. But he had got on at City Dyers. Got a better job, really. But he was a different bloke. A different kind of bloke altogether.

He turned into the second aisle. The heavy cloths were warehoused here. Hughie felt the rolls and thought of the colours he would like to see on these textures. Rich, warm colours.

At the end stack his fingers closed over something foreign. Oblong cards. There were half a dozen of them, the PG cards that Patty had left on the bench the day she came up to speak to Renshaw. Hughie picked them up and ran them through his fingers. He wondered briefly what they were doing here. Whether they were important. He shuffled them through his fingers, then placed them back beside the stack.

There was a trolley already loaded, waiting at the lift-well. The tickets had been taken off. Patty Nicholls had probably written them in and totted up the weight.

Cloth for the vats! He had already weighed up the dyes for it in the lab. Strange, that. The rolls picked out, the tickets written in, the dyes weighed up. He began to laugh again.

The wires sang as he hauled up the crane. He pushed the wire door open. He stopped laughing. Far below he could see a round patch of daylight. He looked at it, bending over.

Then his arms shot out and the floors rushed together as he passed to the bright circle that proclaimed the new day.

CHAPTER TWENTY NINE

John Thompson was late.

There had been a holdup on the line and the trains were running off schedule. It was no use worrying. If he got off the train to hunt up a bus at a strange station he would probably be later still. Better to wait while the train crawled and bumped on its way towards Macdonaldtown.

John had Renshaw's key. Ever since Hughie left, no one had been disposed to accept the responsibility of opening up. Renshaw was loath to come in early every morning. He worked long hours of overtime as it was, and he felt entitled to start work with the main body of the staff at eight o'clock. He had finally decided to give his key to John. John was the logical man. He had to be in early in any case to get steam up. He was honest, trustworthy, dependable.

John glanced at his watch. They were just past Lewisham, and running fifteen minutes late. He picked up his paper and began to read. No need to sit watching every factory as the train moved slowly past.

They were in at last. John picked up his bag. He smiled at some men hurrying off the platform. There would be a good many places without steam for a while this morning. He glanced at the skyline: smoke issued from few of the chimneys. Must be a lot of blokes on this train, he thought, and grinned to himself. Still, he had better hurry.

It was almost 7.20 when he reached the Dyehouse door. The barricading was unlocked, but pushed to. The main door was on the latch. He pondered this for a minute. The seal was broken, and no one was about. That meant someone in authority was in the place. Perhaps Bob Mayers. Perhaps Cuthbert or Harvison had come over on a lightning raid. He cursed under his breath. Well, they could go take a running dive off Ben Buckler. He'd clocked-on on time every morning for twelve months or more. He pushed the barricading open, pushed the door and hooked it back. They were not on overtime now. The men would not begin to drift in until about ten minutes to eight.

He went straight to the boiler-house. He did not change. He worked quickly and methodically. And when everything was under way, he picked up his billy and went whistling through to the tap in the drying area. He noticed the bundle lying under the lift-well, at first absently. It looked strange. From where he was standing in the peculiar light, with the shadows falling here and there, it looked almost like a body.

He filled the billy, still idly looking at the sprawled white mass. He came through to the blinding light under the loading dock.

The water slopped from the billy as he opened his mouth to scream.

The neck was twisted and grotesque, the eyes stared unseeing at a heap of rose swami flung into a corner. Blood had soaked into the white drill of the overalls.

John put the billy on the ground. He picked up a length of yellow silk and flung it over the body.

What to do? Ring for the police! Ring for a doctor! Ring Larcombe, Renshaw. He ran to the office and picked up Miss Merton's Teledex. Dr Sparkes. Yes, the doctor, urgently. Man maybe dead. Man most certainly dead. Now Larcombe. Yes, that's right. Looks like he's dead. Looks like he's had it. What's that? Get the police? Get Renshaw. Keep the men away. He'd be around immediately.

Renshaw was backing out the car when he heard the phone ring.

'Who the hell...!'

He drove to the front door, leapt out of the car and picked up the phone.

Why the hell should Thompson be ringing? Why the hell couldn't he wait? Accident! What sort of accident? Boiler blow up? Trouble with chemicals?

'Hughie Marshall. Looks like he's dead. Looks like he might have fallen down the lift-well onto the loading dock.'

The sunlight was bright on the street. The two peppercorn-trees looked green and inviting through the open window. It looked like a lovely day.

'What's that you're saying?' Renshaw said roughly. 'You must be mad. Hughie Marshall? But he doesn't work there any more. Why would Hughie Marshall be lying dead on the floor? You must be drunk.'

He waited, looking at the trees in the street, at his car parked at the front gate.

'I reckon I'd know him,' John Thompson said. 'Even now I reckon I'd be able to tell Hughie Marshall.'

'I'll be over,' Renshaw said.

He put down the phone. In the space of a few minutes, how the morning had changed! Hughie Marshall was dead, with unpleasant implications. How did Hughie get into the Dyehouse? There were the keys. The keys that he had thought about only yesterday. The keys that he had intended picking up, perhaps today. He pictured Larcombe's face, Harvison's cold anger. Well, they had got him. He was right out on a limb. They'd caught him with his pants down, this time.

The police were already there when Renshaw pulled up before the Dyehouse. They had cordoned off the section and were talking to John Thompson. Looking at his keys. Glancing at the open barricading. Miss Merton, coming through the vestibule, stopped.

'Don't let anyone through this way,' a policeman said. 'The bundy's in this area? Too bad. You'll have to take a risk on who's late.'

The doctor and police had spoken together. There were no suspicious circumstances. The time of death was established. They had tracked Hughie through the warehouse, into the boiler-room, down to the lab and up to the fourth floor.

In the lab, Larcombe had stood looking at the weighing-up that Hughie had done, and at the colour swatch for the new green.

'I see you have that green right,' he said. He indicated the colour pattern and the swatch that Hughie had dyed. Renshaw looked at it too. The green. The new green. They had worked on it most of the previous day without result. He laid the swatch beside the pattern. It was exact.

He didn't lie to Larcombe, this time.

'Poor bastard,' he said.

But there was more to be faced. The police interviewed Cuthbert and Harvison at Head Office. The story might provide evening headlines. It was not good for business.

'Is it common practice to allow keys to remain in the possession of persons no longer in the employment of the Company?'

It was not the practice or the policy of the Company. By no means. And those responsible for this oversight could expect to be dealt with severely.

Mr Harvison looked at Mr Cuthbert. Well, it was his department. Instructions to personnel. Did that rattle-brained Renshaw understand the importance of calling in keys? Of having locks changed if keys should be lost? Was he so lacking in common nous as to be unaware of the value of the stock lodged at Macdonaldtown?

'We should do something about Mrs Marshall,' Cuthbert said suddenly. 'I think we should write to her.'

Harvison's mind swung back from the Company problem. Mrs Marshall. Well, yes. There was a Mrs Marshall. The quiet little figure that he remembered vaguely had a wife. It had married someone. Had set up a home somewhere. No doubt this Mrs Marshall was prostrate with grief over this little man in the white overalls whose face he scarcely remembered.

'With us thirty-five years,' Cuthbert said.

'Got all that was coming to him,' Harvison said bluntly. 'You paid him up when he left.'

'Got all that was due to him,' Cuthbert said. He felt irritated.

'Well, suit yourself. He's caused us enough trouble. I'm going to root that Larcombe along over this. God knows what else is going on at Macdonaldtown. Do what you like, as long as it doesn't cost us dough.'

Harvison leaned back in his chair. He rattled his papers. The interview was over. Cuthbert gathered up his books. He was feeling strangely shaken by Hughie's death. There was something not quite straight about the whole thing. He thought of Larcombe coldly, and with increased irritation. He let Renshaw ride over him.

He went into his office. The day's work was waiting. Decisions to be made on this and that. He plunged into it, and presently he forgot about Renshaw, about Hughie, about the Dyehouse.

There was little work done at the Dyehouse that day. Renshaw was tied up, first of all over Hughie, and then over the keys. The police had questioned him again and again. They would be sure to mention the matter to the old man. It would have to come out. There was no other explanation for Hughie's presence in the Dyehouse. Larcombe was not helpful. In one flash he saw everything that he had worked for swept away. He had trusted this fellow, Renshaw. He had depended on him. Now he was cold to his explanations and pleadings.

'You know the rules,' Larcombe said. He looked with aversion at Renshaw. He had climbed slowly and painfully to his present position, and God only knew just when Harvison might decide to cut his water off.

'It was easily done,' Renshaw said. 'You saw it yourself. I was unconscious when he walked out. You know what the score was. You saw him hit me. I didn't make up his money. I was out like a light when he left. Cuthbert saw him at Head Office. He should have asked him about the keys.'

'Cuthbert was out,' Larcombe said shortly. 'Miss Uliffe made up Hughie's money. Cuthbert left an instruction. It's no good trying to sidestep it. It was your job to get the keys or report them missing.'

'I've told you. I was thinking about it only yesterday. Thinking I'd send Sims around. I wasn't worried. Not really. You know yourself Hughie was honest enough.'

Larcombe turned around. He looked slowly at Renshaw and sneered.

'Your tune's changed a bit today.'

'I mean honest. About money. About things.'

'He wasn't a bad dyer, either,' Larcombe said suddenly. 'He tied up that green that had you tossed. I tell you, Renshaw, if anything comes of this you'd better be watching yourself. You'd just better be on your toes.'

Sims and Collins had not started the vats up early. The weighing-up was done, but they were uncertain whether to use the dyes. The way Hughie was he could have put anything in.

'Seemed all right with the green,' Sims said. He lifted it up, holding it to the light. 'Couldn't be closer.'

'He really liked it,' Collins said slowly. 'Liked mucking about with the bloody stuff. You wouldn't read about it.'

'No,' Sims said.

'I'm not cut out for this game,' Collins said suddenly. 'You'd have to really like a job to put up with this for years. Water dripping from the ceiling. Floors always wet and cold.'

'What about your Tech? That'd be down the drain.'

'It's my life,' Collins said. 'I've only got the one. First job that suits me I'll be right out of this dyeing game. Out of the textiles altogether. First thing that looks like really fitting me I'll be shooting through.'

Oliver was standing on the edge of the crowd, just outside the cordon. He could see nothing more than a shapeless mass in the centre of the loading dock. He caught Barney's eye and went across to him. They had not stripped down for work. The throb of the machinery told them that no vats were under way. Very little machinery was turning in the building. In the boiler-room the two Colonials were panting slowly. The steam was there on tap, waiting for the operators.

Barney and Oliver walked upstairs slowly. It was hard for Oliver to understand Hughie. Only yesterday he'd had a word with Alice. Advised her to talk to Hughie. To get him to take a fill-in job for a while. What was there in jobs that got blokes that way? In the big groups, the professions, men often got like that. But for a bloke in an ordinary run-of-the-mill job...

'Must have been a bit off,' Barney said. 'But I've seen blokes really wrapped up in their jobs before. There's Bob Mayers. There's a bloke really likes his job. Got a feeling for metal. Likes nutting things out and then making them.'

They were quiet for a while, thinking.

'But there's plenty of jobs in Bob Mayers' line. Plenty of scope too. The trouble with Hughie was, he liked this dyeing. He could do it and he knew he could. But it's a pretty close field. How often do you see blokes advertising for dyers? Not too bloody often. And then Hughie hadn't qualified. I think he felt he'd reached the end of the road.'

'He got it pretty rough here too,' Oliver said. 'Renshaw always bouncing him.'

They changed soberly. There was no hurry. Renshaw was still running around in circles, Collins uncertain about the dyes. Presently, someone gave the signal. The machines were turned on and the men moved slowly to their positions.

After Hughie's body was removed and the cement cleaned and hosed off, Mr Mayers went through to the boiler-house. He had been late in, that morning. Larcombe, petulant and full of complaints, was in the office with Renshaw. There had been a constant stream of visitors to the boiler-house, and John had told and retold the story. About picking up his billy; about whistling as he crossed the warehouse floor; about standing at the tap and watching the water flow into the billy; about watching the heap of white under the lift-well. Re-enacting the drama, to the moment of realization: the spilled water, the sharp cry, the running steps. The realization that this was no heap of clothes, but a human body.

'Can't understand it,' John said. 'He could have done anything for a while. While there's life there's hope. He had a happy little set-up. Good wife, nice home. Never owed a penny.'

'Hard to get inside another man's mind,' Mayers said. 'I don't suppose we'll ever know just why or when he decided to do it; whether he was thinking about it when he walked down the street; whether it was in his mind when he opened the door.'

'Gives you a weak feeling round the guts,' John said. 'Maybe he slipped. Maybe he went to grab the hoist and toppled over. Maybe he thought he'd hook the trolley onto the crane.'

'There's not a chance. There were no ropes there, anyway. Nothing to hook onto. Goodwin dropped the ropes down the lift-well the night before. He was going to take them up first thing in the morning.'

They sat back, silent, looking at the boilers.

'Bit of a backhander for Renshaw,' John said. 'I think those coppers really shook him. He looked wrung out when I saw him. Scarcely able to curse the men for standing about, or Collins for not getting the vats under way.'

It was hot and oppressive in the boiler-house. John opened the window and the fresh air came streaming in.

'Gave me a bit of a jolt when I saw the door open this morning,' John said. 'I thought old pussy-foot was over. Old Sneaking Jesus, checking up on the quiet.'

John looked at Mayers. But he didn't rise to the bait.

Clashes between Harvison and Mayers were not uncommon.

Leaning back in his car as it sped through on the way to the city, the Chairman of Directors never failed to glance across at the Dyehouse, to take comfort in its great sprawling breadth, in the imposing height of the chimney-stack rising from the boiler-house, and to trace the track of the smoke as it eddied into the murky air that blanketed Macdonaldtown. On odd occasions he had accosted the engineer, intimating that excessive belching of black smoke meant cash lost to the Company. The BTU's had fallen.

Mayers was not the man to be outdone by a mere Chairman of Directors. He reasoned, fairly enough, that old Harvison had made his way up via accountancy, had never served his time, and was sketchy on the British Thermal Unit. Mayers would hold forth and endeavour to dazzle old Harvison with science. But he was a cagey type, was old Harvison. He only saw the black smoke, and black smoke meant that the Company was paying out money unnecessarily.

It was half-past three. The children were beginning to pass on their way home from school. Their shouts drifted through to the boiler-house.

'New crop coming up,' Mayers said. 'Another year or so and some of these kids will be working here. Starting out. Makes you think a bit.'

The phone rang. Collins was calling from the laboratory. Two more vats. John moved to the boiler and opened the door. The heat rushed into the boiler-room. He closed the door, walked to the pump, checked the gauges.

'Be the last vats tonight,' he said to Mayers. 'Patty Nicholls won't get corns on her behind writing up all the tickets that will come off the production bench today.'

CHAPTER THIRTY

At four-fifteen the phone rang. It was Cuthbert. His voice was curt, colourless, but polite.

'About those bundy cards.'

'Yes,' said Miss Merton.

'I want you to make sure every man bundies off. Not much chance of checking up on the latecomers today. Will you see to that? You might make a point of waiting until the last person bundies off. They'll have to pass your office.'

Miss Merton put the phone down.

'What did he want?' Renshaw asked. He was leaning against the door-jamb, looking moodily into Miss Merton's office. 'Did he want to know anything about Hughie Marshall?'

'Just rang about the bundy cards. Wants to make sure everyone bundies off.'

Renshaw had the evening papers in his hand. There was a picture of the Dyehouse, and in a circle a picture of the loading dock. And at the top a picture of Hughie, stiff and unyielding in his best navy-blue striped suit. It was a younger Hughie, taken more than fifteen years ago. Alice had taken it with an old box camera that had been a Christmas present.

'I wonder what the old man's going to say when he reads this,' Renshaw said. 'But I can't see how I can be held responsible. This was Cuthbert's pigeon.'

'We got an instruction,' Miss Merton said. 'The advice was printed and underlined in red. They pay a lot of attention to the loss of these keys.'

Miss Merton picked up the paper and began to read.

'What can they do, when you really come to think about it?' she said at last. 'You're the only one who understands the dyeing. Collins is only starting. There's really no one else.'

'That's right,' Renshaw said. How right you are, sister. Right on the bullseye. Who else is there? When you get down to taws, who else? He was in a better position than Larcombe. A stronger position. The more you considered it, the stronger his position looked. Still, he was not anxious to cross swords with Larcombe. Not yet. But the time might come.

If the papers would let well alone, the thing would blow over.

He walked suddenly into Patty's office.

She saw him coming, and sat quietly transferring figures from the Shipping books.

'You haven't let up for a long time, Patty,' he said.

She pointed to the pile of books and smiled.

'It's always at my heels,' she said. 'I scarcely clear up one book, and another's ready.'

He noticed that the old books had been cleared from the shelves.

'You got rid of the rolls,' he said slowly.

'I thought I'd take a risk. Make out cards if the rolls come through.'

The day wore itself out. At twenty to five the men began to troop up the stairs to the showers. Some stood for a while in the loading dock, talking and gesticulating, looking at the spot where Hughie's body had rested. But finally it came, the long-drawn-out whistle, the two shrill screams that denoted the end of the day's labour. The men and women passed slowly. The bundy whirred. In the outer office, Renshaw was still talking to Patty Nicholls, his head bent low over her. They seemed to be enjoying the conversation. Now and then Patty smiled.

Oliver, coming from the showers, saw the two heads close together. He smiled fleetingly, but his face darkened. She'll cop what she's looking for, he thought. If you really hunt it up you get it. And Renshaw's just the chap to push it along. You don't play games with a tiger-snake.

He shoved his card into the bundy and clocked off.

CHAPTER THIRTY ONE

The days that followed were not easy ones for Renshaw. The inquiry into Hughie's death took place. Cuthbert wrote to Alice. The men took up a collection. Miss Merton bought a wreath and a card. Life settled down again.

Harvison had not spared Larcombe over the matter. He had no defence. There was nothing to do but stand listening to Harvison's cold summing-up of the situation. It was no good blaming Renshaw. Who could have foreseen the result of Renshaw's carelessness over the keys?

But he'd better start getting a grip on the reins. One or two blues of this nature and he could be out. He'd better really start gathering up those reins, see that they were eased out of Renshaw's hands. He could find himself in the cart if he didn't pull up his socks. And no one had ever accused old Harvison of being a sentimentalist.

Harvison leant forward in his chair. He was not

shooting up his eyebrows. He was not smiling. His mouth was set in a thin, hard line.

When it came to a showdown, Larcombe was right out on a limb. And Harvison wasn't the man to scruple about cutting him down.

'How often do you go to the Dyehouse?' Harvison asked coldly.

He went often enough. Whenever he thought it necessary. Was there any need to sit on the bloody doormat? Watch every piddling little job? Why did they have Renshaw there? Did he have to supervise every vat? Direct every load that hit the presses? Dot every i, cross every t?

'How often?'

Larcombe raised his eyes. He looked warily at old Harvison leaning forward in his chair. If he said this, or this…He ran his tongue along his lips.

'How often have you been out during the past month?'

'Well—I ring. I ring pretty often.'

'How often have you been out?'

'Once—maybe twice a week.'

Harvison put his hand into a drawer. He drew out a folder. It contained a list of the names of all senior Staff personnel, together with their salaries.

'This be you?' Harvison asked. He looked at Larcombe with fury, almost hatred. 'This bloke here—the one drawing down this figure? Do we pay you that for going to Macdonaldtown once, twice a week and attending a party with Best-Yet?'

Larcombe was silent. Thoughts tossed through his mind. There was plenty he could say. If he wanted to, he could lean forward and grab the small, lean neck between his fingers. He could shove a few home truths down his neck. He could tell him a thing or two. This little Caesar in this piddling little backwater, thumping the desk and yelling. But instinct warned him to be quiet.

'I could have your money made up now. Maybe you could find a better job. One more suited to your peculiar talents.'

The blood drained from Larcombe's face. He lifted his eyes and looked at the old man. The old man looked back at him, his eyes cold and implacable.

'How do you think this company was built up?' he asked. 'By chaps going to Macdonaldtown once or twice a week? We've got more useless ornaments on the payroll than we can carry as it is. Too many tall poppies waiting to be cut down. Too many people wasting their time drinking tea.'

Suddenly his face changed. The change was subtle. He placed the folder back in the drawer. He put his hands together.

'All right,' he said. 'I'm prepared to accept that this was an accident. I'm prepared to accept your explanation. What I'm not prepared to accept is your loafing about, letting things drift along in the hands of an imbecile like that Renshaw. There's going to be changes, you can mark my word.'

Harvison picked up a pencil and wrote briefly on a sheet of paper.

'I want you at Macdonaldtown at least once every day. Understand? I expect you to have a grip on everything that's going on. Is that clear? I want these tea parties kept to a minimum. I don't want to be told every time I ring a bell, or get onto the phone, that you're drinking tea with Best-Yet, or Newtogs, or Smith's Worsteds. And I want you to exercise some control over people like Renshaw. Right. So Renshaw knows the dyeing. That's what we want. He can handle the Macdonaldtown people. Knows them. Right again. But never let the day dawn when he runs you. We pay you big money to have everything at your fingertips. So you get on well with the customers? So what? We all do. We've got a quality product, and they know it. I'm paying you big money, and I want results. You're not going to get them going to Macdonaldtown once a week. And I don't want to see you shining the seat of your pants on that chair every time I come in. If we want you, there's always a line to Macdonaldtown.'

Larcombe drew his breath. It was over. He had survived it. He lived again.

Harvison threw down his pencil.

'All right,' he said. 'You can go.'

Larcombe stumbled from the room.

He had scarcely said a word.

CHAPTER THIRTY TWO

At the Dyehouse things settled down gradually after
Hughie's death. Collins was tired of the laboratory. The
wet, dripping ceilings and the constant clanging of the
experimental vat oppressed him. But most of all he hated
mucking about with the dyes, hated weighing-up, hated
thinking about colours, hated the constant care and watch-
fulness involved in the processes.

Renshaw was edgy too. With Hughie out of the way
and Collins openly uninterested, he was obliged to spend
more and more time in the lab supervising the work.

Larcombe was terse and disinclined to be friendly.
Still, he had said little enough about the keys, in the end.
He said he could see Renshaw's point, but that they would
have to tighten things up.

'Who opens up now?' Larcombe asked. Renshaw
watched him warily.

'John Thompson.'

'Not a Staff man?'

'No—but he's got to be in early.'

Larcombe pondered this. Yes, someone had to be in. Someone had to get up steam.

'He break the seal?'

'I suppose so. How the hell—'

'He give the code?'

'Well, what would you think?'

'We had an instruction about this,' Larcombe said.

'About what?'

'About passing on the code. Remember?'

'I'm not Jesus Christ,' Renshaw said. 'I can't be in two places at once. I work back every night, and I'm not coming in early to open up.'

'What about Bob Mayers?' Larcombe said. He was thinking slowly. If anything went wrong with this they could all be in the cart, every man jack of them.

'For Christ's sake,' Renshaw said. 'John's been here for years. He's no fool. Do we have to dig someone out of bed?'

'Oh, well. Let it stand,' Larcombe said.

He would mention it in his report. That would put him in the clear. If Harvison thought fit to question it, he could soon change the set-up. He would toss it right back into Harvison's lap.

'Don't you ever watch what you're doing?' Renshaw said to Collins. 'Haven't I told you over and over again that a dyer has to be extra careful, and clean? Clean overalls. Clean hands. No dye lying about on benches. Back of every good dyeing job everything is like that. Wash. Everything. All the time. Benches, jugs, stands, test tubes, pipettes. You've got all the gear, all the hot water. Even a girl to help you. Yet look at this!'

Renshaw took the pipettes from the stand. 5 cc, 20 cc. All dirty, all clogged with dye.

'You've been using them as stirring sticks. Haven't I told you to use the rod?'

Collins looked from Renshaw to the metal jug on the bunsen burner. There was a pipette lying beside it. It was thick with dye. Renshaw had put the dye in the beaker. He had been stirring it with the pipette.

'I'm telling *you*,' Renshaw said coldly. 'When you've been dyeing as long as I have, you can please yourself. I want those pipettes cleaned up, and if I ever come in and find you using one for a stir stick, you'll cop plenty.'

Collins was not going to make it. He hated the work. As long as he had him in the lab, he'd never be free from worry.

Sims was doing well on the vats.

Renshaw thought of Collins again. What was wrong with the kids of today? He'd given this bloke a chance, and here he was throwing it away. Probably wanted to be a postman, or an engine driver, or a mechanic.

'Do you like the work?' he asked finally. 'Do you find even the least amount of interest in creating these colours? Any sense of satisfaction at all? Does it mean anything to you to watch a length of cloth change from greige to crimson?'

Collins stood woodenly beside the pipette stand. He was not going to commit himself. He was not going to make statements about this and that. But when the time was ripe, he would be out. In the meantime there was this cleaning and scouring; this careful measuring and weighing; this collecting of data and writing up of books.

He took out a clean set of overalls and put them on. He ran the squeegee over the floor. He stacked the beakers in the stainless-steel sink; the test tubes, the pipettes, the enamel jugs. He collected the soft brushes for the cleaning. He scoured the beakers and jugs. He worked for a long time on the pipettes. Those that would not clean he threw into the garbage disposal. He wiped the laminated plastic tops of the benches, scrubbed the pipette stand.

And as soon as this was finished, they'd expect him to start organizing the dye stocks. To work on the labels. To try to keep the rusting old tins neat and clean.

He wondered how Hughie had faced it day after day.

CHAPTER THIRTY THREE

The new girl reported for the wrapping table.

She was tall, with a plain, humorous face. She was no beauty, but she knew her way about, and there would be no nonsense from the men. And none from Renshaw either.

Gwennie was gone. No one had seen her on the streets. After a while the news got around that she was working in the city. Renshaw had been uneasy for days. It was not beyond the bounds of possibility that Verrendah would go to the police. Then Hughie's death intervened. After the strain lifted, Renshaw had forgotten Verrendah, and Verrendah's fear of scandal had prevailed. He had done nothing, after all.

But the event had shaken Renshaw. He must be getting clumsy. Losing his touch. He could scarcely remember when the last girl had run out on him. He remembered plenty with fight in them. Girls with pretty good technique at that. And he couldn't say he really liked a pushover. Well, it would be a lesson to him. No more kids out of Sunday School. No, sir, not for him.

He stood watching Annie as she slapped the gummed paper onto the rolls. She could certainly handle that cloth. He noticed the length of her arms. Should have been a boxer, he thought. Colossal reach. Even for a man.

She upended a roll, and with one toss it fell into place on the trolley.

'Hey—you want to be careful,' Renshaw said. 'We don't want that paper splitting on us. It costs us money to re-roll that stuff.'

Annie turned the roll over. The covering was neat and whole.

'When I do something wrong, suppose you tell me?' she suggested. 'I've been wrapping rolls ever since I was in napkins. And I don't like you standing there all the time. I'm not used to being stood over. I been used to getting a sheet. I never went to no High School, but I can read and add up. If I had a sheet I could check, and there'd be no need for you to stand there, watching me all day. Gives you varicose veins, just standing still watching people.'

Renshaw moved to the presses.

Well, there was no doubt about old girl Merton. She certainly was a picker. No great believer in placing temptation in a man's way.

'Doing any good with Annie, Renshaw?' asked Darcy Harrison facetiously. 'The boys won't be wearing a track to the wrapping bench, asking silly questions. I reckon she might be handy with her fists.'

Renshaw looked at her. Could be handy at that. But never fear, lady, it would be a brave man to front that citadel. There could be blokes, of course. They say there's a bloke for every woman. There could be one lined up for Annie.

'Be a bit of an armful,' Darcy said.

He was a harassed little man in charge of the presses. He looked at the fixtures beside Annie. They were empty.

'She keeps us rocking along,' he said. 'Must be about the best wrapper we've ever had.'

Renshaw moved on down to the drying area.

He stopped to speak to Barney. The cloth was feeding slowly through the dryer. Not too much spark in Barney these days, he thought. His missus had really got him tossed.

Bluey was packing down the hydro. Pulling the cloth as it flew on the winch, stacking it in expertly.

But the vats called. Standing outside the entrance to the dyeing area, he thought suddenly of Hughie; of the trouble over the instructions for the elasticized cloth for Best-Yet. If he could have seen ahead, got to understand a little bit more about Collins, he wouldn't have moved so quickly over Hughie. In a rare moment of honesty, he asked himself why he had pursued Hughie. Yes, persecuted him. But it's not me, he thought. Not really. It's the way things are. Dog eat dog. The kind of thing that makes Larcombe circle warily around me. No one likes to look on the face of the rival. It feels safer with Hughie gone, even if the work's harder.

But he'd better be careful. Not get too clever. Larcombe might decide to pull a few tricks, too. But he'd have to learn a bit more about the dyeing, and you didn't learn that in a few weeks.

The mists reached out from the dye vats. Renshaw moved on and the mist closed in around him. He shouted a greeting to Oliver Henery, who stood like a shadow, stripped down beside the indicators. For a moment time was still. Everything was unreal. The clatter of the harnessed arms as they turned in the vats, the vapours, the apparitions that were less than men. Nothing existed. Only the wet floor, the walls of mist and the power and drive of the throbbing machinery as it turned the cloth in the vats.

He opened the door of the laboratory.

Here the mists were gone, but the air was damp. Water hung from the ceiling in beads, ready to fall. The floor was wet.

He opened up the daily production book.

The dyers' instructions were shoved into the back of it. They were clamped together with a safety pin. Nothing had been written up for days.

'What do you do?' Renshaw said. 'How do you find ways of filling in your time?'

He flicked the pages back. Here in Hughie's slow, careful hand was a record of each day's dyeing, and at the side a weekly total balance of the weight of cloth dyed.

If Collins saw the year out, he'd be lucky.

'There's nothing to this,' Renshaw said evenly. 'Can't you write in a few figures and add them up?'

He was trying not to lose his temper. He'd have to put up with Collins for a little while, until he got onto a suitable boy.

'All the work that's gone through the last week wouldn't give you writer's cramp. In Hughie's day he'd make this a snack.'

Renshaw looked up. Collins hadn't budged from the sink. He stood stubbornly, head averted. But suddenly he turned around. He began to smile. He looked steadily at Renshaw, and the smile broadened.

When he spoke his voice was low but clear.

'But there's a difference,' he said. '*In Hughie's day*. Now, you know where you can shove it.'

All right, son, Renshaw thought. There'll be a one-way ticket for you soon. You've had it coming, and you don't want to be surprised.

He'd have to get old Merton or Patty to help out. He picked up the phone. He heard the click, and then Patty's voice. It sounded clean, fresh and remote.

'Very busy up there?'

'Well, I've got enough. Never really seem able to catch up.'

'Records in one hell of a mess here. Nothing written up for months. Collins either can't or won't. I don't like calling on you, Patty, but I'll have to get topside of this mess somehow.'

There was silence. What did she think she was doing? Who the bloody hell did she think she was? Well, he could try another tack with her: I want you down here, pronto.

But he waited.

'Oh, well,' reluctantly, 'I'll be down.'

She placed the phone on the hook and picked up her

208

pen and pencils. The colour had risen in her cheeks, dyeing them pink. Her eyes were bright.

'Mr Renshaw?' Miss Merton asked briefly.

She glanced at Patty's flushed cheeks and bright eyes. They never learn, she thought. Men like Renshaw draw them like a magnet.

Renshaw had the sheets on the table when Patty came in to the lab. He was sorting them up and arranging them under date headings. Collins was weighing up the dyes. Marj Grigson was busy stirring squares of cloth in a beaker over the bunsen burner. They had dyed several squares for the new mulberry, but none had really satisfied Renshaw. He had taken Collins off the experimental work, putting him on the more mechanical job of weighing up.

'I suppose you could find a way of making a mess of that too,' Renshaw had said.

Marj Grigson worked conscientiously, if unimaginatively, on the experiments. She recorded carefully.

When the business of Hughie had blown over, Collins would be out. It might be policy to wait a while. After all, he had given Collins a pretty big boost to Larcombe, in the days when he was trying to ease Hughie out. But he'd keep his eyes open. He needed a conscientious youngster with some feeling for the work.

'Best part of a month. Nothing written up at all.'

Renshaw handed the papers to Patty. 'I'm really stuck with it. No reason for you to stick around in this wet hole, though. You could cart the whole lot up to the office.'

They walked together to the storeroom. Here Renshaw

stopped. He placed his hand on Patty's shoulder, holding her off at arm's length.

'You sure are a pretty kid,' he said. 'Aren't you, Patty?'

She moistened her lips. She expelled her breath in a low sigh.

Yes, she was a pretty kid. She knew that. The appreciative whistles from the men told her; the wavy mirror on the dressing-table at Wentworth Parade assured her of it.

Renshaw's hand dropped to his side. They began walking again. At the office he placed the records on the table.

'It's pretty straight-ahead work. Make up a date heading. Let's see. What was the last number recorded? 1793. Number each vat. Make the next one 1794 and so on. It's really pretty simple.'

He stood while she wrote in the headings and lifted out the first instruction. She began writing it in.

'You could extend the daily weight total over here.'

Patty wrote in the extension.

She raised her eyes suddenly and looked at him. The bruise was gone from his eye, but just above his brow there was a fine white scar where Gwennie had hit him with the stone. Renshaw looked back at her. It was a long look.

'What do you think of me, Patty?' he asked. 'I couldn't rate too high with you. I don't know what came over me. It's not much use saying how sorry I am. But that's the way it is.'

He was sorry. She thought about it. She thought of all the things she had talked over with Oliver. He'd have no trouble laying you on your back, Oliver had said. It was easy to say you were sorry. She picked up her pen and began to work. She felt suddenly embarrassed.

Renshaw turned around. He encountered Miss Merton's steady gaze. Sanctimonious old busybody, he thought. But he backed out of Patty's office. Well, the paper work was under way. And when things settled down he'd have a new kid in the lab. He'd nut that out as soon as he possibly could. The future began to look rosy again.

CHAPTER THIRTY FOUR

Barney grew more thoughtful as the time of Esther's delivery approached and she entered the city hospital.

At the Dyehouse he was moody and irritable. Goodwin's sly jokes and leg-pulling went over his head. He began to think of the future, of the fretful child wailing in the house, of Esther harassed and weary. It wasn't as though they had wanted the child, had planned for it. It seemed incredible even now that the thing could have happened.

'Be a lot of comfort to you when you're older,' Goodwin said. Barney grunted. He didn't think kids were a comfort in a man's old age. Selfish little brutes, usually stuck up to the ears in their own affairs. Couldn't care less whether you sank or swam.

'Never noticed it,' Barney said.

He bent over his work. His mind was active, totting up the hospital bills, the cost of the new clothes to keep the kid warm, the special foods it would need for the first eighteen months of its life.

And at the back of his mind a secret thought had taken root. He brushed it aside, ashamed to have harboured it. But it came again and again. Sometimes, waking in the darkened house with the untidy kitchen, he felt the thought tapping away, like Morse code. He thought of fingers relentlessly sending out the message. On such occasions he would struggle groggily back to consciousness and light the lamp. He would sit up in bed with his arms crossed over his knees and his head leaning on his arms. But the thought persisted of itself. It was never put into words; never spoken of. It came unbidden. While he was pulling the cloth through the hydro, picking out the vats, helping on the mangle, it would suddenly be there.

What if the child died? What if it was stillborn?

He would put the thought aside. Concentrate on the vats. Call the numbers aloud to himself. Call out the weight of each number. Think of every action. The way he lifted the roll and flapped back the cloth. The way he stripped off the tickets. The way he placed them into heaps. The noise of the rubber bands as they snapped around the tickets.

He began to think of the day when Esther would come home. What he would do. How he would polish up the house. And again, how nice it had looked when Esther was home. The bed always made. The stove polished. The dishes washed and gleaming on the shelves. The curtains stiff with starch at the open window.

'Certainly be a bit of company for you,' Goodwin said. He was needling Barney gently. It was no good Barney pretending that he wanted the kid. Not to him. He knew better. But he knew, too, that kids had a way with them. Put one in a house and things were different.

'Knew a bloke once,' Goodwin said, 'couldn't stand kids at any price. Got one himself. Little sandy-headed rat of a kid with weak eyes. Different tale altogether. Couldn't get home soon enough. Used to drive us crazy talking about it. So help me, you'd think no other kid ever grew teeth or hair before.'

Barney let go of the roll and straightened up. There was a steely glint at the back of his eyes. He looked levelly at Goodwin for a long time.

'No offence meant,' Goodwin said hastily. He retreated a little. 'Just passing a remark. Just wondering.'

'I wouldn't wonder out loud too much, if I were you,' Barney said coldly. He felt a sudden sense of fury. It was almost as though Goodwin had read his thoughts. As though he knew.

'Well, I did you a good turn once. You were pretty glad to come and ask me. And after you backed out—not that I blame you altogether—you haven't got a civil word for a chap.'

Goodwin walked towards the vats. Then he turned and stood for a moment, gazing nonplussed at Barney. He felt rebuffed and aggrieved. He had worked along well with Barney. They had been mates, in a way, for a long time. Something was eating Barney. The kid was there. There was no good feeling sore about it now. Nothing could alter things at this stage. If Barney had any sense, he'd stop this useless worrying. The time for bellyaching was gone.

214

But there was no time for further puzzling. Oliver was calling from the vats. The demanding labour was there. The work was coming off the hydro ready for the dryer. He walked back towards Barney.

They'd cracked it for the dryer. Maybe they could take it easy. Drag the chain just a little.

The tickets were thrown on the bench. The cloth was coming through. Piles of it. Rose swami, pale green swami, buttercup swami. Barney sorted the tickets, picking out the quality numbers and sorting out the roll numbers and the widths. He dragged up the trolley. The cloth was folding automatically into heaps on the table. Now and then he stretched up, straightened a fold, and the cloth fell into a heap of pale gold. I wonder why we do it, Barney thought. Every day. When I get a bit of money I'll try for a boat. He thought of the fishing fleets that he had seen one year down the south coast. But it'd take a lot of money to buy a boat, a good boat. He looked up suddenly and caught Goodwin's perplexed glance. His face cleared. Goodwin walked slowly across to him.

Everything was sorted and under way. He moved over, and Goodwin took up his position.

'Nice bit of cloth,' Goodwin said. He looked at Barney. 'Wouldn't mind a bit of this myself. Want to make sure you get a bit for the missus.'

He waited. He was friendly and apologetic.

'No offence meant,' he said to Barney. 'I mean, about what I said. We've all got our touchy spots.'

'That's OK.'

Barney looked at him. At his lanky arms pulling at the

cloth; at his shrewd, ferrety face; at his mouth, strangely and surprisingly generous.

They worked in silence. Goodwin was elaborately interested in the cloth as it fell to the table. Barney listened to the throb of the machinery. He isolated and identified every sound. Above the clatter he could hear the shrill voices of the laden women, the cries of the boys skylarking at the presses, Sims' voice calling as he lowered a truck full of greige stock for the vats, Harrison calling from the presses.

Barney and Goodwin wheeled the trucks across the floor. The pressers reached out for them. They pulled the spreaders from the wall. The cloth was stretched to the spreaders and began to run smoothly. The steam rose. The operators bent to the presses.

Goodwin tossed the bundles into the truck. He winked at Barney.

'Know a good mate when I got one,' Goodwin said.

Barney smiled back at him. But the thought was still there. Still there, ticking away at the back of his mind.

He began working hard again, pulling at the cloth, ashamed.

CHAPTER THIRTY FIVE

The hospital was calling.

The phone rang in Miss Merton's office. She let it ring while she finished writing up her report. People had been ringing all the morning and the work was piling up. The line was getting so busy lately that they could almost do with a permanent switch operator. But there'd be ructions if anything of that nature was suggested. She folded the report, picked up a sheaf of papers and took them into Renshaw's office. Most of them had to be countersigned before they would be accepted by Mr Cuthbert's staff.

She leaned over absently and picked up the receiver.

'Southern Textiles Dye Works.'

'Have you a Mr Monahan on your staff?'

'Yes,' Miss Merton said. It must be the call about the baby.

Miss Merton put down the phone and walked to Patty's office. She was smiling.

'Would you mind?' she asked Patty. 'It's for Barney. I think he's working near the hydro. Probably about his wife.'

She sat down at her desk.

Barney was working on the mangle. It was an easy job, merely guiding the cloth through. Barney didn't like it. Time dragged. It was easy enough, but you'd want to be a zombie. It was exactly as Oliver Henery said, he thought. A man must get some interest out of a job or he'd go mad. Maybe there were blokes who liked to stand all day with their eyes almost shut, but not him. He'd almost rather be on the vats. Although the work was hard, there was interest and action. He watched Patty Nicholls as she walked across the drying area. She had changed a bit over the months, he thought. Lost a lot of that cheap, brassy look. She'd thinned out too. In some of those clothes that you saw on the pictures she could be quite a sort.

'There's a call for you,' Patty said to Barney. 'From the hospital, I think.'

Barney leant over mechanically and pressed the switch. The cloth ceased to flow.

He felt weak as he walked past the dryer. This was the moment he had been waiting for.

He picked up the phone. In the very act the thought recurred to him. The thought. The constant, nagging thought. He thrust it down, disowning it.

'Hullo,' he said.

The line crackled. There was no answer. He could hear a low, buzzing noise.

218

'Hold the line please.'

'Yes, sure, sure.' Hold the line. Sure he'd hold it. He began to feel panic. How much longer were they going to keep him? If there was something to say, why couldn't they say it quickly and have done with it?

And now a new thought thrust itself into his mind. Suppose it was Esther? Suppose Esther didn't pull through?

He could feel the sweat on his face and fingers. The line suddenly came to life.

'I'm putting you through now.'

'Hullo,' Barney said. His voice was thin in his own ears.

'Good news for you, Mr Monahan. Mother and son both well.'

Barney held the phone with both his hands and leant against the desk.

'My wife,' he said. 'Esther. How is she?'

'She's well. She's very well. She surprised us.'

She was well. He felt a sudden wave of exultation. Esther was well. In that second the cottage sprang to life again. Esther would be home. There would be a heart in the house. He hung onto that joyful moment.

'She's been a very sick girl, of course. You'll have to take special care of her for a while.'

Take care of her? He felt suddenly strong. Only let Esther come home. Poke about the cottage. Only let her be there at night with the lamp lit, and the fire. Let her be there to welcome him home. Nothing else mattered.

'And the boy,' Barney hesitated. 'My son?'

'Seven and a half pounds. Doing well.'

Seven and a half pounds and doing well.

Barney put down the receiver. He slid down onto the chair, and ran his fingers through his hair. Wife and son both well. How many generations of men had been gladdened by those simple words? He buried his face in his hands and sat, suddenly weak.

Miss Merton turned from her desk and looked at him.

'Are you feeling all right?' she asked kindly. 'It's a big strain, that kind of thing. Even for the fathers!'

'A son,' Barney said slowly.

Miss Merton folded her hands together and looked at him. Patty Nicholls came to the door. She stood with a happy smile on her lips.

'It must mean a lot to a man to have a son,' Miss Merton said.

'Yes,' Barney said slowly. He thought of the hours he had spent in the cottage. The scene with Esther when she had first told him. The dark, secret thought that had tormented him. Well, it was over. It had resolved itself. The problems that remained did not seem insurmountable today.

There might be battles ahead for the kid. But he had braved the biggest adventure of them all. The adventure and hazard of being born.

Barney walked back to the mangle. But he didn't switch it on. He stood in the mist that swirled through from the vats, thinking of Esther. He would take the afternoon off. He remembered the delicate flowers Esther and he had admired one day. Hyacinths. He would go down to Martin Place and get some of them for her. He looked at the clock. A quarter to eleven. Oliver Henery walked through from the vats, carrying a large white enamel jug. Barney beckoned to him.

'Good news,' he said. 'Just had word from the hospital. It's a boy.'

'Good on you,' Oliver said. 'Going to wet its head?'

'Not tonight. Going walkabout after lunch. Might have a few tomorrow after work, if you'd like to be in it.'

'Goodoh. I'll clock you out tonight.'

After Barney left the office Patty sat down before the switchboard. It was a rare thing for her to sit there uninvited. Something of the gladness of Barney's news seemed to remain in the room. Miss Merton leaned back in her chair, a smile on her face.

'It seemed to mean a lot to Barney,' Patty said. 'You wouldn't think a man like that would be so affected. I've always thought of Barney as a pretty tough sort of chap.'

She was searching around in her mind. Thinking back over the last couple of years. Of her own infatuation for Renshaw.

She looked suddenly at Miss Merton. At her neat hair and her trim features. It seemed funny that no man had married her. Yet she must have been a very pretty girl in a way. A question trembled on Patty's lips.

Did anyone ever love you? Were you ever in love? You couldn't just ask Miss Merton that. Or could you?

'I've often wondered,' Patty said. 'Whether you have ever been in love. When you were young.'

It was very quiet. Miss Merton turned around quickly and looked at Patty. This pert little girl with the unsavoury involvement with Renshaw was asking about Stephen. The picture of the river flashed across her mind. Stephen holding her in his arms the day she had gone to his hut. The long, empty summer days after he had gone.

She brought her mind back to Patty. She was watching her intently. Miss Merton smiled almost coldly.

'Once,' she said, 'when I was young, I believe I was in love.'

'What happened?'

'Oh, I was young. He went away. I never saw him again.'

'Didn't you try to see him?'

'You don't understand. He went away. Right away. I don't even know where he went.'

'Did he love you?' Patty asked. 'Why didn't he write? Why did you never hear from him?'

Miss Merton was still. She tried to recapture the reality of that summer. Did he love her? She remembered her sudden tears. The way he had talked politics the day they parted.

'I think he loved me,' Miss Merton said to Patty. 'Although he never told me so. There would have been no future for us.'

'Why not?' Patty asked.

'Well—there was no work around at the time. He had nothing.'

'But people kept on getting married,' Patty said. 'Even when there was no work. I've heard people talking about it. Women lived in huts. Some of them tramped the roads, too.'

And that was it, Miss Merton thought. Some women had battled it out beside their men, sharing the bitter struggle of the time. Stephen had not asked her. Perhaps he had judged her well. Stephen was a blade shaped for battle. She thought of the quiet tenor of her days. She was not a woman meant for struggle; perhaps Stephen had understood that. Perhaps he had known. And because of it he had walked out of her life that last warm summer's day.

'Lots of women tramped out beside their men,' Patty said.

'Would you do that?' Miss Merton asked suddenly.

Patty considered. Her life had always been hazardous. The room in Barrington Terrace was a rare and cherished form of security.

'If I loved him. Yes, I would,' Patty said. 'I would.'

She looked at Miss Merton. At her neat frock, her trim ankles, her plain sensible shoes. And all the time there was this love story, fragrant as lavender and somehow unreal.

'I've been thinking about Mr Renshaw,' Patty said suddenly. It was out. It was said. The unspoken thing that had earned Miss Merton's constant disapproval lay between them. The smile slid from Miss Merton's face. A cool, polite look of interest replaced it.

'When I first came here,' Patty said slowly, 'I was young. I thought he really was in love with me. I used to go home at night thinking about how he looked and what he said. Then one day he asked me. He said we'd get married. I must have been an easy mark. He didn't mean it, of course. He didn't mean any of it. Then Gwennie Verrendah came. I used to walk past the wrapping to see if he was there. I used to be

223

glad that Gwennie was so straightlaced. I used to think the time would come when she'd knock him back and he'd come looking for me again. I got that way I hated Gwennie so much I used to wish she'd step under a train. Then one day I went up to the stockroom. You remember? It was the day we talked about the old cards in the PG Control. He had his arms around Gwennie. He was kissing her. I wanted to remind him of his promise, but it was no good.'

Patty stopped. She was thinking of Renshaw. His arms on her shoulders, the open gate, the gaping lift-well. The black look on his face when he had threatened her. She thought of Hughie's crumpled body and shivered.

'I felt I didn't want to live. And then something happened. Gwennie was a match for him. She wasn't so easy and she got away. And after a while he began thinking about me again. He began talking to me again. Being friendly, like he used to be.'

'Yes,' Miss Merton said. She was interested, despite her disapproval.

'I think he's getting ready to ask me out again,' Patty said. 'But now I know. Things will never be the way they used to be.'

Patty drew in a deep breath.

'I can think about him now, and it doesn't even matter. It doesn't seem to hurt. All at once I can see him the way he is.'

'It must be a sad thing to be so disillusioned,' Miss Merton said.

She felt suddenly moved. She bent over and her hand rested on Patty's for just a second.

'It doesn't matter now, of course,' Patty said. She got to her feet. She had stayed a long time talking to Miss Merton.

Barney had finished up and was heading for the showers.

'Good luck,' Patty called. Her voice sounded young and vibrant.

Miss Merton picked up her pen and began working again.

A son, seven and a half pounds, she said to herself. She began to think again of Stephen. She wondered what would have happened if she had left the house on the river. Or maybe if Stephen had stayed. They might have made out on the property. They could have worked together. Well, it was over and decided. Patty would have tramped off beside him. Patty would have taken up the challenge. Miss Merton smiled.

CHAPTER THIRTY SIX

Barney waved to Miss Merton as he passed her office.

He walked across the vestibule floor and out the front door. Word of the baby's arrival had spread through the place. There had been a lot of good-humoured chaff and chiacking and hooraying.

The burden that had lain so heavily on him seemed suddenly to have lifted.

All the way down the street onto the station and into the train he thought about the child. A boy.

In the city he walked along the street, looking into the shop windows. He stopped for a while before a big window of toys. The window was well-lit. He stood with his face close to the glass. There were trains that ran on looped lines. He remembered suddenly how he had envied other kids when he was a youngster. The ones who were lucky enough to own a clockwork train.

He looked at the tricycles, the rocking-horses, the dolls that walked and talked. The doll reminded him of Kathy and he smiled. He had received a humorous letter from Kathy and her husband. She would like to have got across, but it was a long and expensive trip. If it became necessary, they would manage it. They were saving up anyhow, and next year if everything went well they might get over. In the meantime John had a promotion. More money. They were making out all right. And he'd better not get too puffed up about that new baby. They could be thinking of making him a grandfather any time. It was funny, he thought. Little wonder the blokes were amused. Oliver said his blood was worth bottling. And it could be, at that.

He looked at the rocking-horse. If he had the money he'd go straight in and buy it. He pictured it on the verandah. But he didn't have the money. He walked on, whistling to himself.

Outside a lingerie shop he stopped again. Here were fluffy nightgowns and negligees, fine cambric petticoats with hand-made lace. His face softened. Esther would like these things. In all their married life Esther had never had clothes like these.

He walked past the shops and turned into Martin Place. The flower stalls were open. He looked for the delicate waxen hyacinths. There were none on the first stall. He walked along in front of the post office steps. On a bench in the second stall was a low enamel bowl. The hyacinths were in tight bunches. White waxen bells, soft blues, mixed colours, delicate pinks.

'I'll have these—the pink ones,' Barney said to the girl.

After she had wrapped the flowers he walked back down the street. He looked a long time at the lingerie. He remembered his bitter rejoinder when Esther had told him about the baby. He thought of his visit to the woman that Goodwin knew, of the recurring wish that the baby might die, of his struggle to free himself of this extra responsibility. He began to wish there were some way of making Esther understand.

Perhaps the horse? No, it was too expensive. And it wasn't what he needed. Not the horse. He looked down at the flowers. His face softened. He needed something to tell Esther. A letter. Or one of those cards. He could buy one and put it with the flowers. He could write something inside.

The woman at the little shop was helpful. She brought out a box of congratulation cards. They looked cold and were mostly printed in gold and white, or silver and white. They were not what he wanted. She bent down and pulled a small shoe-box from under the counter.

'You might find something in these,' she said to Barney.

They were samples and oddments. There were small handpainted cards, cards printed on crafted paper, end-of-range cards. Barney picked out a small card. He looked at it for a long time. There were two gum-trees, a small cottage and some pink flowers in the foreground.

'What do you think of this one?' he asked.

The woman picked it up.

'Well—of course—for myself now, I like something plainer. Bit too much in it, don't you think?'

She rustled through the cards and picked one out. It was plain, with a simple motif arranged at the side.

228

'Or even this.' A bunch of flowers and a long verse inside. 'Or this?'

He looked at the card he held and opened it out. There was no verse inside. Just the blank space for him to write on.

'I like this one,' he said suddenly. He didn't like the one with the motif. This was the one that Esther would like, the one with the trees and the house and the pink flowers. The woman made a hole in the corner of the card with a stiletto and threaded a length of silk through it. Barney walked to a quiet corner of the shop. He wrote clumsily, in the hand of a man not accustomed to shaping letters. He covered the words up quickly. He felt suddenly embarrassed. He smiled at the woman and walked into the street.

When the bell rang Esther sat up in bed. She was looking bright-eyed and younger than she had looked for years. Her cheeks had filled out a little. She had brushed and brushed her hair until the unruly mass shone like dull silver and had fixed it close to her head. The plaits were massed in a knob at the back. In her weeks in hospital she had knitted a new lavender bed-jacket; the young mothers had helped her choose the colour. Lilacs and lavenders, soft mauves and pinks, was their verdict. Keep away from those steely blues. Someone had made a flat velvet bow in a deeper shade, pulled it through a slide and fastened it at the side of her hair. Her nails were shining and she had a faint dusting of powder over her nose and wore a trace of pale pink lipstick.

The visitors began to flock into the room. The young boy was bending over his girl wife in the next bed. Esther looked quickly away.

She looked up and saw Barney tiptoeing down the

ward. He was neat enough. His trousers were pressed, his shirt clean, his tie straight. She lifted her eyes until they met his. He came swiftly to her. The flowers were on the bed. He put his arms around her and kissed her, holding her head against his chest. He held her so, running his hand up the back of her neck, feeling the great weight of the knot of hair. He had not seen Esther look like this for years. She looked pretty. Her hair was thick and silver; her eyes were smoky. Her skin had changed from a sullen, muddy yellow to a soft, glowing cream. He sat beside her, holding her hand and looking at her. There were lots of things he wanted to say. But he just sat holding her hand and thinking.

He wanted to tell her now that he understood how long and bitterly she had laboured to bring this life into the world. That things would be different. That now he thought differently about the boy.

But Esther knew him. There was no need for words.

'And the boy,' Barney said suddenly. 'The baby.'

Esther lifted her eyes.

There was no anger on his face; no resentment. She began to laugh. She looked at his face. The strong line of his jaw; the set of his eyes; his nose.

'When he's older he's going to look just like you. He's got that-sort-of-shaped face.'

He bent over quickly and kissed her on the lips.

When the buzzer went, Barney rose with the other men and walked out of the ward, to the nursery. Behind the plate glass the babies were displayed. There was no handling them. They all seemed to look alike. Yet you never saw two people really alike. That is, excepting twins.

'Monahan.'

Barney walked to the window. He was the oldest of the men waiting outside the nursery. Most of them were in their late twenties or early thirties.

The nurse wheeled the crib to the window. Against the pillow Barney could see the new red face, the dark hairline, the carved nose and the sockets of the eyes.

He stared quietly at the baby. He remembered his exultant roar when he picked up Kathy the day that she was born. No plate-glass windows. Kathy in a crib beside her mother. And Esther had said, 'Careful, careful now, Barney, you'll drop her.'

A lot of the sting had been taken out of him over the years. A lot of the bluster and the ballyhoo.

He looked at the sleeping child.

There was a long way for this kid to go. A long, hard, bitter way. Sometimes the going would be good. Sometimes a chap could be lucky and meet a girl like Esther, and there would be days that stood out like jewels. Pictures of Esther laughing. Pictures of her in a straw hat she used to wear. Days when a man would choose a plot of ground on which to raise a house. The long, long golden days when hope was high in the heart. Days when a man would look at the face of his first-born. Days when a man would look and say, 'This is my son.'

He stood for a moment moved and shaken.

He had little enough to hand on. What he had was already given. On the way back to the ward he pondered this. The slight thread of life.

He could hear the voices of the men as they trooped

back. Nine and a half pounds. Got a couple of boys. Cracked it for a girl. They were laughing and happy.

The men passed and he stood for a moment outside the door. Life was moving swiftly, now. Changes coming one on the heels of the other. Only in the Dyehouse the changes were slower.

He thought of the boy lying in his cot; of the strange, complex world into which he was born; of the struggles and battles that would confront him.

And he thought of the house, of the early train, of Renshaw, of the hydro and the cloth.

It might be easier for the boy, Barney thought. Sixteen or seventeen years is a long time. And the future could be different. Yes, a man could bank on that. The future would not be the same.

He pushed open the door. The boy would deal with the future. In a few years the boy would be striding through the world, pushing the future about.

CHAPTER THIRTY SEVEN

At the Dyehouse the work was beginning to slacken off. Orders were still coming in, but the tempo was slower. There would be a breathing space before the year exploded into a last frenzy of labour for the Christmas stocktake.

The stand-down had not amounted to anything. One or two men had pulled out and Renshaw had not replaced them. The work had held, and he had been able to maintain the present staff. But he felt no real ease at the Dyehouse. There could be no real slackening for himself until he had replaced Collins.

He mentioned it to Larcombe.

'That kid Collins looks like he's not going to make the grade in the lab. I don't know what's come over him. He seemed keen enough at first.'

Larcombe looked at him.

'He's been doing pretty well at Tech.'

'Maybe. Seems all right on paper. There's more to this job than paperwork. He doesn't like the manual work, mixing the dyes. I don't know what it is. And I think he's got a blind spot where colour's concerned.'

'We spent a bit of money on training him,' Larcombe said. 'Best part of twelve months down the drain. And I don't know how Harvison will feel about it. He's begun to take an interest in these kids going through the technical schools. I don't think he'll like it at all.'

'Well, he can please himself,' Renshaw said shortly. 'My guess is that Collins will shoot through any time. He won't be considering what Harvison thinks about the matter.'

'Maybe we could talk to him. I think I'd let the matter ride. See what happens in the new year.'

Larcombe moved off. Renshaw watched him for a moment. Well, he'd met a few gutless wonders in his time. A few blokes that liked to be on both sides of the fence. Well, he'd told Larcombe. Let him know what was cooking. He could do what he liked about it. But the first likely-looking kid would be in there, weighing up the dyes. Larcombe could dither about like a piddling pup, but when the time came he, Renshaw, would act.

He walked across to the office, whistling to himself. Through the glass he could see Patty Nicholls. He picked up a pencil and began tapping his teeth with it.

During the winter and the busy season after the stock-take he had scarcely given her a thought. Scarcely noticed her. And when he had, she'd been looking pale and uninteresting. Beside Gwennie Verrendah's dark, vivid colouring she had seemed insignificant.

But with the spring there was a change in Patty and not a subtle one. She had changed almost overnight from a tousle-headed youngster to a poised and thoughtful woman. With just a bit more grooming she could be arresting, almost beautiful. He would have a bit of back-pedalling to do to straighten out the Gwennie Verrendah affair. He must have been a bit soft to have fallen for that line. It might take a little time to get on-side with Patty again, but he had worked things before today. And he could wait. When it suited him, he could certainly wait.

Around the Dyehouse he let it be known that he regretted the interlude with Gwennie Verrendah. He talked about it to Goodwin in a sudden burst of confidence.

'If you didn't know the flaming cow,' Goodwin said, 'you could almost believe he meant it. I'm tipping he's getting the stage set to make up to Patty Nicholls again. It's as plain as the nose on your face. If she hasn't had time to sum him up, she's a lot slower than I think she is.'

'Can't altogether tell with women,' Harrison said. 'They seem a bit slow on the uptake sometimes. Try to do them out of sixpence and they're awake-up straight away. But blokes like Renshaw seem to go down well with them.'

Renshaw gradually assumed an air of remorse. While the mood lasted he walked slowly past the workers, rarely criticizing, often inquiring after wife or children, handing out fatherly advice to the youngsters. Even Collins, trying to line up a job for the next year, came in for his share of assistance.

'It can't last,' Collins said. 'And I don't want to be around when the bust comes.'

Renshaw's interest in Patty was not the kind to include marriage. Marriage was a long way from his thoughts when he called through the door to Miss Merton.

'Send Patty Nicholls in to me.'

Patty moved in quietly. She stood before his desk with a pencil and pad in her hand. She wore a smooth linen frock. It was longer than he remembered her frocks to be. And she had tied her hair back. He decided that the smooth, sleek hairdo had contributed most of all to her changed appearance.

'Sit down.'

There was a chair in the corner and she drew it up. She sat down opposite Renshaw.

His eyes flicked over her. He remembered the nights in the corner of the park and smiled faintly. It had been a different cup of tea then. Well, maybe those days were not all over, either. If he did the right thing, maybe they would not be all over.

He picked up a sheaf of memos. They were all queries from Head Office. Renshaw was not really a paper-work man. The checking, querying and confirming of small, unimportant details infuriated him. More than once he and Cuthbert had joined battle over some detail that had not been double-checked or countersigned.

He picked up the sheaf of papers. He tossed them across to Patty.

'Few wrong numbers recorded. Think you could trace them?'

Patty wrote in the particulars. She raised her head and met Renshaw's steady, faintly smiling eyes. It was the old look. The dear, remembered look. She felt her heart suddenly thump in her chest.

'They could be old numbers,' Renshaw said slowly.

Old numbers. Patty wrote the words in carefully.

'We went through a lot of old stock about the time that particular vat was dyed.'

Patty finished writing. She waited in silence with her heart thumping, and the colour high in her cheeks.

Renshaw picked up dye samples and weighed them in his hand.

'What do you think of those?' he asked abruptly.

He threw a handful of samples across to her. They were the colour swatches for Smith's Worsteds.

'The blue's lovely,' Patty said.

He looked at the cloth.

Suddenly he looked up. His eyes were appealing.

'Are you still mad with me, Patty. Are you?'

She dropped her hands onto her lap. She knew what to say. She had thought of this opportunity over and over again. But her lips refused to frame the words.

'It's not enough to say that I'm sorry. I don't know what got into me. I've got around to wishing lately that we could be friends.'

He said it slowly. Even in his own ears it sounded sincere.

But he waited like an actor for the effect of his words. Patty raised her head and looked at him. It was a long, steady glance. Once before she had tried to sum him up. She should be saying all the words she had prepared. Letting him know exactly what she thought of him. What did she think about him, even now?

'I'd really like to tell you something,' Renshaw said. 'This Gwennie Verrendah. There wasn't anything really. There was nothing. It was just a night…'

'But Gwennie. I think it meant something to Gwennie. I think she might have really liked you. Perhaps she even loved you.'

Renshaw laughed suddenly.

'Perhaps she did. My guess is that she didn't. What do you think this being-in-love is anyway? Sitting down playing ladies? D'you reckon getting together isn't part of this being in love?' His face hardened, remembering Gwennie.

'I was worried at the time. The work was piling up. It wasn't serious, Patty. No more than a passing distraction. No more than other blokes are doing all the time and getting away with.'

She watched him steadily.

'I don't trust you,' Patty said suddenly. Her voice was unsteady.

'But you like me? Just a little bit? You don't trust me, but you like me? Not a lot. But a little bit? Is that it, Patty?'

There was a weariness in his voice. The expression of his face altered. It was almost sad.

'It's a lot to ask, I suppose,' he said.

He glanced down at the papers again.

They began to work.

And as the work proceeded, Renshaw kept bringing his mind back to Patty's answer.

There was no real hurry, and he was good at waiting. They worked through the lists together. When the last query was straightened out he looked up and smiled.

'Pretty smooth.'

Patty laughed. She felt suddenly easy. Her heart had ceased to pound. There were times when she enjoyed working with him. When his temper was under control he worked quickly and efficiently.

He stretched his arms above his head.

'Things are hanging on,' he said suddenly. 'Orders still coming through. Bet you haven't started to slack off on the records yet.'

'No.'

She picked up her pencil and pad.

She was glad it was over. The opportunity had come and she had not availed herself of it. The carefully prepared lines were stillborn. And for Renshaw the first round was not altogether lost. He had talked to her about Gwennie. This alone had placed their relationship on a new footing. Not a lot of headway, but some.

At the door he called to her.

'Patty.'

There was a look of amusement and tolerance on his face.

'Yes?'

'I forgot to mention. I've been hearing some pieces of interesting gossip.'

'Gossip?' Patty said. 'About me?'

'Well—about a certain young lady. Could be you. And a young cock on the dye vats.'

He means Oliver, Patty thought. She began to laugh.

Renshaw laughed too.

'Just thought it seemed funny.'

Patty stopped laughing. Why had she laughed like that? She had a sudden sense of guilt. But there was something so droll about the idea of Oliver Henery.

'He was kind,' Patty said. She felt, suddenly, thoroughly ashamed of herself. 'He was very kind to me,' she repeated. She turned to go. She should not have laughed like that about Oliver.

Renshaw made no attempt to stop her. Things had gone along well enough. She had been flushed and embarrassed but she was not going to put him into the discard. He would keep out of her way for a couple of days; give her time to digest this day's work. A week or maybe less. The thing to do was to avoid her for a while.

He picked up his pen and began to work.

CHAPTER THIRTY EIGHT

In the street outside the maternity hospital, Barney came suddenly face to face with Cuthbert.

Cuthbert smiled immediately. The rule by which he lived included something about the recognition of men in the employment of the Company. He never forgot a face, and he never failed to show his recognition by a brief, impersonal smile.

For a second the men glanced at each other. Cuthbert noted in an almost clinical way Barney's cheap coat and trousers, his shirt and tie, his thinning hair. The men passed and drifted along with the crowds leaving the two hospitals which faced each other.

As soon as Cuthbert was alone he glanced at his watch. It was four thirty-one on Thursday afternoon. If he walked smartly he would be back at the office in time to put through a call to the Dyehouse, before work finished for the day. His own visit to the general hospital was in the line of duty. He had been to see the Chairman of Directors, who was recovering from a minor operation. Harvison was feeling better, and after lunch he had phoned Cuthbert and asked him to come over with certain books and figures.

Cuthbert walked along smartly. There was nothing unseemly in his haste. His even gait brought him to the office door at twenty-two minutes to five.

'You might get Macdonaldtown for me,' he said to Miss Gregory as he passed through the outer office. He placed his hat on the rack. He took out the keys and unlocked the safe. He placed the documents in their correct order, then closed and locked the door of the safe.

The phone rang. The Macdonaldtown call was through.

'Just checking on a bundy card,' Mr Cuthbert said. 'Number four seven three, B. Monahan. I would be interested to know just what time he checked out today.'

In the Dyehouse office, Miss Merton hung onto the phone. She glanced at the clock. Just on twenty to five. Five minutes to go.

She thought for a moment of Barney sitting before the switchboard, of the deep tone of his voice as he answered the phone, of the brief moment of happiness when Patty Nicholls had looked in at the door. Barney had left the Dyehouse about one o'clock. And now here was Cuthbert, cool, polite and courteous as ever, waiting on the end of the line. He was asking questions about Barney. As though he knew something.

'Barney Monahan?'

'Yes—what time did he clock out?'

'I'll have to check. I didn't notice.'

She walked to the bundy. Number 473 was empty. No card on the Ins, none on the Outs. She found it at last, pigeonholed with Oliver Henery's. She smiled to herself. Renshaw must know about this, too. She stood with the two cards in her hand, pondering. So Renshaw had turned a blind eye to Barney's afternoon off. It was ironical that Cuthbert should have got to know about it. She saw Renshaw walking across from the mangles, and she beckoned to him and waved the cards. He came up slowly. He looked tired. His fair hair was dishevelled.

'It's Cuthbert,' Miss Merton said. 'I think he must have met Barney somewhere. He's on the line. Wants his card checked.'

'OK. Put him through to me.' He took Barney's card. Miss Merton slipped Oliver's card back into its slot on the In section.

'Good day,' Renshaw said good-humouredly. 'Don't you blokes have anything to do in there but ring up checking up on times? It's nearly time for us to knock off.'

Cuthbert made a thin, cold noise. It was the closest he ever got to really laughing.

'Ran into that chap on the vats and the mangles. Monahan. Struck me as being funny that he should be about at four thirty-one.'

There was silence while Renshaw thought.

'Where'd you see him?' he asked finally.

'In Missenden Road. Near the hospital. Couldn't be mistaken. Recognized me, too.'

'Yes,' Renshaw said guardedly.

'What time did he clock out? Take him a while to come from Macdonaldtown.'

Yes, it would take a while to come in from Macdonaldtown. But not all that long. If a chap cut along, tied up with a train, jumped a tram, he'd be at the hospital in thirty minutes. He could be running down the steps from the stockroom at three o'clock and walking up the hospital steps by three-thirty. He could spend an hour with his wife and be leaving at four-thirty. Renshaw picked up his pencil. He totted up the times on his blotter. Then he wrote 3 p.m. on Barney's card and initialled it.

'I marked him out at three o'clock. Noticed the time as he went through.'

'You want to crack down on them if they fail to clock off. Lucky you noticed. Get away with murder, some of them. Don't suppose he'll make a sick-pay declaration?'

'Not likely,' Renshaw said slowly.

'Well, I just thought I'd let you know,' Cuthbert said. 'How are things with you?'

'Never any different. Seems to be holding. Orders still coming in.'

Cuthbert put down the phone.

Renshaw sat holding the card. He had done what he could for Barney. He'd lose about a couple of hours' pay in any case.

Oliver Henery put his head inside the door.

'You see Barney's card?' he asked.

Renshaw picked up the card and handed it to him.

'Put it in the bundy and don't bother to clock it,' he said sharply.

Oliver noticed the pencilled figures. Three o'clock. Must have left about one, Oliver thought.

He joined the men at the queue near the bundy.

CHAPTER THIRTY NINE

It was late when Miss Merton reached her cottage.

It had been a warm day, almost oppressive. Out to sea lightning shimmered behind the clouds. The thunder was muted by distance.

It had been a heavy enough day, despite the interlude with Barney and Patty. Renshaw had been chasing figures, working out comparisons, turning up dye and chemical consumptions for the previous year. The costs were up; there was no blinking the fact. Prices had been rising steadily, but the consumption was up, too. With Hughie's hand off the helm the wastage had risen steadily.

Miss Merton took out her key and opened the white mailbox set in the low picket fence. She took out the letters and carefully clicked the lock. Then she opened the front door and stepped into the darkened living-room.

Far below, the little neck of water lapped onto the sandy

beach. Across the gully the lights were showing through the darkness. They were beacons, isolated on the steep sides of the hills. She flicked on the light and glanced briefly at the envelopes. Account for papers. Invitation to attend a meeting at the local school hall. A letter from Aunt Ethel.

Outside, the air was still. The leaves hung motionless from the trees.

Then suddenly the wind came with a mighty roar. It swept in from the sea. It lifted up the waves and tipped them with white. The clouds darkened and spread. The rain fell onto the sandy beach and lashed at the houses clinging to the craggy hillsides.

Miss Merton stood for a moment listening to the fury. The long bough of the gum-tree was almost hitting the roof. The branches swished and slapped at the tiles.

I'll have to get someone soon, she thought. I should have that bough lopped.

She went to the bedroom and took off her hat. Then she switched on the jug to make a quick cup of tea.

She turned over the letter from Aunt Ethel. For a brief moment she pictured the cottage. The sloping roof. The circle of pines. The long row of hoary pears. The wistaria on the front verandah. And beyond, the whitewashed stable, the isolated japonica in full scarlet bloom, the cherry trees, the cultivation paddock and the rolling hills.

She put tea into a pot and poured boiling water over it. Then she ripped the envelope and settled down.

It was a gossipy letter, full of dear, familiar chatter.

Alice Weatherby was having a baby. Jan Easton was going to be married. They'd missed out on the best of the fat-lamb market. Ena Henderson was planning a trip to the continent. There was a lot of gossip about Mark Wilson marrying Hilda James. People were wondering if it could be a shotgun affair. Mark was eighteen and Hilda old enough to be his mother. But everyone was hoping it would turn out for the best.

'I wonder if you would remember that strange Stephen Forrester?'

Miss Merton held the letter, suddenly still.

'He used to wash for Gold on the banks of the River at the old House. He turned up here about a Month ago. Your Uncle put him on to helping in the Sheds. He doesn't seem to have changed much over the Years—he still talks Politics as much as he used to. A bit greyer in the hair, like most of us, though. He is a good Worker, and I think your Uncle would like to have kept him on. But he packed up yesterday and drew his Money. He's still on the Track. I think he's drifting up North to the City. I must say we found him very agreeable Company, and your Uncle seemed rather put out when he left us.'

Miss Merton scanned the letter. There was no more mention of Stephen.

He had turned up a month ago, and now he was gone.

She placed the letter carefully on the table and sat thinking. In her mind's eye she traced the track from the cottage twisting down through the orchard, across the paddock to the white gate. And then the highway. The wide country road. The rising hill. The man breasting the rise. The long track from the cottage.

Outside the storm increased in fury.

248

Miss Merton walked to the window. The rain fell in sheets. The lights across the gully swung and flickered. She went abruptly to the bathroom and turned on the water. She stripped off her frock and brushed her hair. She glanced fleetingly into the mirror. The woman looked back at her, strange yet familiar. She looked at the ageing face inquiringly. The hair was neat, and in the light strongly marked with silver. The eyes were good, but the lines were etched at the corners. It was a middle-aged face. More. It was the face of a woman getting well on in years. She wondered briefly what had become of the girl who had run so lightly down the track towards Stephen's hut. The years had dealt with her. Slowly but surely they had dealt with her.

But after her bath and her quickly prepared meal she felt no more relaxed. She had a sense of waiting. It must be the storm.

She picked up the letter and began to read it again.

'He packed up yesterday and drew his Money.'

It was intolerable in the living-room. Miss Merton went slowly into the bedroom. She undid her hair and sat brushing it down before the mirror. She was listening to the storm. The thunder rolled along the hills. The house shuddered. The trees bent almost double.

And suddenly she had a vision of Stephen.

He drew his money yesterday. That would be Tuesday. If he walked at a good swinging pace he would be over the mountain. But if he stopped to pick up stones, to look at them, to loiter in the cool shallows above the spot where the platypus nested, he would still be on the Monaro. She pictured the wind-lashed road and the figure reeling through the dark. Perhaps he would be lucky and reach the bridge. High on the rocks above the bridge there was a cave. A dry, warm cave. One summer's day they had walked to it and sat watching the sun on the distant hills.

There was no rest for her tonight. The wind clamoured. The leaves beat and beat upon the roof. All living things would be seeking shelter tonight. But the road ran bare, with sparsely timbered paddocks fringing it. There was no dense scrub. None till the road climbed the stony rise above the river. Here the scrub was thick and matted. Here a fox might creep for hiding and shelter. Here a man might crawl on hands and knees to seek shelter from the elements.

She picked up a book and began to read. The sentences were unintelligible. She began reading them aloud in an effort to concentrate. She read the page once and then again. Finally she closed the book, put a marker carefully between the pages and placed it on the table. She began reviewing the next day's work. Thinking about Renshaw. Of his surprising gesture over Barney, of Cuthbert's phone call, of her conversation with Patty Nicholls about—Stephen.

She put his name out of her mind. Tomorrow she had a new set of figures to produce. If she got a good start, with a little luck she might have them out by midday.

After she had gone over and over it, planning the methods she would use, calculating the probable times, mentally checking folders for relevant material, she was back again with the night and the thought of Stephen.

It was no use trying to rest. She picked a soft green cotton dressing gown from the wardrobe. She pulled it over her nightgown. She smoothed it around her slender figure and tied the girdle in a heavy knot.

It would be better in the living-room after all.

She switched on the lights. The flowers caught her attention. She picked out two withered leaves. Then she lifted them all from the bowl. She wrapped a handkerchief around the stems to prevent the water from dripping. She carried them through to the kitchen. Here, she cut the stems back an inch and rearranged them all in the bowl. Tomorrow she would buy more flowers. The heat really had played havoc with them. She carried the bowl back to the living-room and placed it on the table.

She drew the curtain back and looked out into the night. The trees were a dark, seething mass, dense shapes in the darkness. The rain came, driven by the wind, and hit the shuddering roof in great sheets. Across the gully the lights were grotesque. The lightning split the sky. For a second she saw the road far below her, the alien pine-tree, the gabled roof of the darkened house.

It would pass. It must soon reach the peak of its fury.

She let the curtain fall. The soft folds slid into position.

The storm must surely pass. She covered her face with her hands.

God grant him shelter, she said. A bridge, a cave, a friendly door. God grant him shelter tonight.

CHAPTER FORTY

The stock sheets had come over from Head Office.

The sight of them stacked on the floor gave Renshaw a sudden sick feeling at the pit of his stomach. There would be no let-up now. From this minute until the last of the auditors were out of the door, the tempo would quicken. They would expect him to organize the stock, keep the production rolling along and find sufficient men and women to arrange the physical stocktaking. He had protested to Cuthbert about it.

'You're doing all right. Production figures going along. You've got all the stock organized on the ground floor. Nothing to worry about.'

'I need four pairs to get this stock recorded before the auditors come in. I need every man I've got on production. You know we haven't been replacing the ones who pulled out. There isn't a man I could take off even for an hour.'

'Better put on some overtime,' Cuthbert said. 'I don't feel like putting on more staff at this time. You've always handled it. I can't see why you won't this year. Do you think four pairs could handle it, working two nights a week? And keep them notified. We don't want any trouble over tea money.'

'Sure.' Renshaw was annoyed. Last stocktaking there had been trouble over Goodwin's tea money. He had kicked up a fuss about it. Cuthbert had OK'd the pay out, finally. Goodwin had taken the matter to the Union. Cuthbert had blamed Renshaw. It was in the award. And it was Renshaw's job to see that they were advised twenty-four hours in advance.

'Two nights a week?' Renshaw said. 'I might. Try it for a couple of weeks and see how I go. If I have to, I'll work three nights during the last few weeks. Don't see how I can handle it during regular hours.'

'Anyway, you take it up with Larcombe. I'm prepared to OK the overtime.'

Renshaw put the phone down. Take it up with Larcombe. Well, that was a bloody farce if ever there was one. But he'd have to put it to Larcombe. Wait while he considered it from this angle and that angle. And finally he'd have to put the words into Larcombe's mouth.

On the fourth floor the stock was being organized. The ground floor was stacked and ready. Rolls were being picked out every day for the vats on the fourth. And all the time the stock was being written in, the production would go on. He'd need to isolate a fair stack of cloth in the greige. It was not good planning to write in the stock and then begin pulling it out.

253

He had been down to the lab and the chemical stock-room. A new method would have to be evolved here. Somehow the usage would have to be split up over the twelve months. It looked as though the December write-off would be heavy.

With the production falling, the work in the office would begin to taper off. He could pull Patty Nicholls out of the recording. Old Merton could hold the fort till the last week, then he'd push Patty back into the office for the last bout with the paper work. The work would flow along now without his constant supervision. With the exception of Collins he had a fair team. He could get Sims to double check all the instructions with Collins. That would give him a break from the lab. With Patty writing in the stock and him calling, they could cover a lot of ground in a day.

'Do what you like,' Larcombe said. The mundane details of the work irked him. He didn't really care how Renshaw arranged the stock. As long as it was all ready without too much fuss when the auditors came in, he didn't want to be bothered with the details.

'Cuthbert thinks we ought to work two nights a week.'

Larcombe considered. He wasn't really thinking about it at all. He raised his eyebrows in a pretence of thinking the matter over.

'Well, what do you think about it? You're the bloke that's going to organize the work.'

'Well I'm not going to handle it with the present staff. The other alternative is to put more men on.'

That was it. The same old pretence. Larcombe bit on a pencil.

'You'd better start them on overtime. It's against policy to put on more staff just now. I wouldn't make the overtime general. See how many pairs you need, and bring them in.'

'Yes,' Renshaw said. 'I think it's a good idea.'

Larcombe smiled. He had tied the matter up in a few moments. He wondered why there was always this fuss every stocktaking.

Renshaw decided to begin work on the ground floor. He had a twofold purpose in choosing the back stockroom as a starting point. To begin with, the room was not overlarge. He and Patty would handle this part of the stock recording alone, working at a rate of three hours a day. This would give Patty time to help Miss Merton out if the work showed signs of piling up in the office. And besides, it would give him the chance of talking to Patty in private. On the fourth floor people were always coming through to pick out cloth for the vats.

He had not had a conversation with Patty since the day he had talked to her in his office. He had judged it best to let matters drift along for a while. With the women in general he had adopted a friendly, but not over-familiar attitude.

'Something's going to bust,' Goodwin said. 'Against all the laws of nature. A bloke like Renshaw can't change all that quickly. I've seen him this way before. When it suits him he could almost fool a parson. But when you know him, you know just where to look for the wolf coming through. For me, well I hope it lasts till Christmas. But I seen it before today. It builds up to a point, then God help the poor coot that's working with him when he blows his top.'

Collins was leaning on the bench in the lab. He had the beakers scrubbed up. The pipettes gleamed in their stand. In the storeroom the tins had been wiped over and the old labels replaced. He had tried to work out a weight for the contents of each tin, but it wasn't very accurate. It was hard to judge the weight of containers. He had done the best he could. If it wasn't right, then Renshaw could do better.

'He can get rooted, for all I care,' Collins said bitterly. 'I wonder that someone hasn't pushed his face in before now.'

'He's a pretty fair-sized bloke,' Goodwin said. 'And he's handy with his fists. Only bloke I ever saw take him on other than Hughie was the mad fireman. That was before your time, when we burned coal. Pretty dangerous sort of bloke, at that. Used to turn the steam off just when he felt like it. Wouldn't have any truck with Renshaw at all. Chased him out of the boiler-room more than once. I remember him chasing Renshaw with a shovel. Followed him around the presses. He was screaming and threatening all the time. He didn't last long,' Goodwin said thoughtfully. 'But it was fun while it lasted. Some blokes reckon it was a pity he didn't catch up with him. But I suppose one bloke's not much different from another. But I could think of lots of blokes I'd rather spend an idle hour with.'

Oliver walked in. He was on his way to the chemical store for sulphuric acid.

The year was running out. Close to December now, and he was still at the Dyehouse, drifting with the tide. He had talked over the possibility of a stand-down with the shop steward, and they had laid down a plan of action in case of a sudden move in that direction. There was little else that he could do. In principle he was against overtime when other men were out of jobs, but reasonable overtime was stipulated in the award.

If he stayed until Christmas he would probably work the year round.

'What do you think about this sudden change in Renshaw?' Goodwin asked.

'I got a lot more important things on my mind right now,' Oliver said, 'but my guess is that any change in him is for the better.'

He was not anxious to involve himself in a discussion on Renshaw. Particularly on Renshaw's attitude to women. He walked through to the chemical store.

In the back stockroom Renshaw and Patty were working on the stock. Renshaw had selected roll No. 1 in each fixture for the location of the auditors' copy of the stock sheet. Patty sat on a tall stool recording, while Renshaw called.

She headed the stock sheet and waited for Renshaw to begin.

Renshaw began to call. Fixture A. Fixture B. Fixture C.

They worked steadily for an hour.

They'd covered a fair amount of ground. There was time for a breather. Renshaw bent over and offered Patty a cigarette. He leant close to her as he lit it. The flame spluttered. He looked suddenly into Patty's eyes. It might be the moment, he thought. Now.

'We had some good times together, Patty,' he said.

She looked at him. They had been good times. They had seemed good then.

'They were good times.'

'The last days of the summer,' he said slowly. 'There'll never be days like the last days of last summer.'

'Things are never the same,' Patty said.

Already the lazy days of last summer had receded from her mind. It was not only the summer, the long golden days. It was the people too. The summer would never be the same. Nor the people. People changed. Already the precious memory of the days with Renshaw was blurred in her mind. Things had changed. Renshaw had changed. She drew a long breath. And along with it all, she too had changed. She thought differently about Renshaw now.

She thought suddenly of the afternoon that she had walked out along the tram tracks. If he had spoken to her then...If he had approached her that day...

'It's true,' Renshaw said slowly. 'But sometimes changes are for the better. Some blokes reckon that all changes are for the better.'

'I don't believe that. Sounds like someone trying to be clever. Terrible things happen to people.'

'I wasn't really arguing in favour of it, Patty. But sometimes it can be for the best. I'd give a lot to be able to undo what I did to you. Over Gwennie. I don't know now why I acted the way I did. I really don't.'

He believes it, Patty thought. He really believes it. He's played the act so long that he's come to believe in it himself. And people have fallen for it for a long time.

'It doesn't really matter. We're still friends. We get along well. It can be fun working together. And I wasn't blaming you, now that it's over. It was my fault too. I've got around to seeing it that way lately.'

258

'What do you mean,' Renshaw said. '"Now that it's over"?'

He put out his hand and grabbed her by the arm. The smile had left his face. There was a slight, spasmodic twitching of the muscle under his eye.

'Did you understand what I was saying?'

'I understand.'

Patty peered intently at him. There was no faltering of her gaze. Her heart was still. Yes, it was over. She looked at him. There was no quickening of her pulses, no rising flood of colour, no wondering. No sense of anticipation. It was over. The summer of last year was gone. She drew a sharp, clean breath of air.

'You're pretty sure of yourself, aren't you?' Renshaw said.

His mouth hung down in a sudden sneer.

'I wouldn't count too much on that "working with me" angle. I could put you onto anything. I could set you to picking out vats. Ever thought about that? About the way I've looked after you? The way you've been sitting up with old Merton while the other women have been slaving out their guts carrying rolls and picking out vats?'

'I came here to help in the office,' Patty said. 'To work on the cards.'

'You came here as a recorder, not a clerk,' Renshaw said suddenly. 'I could put you onto anything. Anywhere. I've looked after you, Patty. You've got it pretty easy.'

He was quiet. So it was the wrong line. He could start again.

'I don't want to hurt you, Patty. I don't know why it

is, but whenever we get to talking together lately we end up fighting. Let's forget the whole affair. Everything I've said or done. I don't want to have to beg. It's not good for a man to have to beg, Patty. And I don't want to hurt you. I've never posed as a saint. But I'm no worse than a lot of other fellows. There was a lot of gossip about Gwennie, I know that. There's always gossip. Even when there's nothing to gossip about, people invent it. But the Gwennie affair is over. Can you understand that? It's over. Finished, done with. If I could, I'd wipe the whole thing clean. What's done can't be undone, it can only be regretted. I can't undo it. But I wish now that it had never happened.'

Patty stood up. She placed the stock sheet on the stool.

'I'm not blaming you,' Patty said. 'Not really. I was dazzled at the time. It all seemed so glamorous. I was so pleased to have you notice me.'

She looked at him shyly.

'But now I've grown up. I understand a lot more. Things like promises. Things about men. Things I wish now I didn't know. I wish it could be undone, too.'

'We could wipe the slate clean. Start again.'

'Do you remember,' Patty said suddenly. 'You asked me to marry you once. I really believed what you said. I didn't know men could act that way. I know now you didn't mean it. Lots of girls that strung along with you would understand that, too. But I believed you. I really believed you.'

'What is this?' Renshaw said. There was an edge to his voice. 'You knew as well as I knew. And now you're another outraged plaster saint. I didn't hear you objecting at the time. You could have screamed for help. You could have offered some resistance. We weren't all that far from civilization.'

Renshaw moved suddenly to the end of the fixture.

'And now you've come all over mealy-mouthed. You knew that marriage act was a game. You were as eager to believe it as I was to dish it out. And now you're Venus torn down and deflowered. You've been brutally set upon. I've been out with a few dames in my time; I've seen a few acts. But I can say this. I don't remember hearing any protests from you.'

'I think I'll go up,' Patty said unsteadily.

'You think you'll go up. Well, before you go I've got a few more home truths for you. You can look down your nose at other people. But I've been seeing plenty. Do you think I go around with my eyes shut? That I'm not awake-up to you? I'm not as dumb as all that. Sliding down the scale a bit, aren't you? Not quite so particular. Playing up with the bucks on the vats.

'You're a bitch!' he said suddenly. 'Do you think I'm going to let you walk out just like this?'

'I don't want to talk about it any longer,' Patty said. 'It was all different to me. I didn't think about it like that. I don't want to talk about it at all; or think about it, ever. I used to think of it like it was a cool fountain, something secret and lovely. It was never anything more than a dirty little pool of scummy water. I wish I could say it had never happened.'

She looked at him quickly.

'And maybe I was lucky at that. We could have been married and then there would be no escape.'

261

'You took the bait pretty well. I'd like to have offered it to you the day you came bleating into the stockroom. You harped pretty well on marriage that day.'

He bent his arm suddenly, and drew her to him. He didn't believe this. He knew more about women than they knew themselves. They'd rant and roar, but with the right technique they always came good. He bent his head.

It was no use screaming. The stockroom was isolated. The sound would be lost in the clatter of the machinery. She slid suddenly down, out of his arms, tearing loose her brooch and scraping the pin on her cheek. Then she picked herself up and began to run.

It was not far.

She could hear Renshaw. The clatter of his feet. The running flow of obscenity.

She pushed open the door of the chemical storeroom.

Oliver Henery looked up as she ran towards him. She put out her arms as she ran.

Her hair was dishevelled. Her frock was torn. There was blood on the side of her face.

Oliver stood up. He could hear Renshaw's frustrated bellow.

Well, it had come to this. He would have Renshaw to deal with after all.

He made a quick calculation. It was not yet December. The year was not over yet. But it was too late for a job in the heavy industries. Bosses would think a lot before they put a bloke on at this time of the year.

He looked at Patty and smiled.

262

CHAPTER FORTY ONE

Collins was working in the lab when he heard the sound of running feet. He left Marj Grigson in charge of the beaker and went into the storeroom to investigate. He was partly hidden by the casks stacked on one side, but he could see Oliver standing near the bags of soda ash and Patty behind him. He heard Renshaw's steady cursing before he saw him.

Just what I reckoned, Collins said to himself. I knew it wouldn't last too long. And it looks as though the bust's going to happen right here in the storeroom. Maybe even in the lab.

Renshaw pushed the door open. He looked like a man who had finally thrown discretion to the wind.

'Did you want something?' Oliver asked.

His voice was hard and level. He put out his arm and drew Patty beside him.

'I could,' Renshaw said. He said it softly. 'A bit of

something I dropped and thought to pick up again. Little bit shopsoiled, but could still be useful.' He smiled broadly. 'It would be safer for you if you decided to get out of the way.'

Oliver bent over and wiped his hands on a piece of sacking. He measured Renshaw with his eye. Six foot one in height, fourteen stone and solid. Gone a few rounds with the gloves. Quick on his feet and handy with his fists.

'D'you reckon?'

The blood flowed suddenly into Renshaw's face.

'I'm staying right where I am,' Oliver said. 'You can throw me out if you like.'

'I don't need to throw you out,' Renshaw said. 'It's easier than that. I can run you out. Sack you on the spot.'

'You could,' Oliver said. 'But I don't think you will. Later, when you've got time to cook something up. But not over this.'

'Look,' Renshaw said. 'I've had enough of this.'

He moved slowly forward. He had a theory. All curs yapped. But a show of force brought them pretty quickly to heel. And Oliver Henery was giving away too much in weight and height to amount to anything. Beside his own bulk, Oliver's slim, brown, near-naked body looked almost puny.

But he stopped and looked at Oliver, suddenly uncertain.

'I'm telling you,' Renshaw said. 'I want that girl in the office. Now. And your days are up too, Galahad. You'd better start reading the positions-vacant column, pronto. I wouldn't be looking so bloody sure of myself if I were you.'

'I'm bloody sure of what I intend doing. This girl gets an escort to the office, and home if necessary. Tommy can take the matter up with the Union and negotiate. You're going to run into a bit of dirty weather over this job, Renshaw.'

'You bastard,' Renshaw said. 'You bloody sneaking, yellow bastard. A man ought to cut you in two.'

He considered the implications. Oliver Henery might back down. If he took a poke at him, he might collapse like a pack of cards. But he might make a fight for it. He might keep going until word got around the factory. Until the men began trooping in from the vats and the presses. It would not be a good thing.

But if he could count on one good knock…if he could flatten him. He stepped forward.

'You said a mouthful,' Oliver said.

He thrust Patty behind him.

Renshaw's weight was behind the punch when it landed. Oliver went down, sprawling over the soda ash. He rolled over and over and came to rest near the jamb of the laboratory door. Collins backed out through the doorway. He had seen the whole thing, and he darted through to the vats to pass the word.

Renshaw had clocked Oliver. They were fighting over Patty Nicholls. It looked as though the fight would move into the lab.

'Could be bloody murder,' Barney said. 'Oliver's no match for Renshaw. He's not even in the hunt.'

'I hope Oliver beats him up so's his mother wouldn't even know him.'

The men pushed the door open and drifted in. The steam rushed in with them. Renshaw had torn off his shirt and was fighting in his trousers and cotton singlet. He was taking it easy. His hair was still plastered down, and except for one unlucky hit below the eye he was unmarked. Oliver's eye was cut and bleeding. The blood flowed down the side of his face onto his throat and chest. Bruises were beginning to show up on his body.

'You had enough?' Renshaw said. 'You know when you're beaten?'

'He's not in the hunt,' Goodwin said. 'Must be giving away about three inches and two and a half stone. I think we should get Tommy to stop it.'

Tommy was the shop steward. He was standing in the doorway. He held a large pair of cloth-shears in his hand.

Oliver was down again. His lip was bleeding and dark patches were showing on his ribs and shoulders. His hair was wet and streaked with blood. He got groggily to his feet. He was almost at the end of his string and he knew it. He gathered himself for the final assault.

The blow when it came sent Renshaw reeling back. He slid through the water, struggling to regain an upright position. Oliver hit him again as he fell. He slid down near the experimental vat and lay in a pool of dirty water and spilt dye beside it.

Tommy moved in from the door. The men crowded round. Oliver slumped on an upturned bucket, his arms sagging.

Tommy picked up a bucket. He went leisurely along to the tap and filled it with water. Renshaw still lay on his back in the pool of red dye as if in a sea of blood. Oliver sat on the tin propped against the wall.

'Better ring through for Miss Merton,' Tommy said. 'Tell her to bring some plaster and bandages and a drop of brandy from the medicine chest.'

He dipped out a pannikin of water and threw it in Renshaw's face. Renshaw struggled to sit up. He shook his head. His jaw was sore and his head ached. He had hit the side of the vat as he went down.

'The fight's over,' Tommy said. He handed Renshaw a pannikin of water.

Renshaw sat up. He fought as Barney and Tommy struggled to restrain him.

'You'd better clean yourself up,' Tommy said suddenly. 'Wouldn't do for Larcombe to walk in right now.'

But Renshaw was beyond reasoning.

'We don't want to have to knock you out again,' Barney said. 'Wake up to yourself.'

Miss Merton came in slowly, bearing a heavy tray laden with antiseptic, gauze, medicaments and brandy. Tommy took the brandy and poured some into a pannikin. He offered it to Renshaw and waited while he gulped it down.

Miss Merton moved down the room. She bathed the cut above Oliver's eye. She began laying on plaster.

'Well,' she said. 'You certainly do look a sight. Are you going to try some of this brandy?'

'There'll be more about this,' Renshaw suddenly yelled.

Oliver stood up slowly. He had swallowed the brandy. He could feel it warm in his stomach.

So he had come to grips with Renshaw, and he had

won. Not without luck, but he had won. He had really flattened him.

Across the room he could see Patty standing in the shadows. Something clarified in his mind. Patty!

He walked towards her, slowly.

When he was within two paces of her he stopped. He knew the men were there. Renshaw still struggling on the floor; Barney and Goodwin, Collins, Bluey, Sims, the men from the presses. It was not important.

She raised her head slowly and looked at him.

In her panic she had run unerringly into his arms. And he had not failed her. He had said once that he was a little man. Not big enough to fight giants.

'It was a pretty brave thing,' Patty said slowly. 'He was a lot bigger than you. He could have killed you.'

'The devil looks after his own,' Oliver said. 'And a man can sometimes get a lucky break. Sometimes the luck really goes with him.'

She raised her eyes shyly.

'I want you,' Oliver said suddenly. 'Come over here.'

He put out his arms and drew her to him. Over her head he could see the men standing in the mist near the door. He bent his head until his lips met hers.

Patty closed her eyes. She put her arms around his damp shoulders. He drew back and looked at her.

'You like me, Patty?' he asked huskily.

She remembered the day she had met him at the corner of Barrington Terrace, the day he had waited outside the church. All the time she had been thinking of Renshaw, Oliver had been there. Not a giant, he had said. Just a little bloke. Like you'd meet anywhere. Any day, in any factory.

He tilted up her chin, so that he could see into her eyes.

'You love me, Patty?'

His arm tightened around her.

'When can we get married? When?'

CHAPTER FORTY TWO

'You don't think this is the end of the episode, do you?' Renshaw asked.

He picked himself up. He smoothed down his hair. He fastened up his shirt. His anger had subsided, but he was casting about in his mind for ways of evening the score.

'I'm going to clean this place out. And the trouble-makers will be in number-one position, right in the shooting line.'

Barney Monahan waited until Renshaw had finished. There were a few things that had to be said. And he waited, half hoping that Tommy would say them. It was Tommy's job as shop steward to say them. But Renshaw's got him in his hand, Barney thought. We want more than a shop steward. We ought to have a shop committee here. A few well balanced blokes that can't be bought off or intimi-dated. A bloke like Renshaw should be stopped.

But it wasn't his pigeon. He had Esther and the boy to think about.

'He'll be out of here quicker than it takes to get his money over,' Renshaw said.

Barney had turned his back. He was walking towards the door. Yes, he had Esther and the boy. But he had something else, too.

'There should be a ruling against that,' he said suddenly.

Renshaw turned and looked at him. He looked at him for a long time, 'You like to go with him—just to show how close cobbers can be?' he asked finally.

'There's a ruling on this,' Barney said clearly.

Tommy moved in reluctantly. He looked appealingly towards Renshaw.

'I'll say there's a ruling,' Renshaw said. 'And it's this. No cock on these vats rushes in with his fists up and lives to tell the tale. Heads have rolled for less. That's your ruling.'

Collins looked up. There was a flicker of amusement at the back of his eyes. I've got him, he thought.

'That's a lie,' he said slowly. 'You clocked him first. You came in like a bull on the heels of a heifer. You hit him first. I saw it. So did she.'

'I think we'd better let sleeping dogs lie,' Tommy said.

'Not till things are straightened out better than this,' Barney said. 'There's a few things want tidying up. I think we should get an organizer out. We ought to find out what steps can be taken to protect the women. Especially the youngsters and particularly the good looking ones. We could get the Union to take the matter up with Cuthbert and Larcombe.'

A crowd had gathered around Renshaw and Barney. Oliver pushed Patty gently aside. He pushed through the crowd until he reached Renshaw.

There were lots of things he wanted to say. Lots of things that had been simmering at the back of his mind for months.

'I want you to know,' Oliver said, 'that I'm not quitting. You'll have to sack me; and if you do, it will be a matter for the Unions. There's going to be some changes. We're going to work for a shop committee. We're going to have a bit more say in the loads these women are humping about. There's going to be more negotiation and less fist play.' He turned and looked at Tommy. 'There's no need for you to be so apologetic either, Tommy,' he said. 'From now on you'll be apologizing to us. You're in the job to watch our interests, and that's the way it's going to be.'

'All right,' Renshaw said suddenly. 'Back to work, the lot of you.'

The men drifted back.

Renshaw picked up the dyeing programme for the day. He put the incident at the back of his mind. He wasn't really that concerned with Oliver Henery or whether he left or stayed on. There were other things to be considered. But his face darkened when he thought of Patty. So she was tied up with Oliver Henery? No doubt the affair had been going on under his nose for months and he had failed to notice it. She had been pretty high and mighty in her time. Well, she was down to her own level now. Down to the likes of Oliver Henery. And he would marry her. The poor sap. No doubt he'd end up marrying her.

CHAPTER FORTY THREE

Some time had elapsed since Renshaw's clash with Oliver. In the long run Renshaw had decided that it was a chancy issue on which to take a stand. It would do him no good if it reached the ears of Larcombe or Cuthbert.

Behind the scenes, Barney and Oliver were negotiating. The idea of a shop committee had been born. They were pushing the idea with Tommy and the men.

'They don't seem very interested,' Oliver said to Joe one morning as they ate breakfast. 'Though not too many blokes take such a lacing as these fellows.'

'They were all worked up the day Renshaw hit you.'

'Yes. The trouble is they forget things. And when things are going along well no one wants to stick his head out and get off-side with Renshaw.'

'It'd stop a lot of trouble if you had a committee there. Something should be said about the ventilation. And the overloading of women. It won't solve all the problems in a factory. But it can be a help.'

'Renshaw's no fool either,' Oliver said. 'Not by a long shot. Patty's still working along with Miss Merton. I'm on the vats. And Renshaw has let us alone. He's built up a bit of prestige for that, really.'

'Well,' Joe said, 'that's all right, too. You blokes were united for once. And things turned out all right. That's as it should be.'

In the evening Oliver and Patty walked down The Crescent. The day's work was finished. The stocktake was almost completed. In a few weeks' time the Dyehouse would close down. For two long, glorious weeks there would be nothing to do but laze about.

'And we could get married,' Oliver said suddenly. 'There's no reason for us to wait. We've no one to consult.'

'There's my mother,' Patty said.

'But she wouldn't mind. I thought she seemed all for it.'

'She is, in a way. But where would we live? I couldn't just walk out and leave her. You do see that, don't you, Oliver?'

They walked slowly down the street. Past the tall, dark terraces until they came to the house with the broken window and the door that sagged on its hinges.

'We could have this house,' Oliver said. 'It's big enough inside. We don't pay very much for it. Not that you'd want to, the condition it's in. But we could fix it up. I've got a little bit of money, Patty. We could do it. Joe would want to stay on, and Brother Martin too. We could give your mother the room on the ground floor near the kitchen. We could have the little attic room right upstairs.'

'Do you think they'd like the idea? You've been happy here together. Maybe they'd think I was pushing in.'

Oliver put his arm around her and squeezed her.

'Not likely. Why, Joe suggested it himself.'

'What does Brother Martin think of it?'

'He's all for it.'

They stood silent for a moment.

'It's not much of a place,' Oliver said suddenly.

They looked at the dirty brown, peeling paint, the torn guttering.

'Doesn't look like the place to be offering the bride. Perhaps we should wait.'

'If we fix it up could they make us pay more rent or take it from us?'

'We'd have to go into that. I don't really know.'

'A house,' Patty said slowly. 'A whole lovely house all of our own. Do you know—I've never lived in a house before? It's always been furnished rooms. Always some old busybody nosing into my affairs.'

She put her arm around Oliver.

'It really looks like part of heaven to me.'

'It's not much, Patty.'

It hurt him to see her standing looking at the derelict with such shining eyes. It was wrong that this dilapidated place hiding behind its tracery of old-fashioned cast-iron railings should come to mean heaven to any human being, let alone to Patty. He felt suddenly abashed. He bent over and kissed her.

'I'd like to have a lot to give you, Patty. A new house in one of the outer suburbs. Lovely clothes. We haven't got much. All our lives we'll be working and just trying to hang on to what we have. Blokes with money will make more and more. People like us will make it for them. And all the time we'll be lucky if we can just hang on.'

'We'll have each other,' Patty said.

Oliver bent over and kissed her on the hair. The sun was setting. The last rays were striking the top of the terraces. In the light, just for a moment, there was glamour in the stiff iron lacework and in the outline of the two trees at the end of the street. Two girls were walking down the road. They wore bright-coloured skirts which flared out at the hemline over heavily roped petticoats.

'We'll have each other,' Oliver said gravely. 'It's a big decision we're making, Patty. I wonder if you realize just how big it is.'

'I don't think it means happy ever after,' Patty said. 'I know you'll have to work all your life, and maybe me, too. I know that even then there'll be lots of things that we won't be able to have. I know you might have another fight with Renshaw and get sacked any time.'

Oliver looked for a long time down the narrow alley that was The Crescent. He had said that these streets would never get him. That he'd be out of this jungle. That by the summertime he'd be striding out, leaving the city behind. He'd be an unshackled man. Not tied down by women and kids. A free man.

'Not afraid of the future, Patty?'

'We've got to take our chances,' Patty said. 'Remember

what you told me that day in the park? About us? About us learning? And fighting?'

Oliver bent down and kissed her.

'We've got to keep a bit of guts for ourselves,' he said. 'All the time. But the future's ahead of us now, Patty. We might even have a hand in its shaping.'

CHAPTER FORTY FOUR

Mr Mayers was going out.

He had changed from his navy-blue boiler-suit into his tweed sports clothes. He stood beside Miss Merton's desk, leaving instructions for possible callers. He did not expect to be long away. He was on his way to a vacant lot out from the city at the edge of the sea. Here, adjacent to a rubbish dump, were a number of dismantled boilers. His commission was to inspect them, and if possible to purchase a suitable one for the Company.

There had been a lot of overhauling and changing about going on at Macdonaldtown lately. Every week some unsmiling VIP from England or America would appear.

When really big VIP's were on the way, Renshaw cleared the vats. The experimental vat was turned off, the wet floor washed and hastily dried. No more than four vats were left in operation. The holes near the vats were swept out, the steam was cleared.

'You'd better put a jacky on,' Renshaw said to the men standing stripped to the waist near the vats. 'We want to make a bit of a showing.'

'These bastards aren't interested in how we look,' Oliver said. 'What interests them is how the money looks. They ought to see it as it really is. Vats going full blast. Air so thick you could eat it with a spoon. Men stripped down with the water running out of them. We shouldn't be putting on a show like this for them.'

Mr Mayers' team had been working hard.

The layout on the ground floor was changed and for weeks engineers and maintenance staff had been uncoupling and moving machinery about.

'I don't know what they're cooking up now,' Mayers said. He was a bit aggrieved that he had not been in on the first conference over the boiler. He was justly suspicious about accountants making decisions that were rightly in the province of the engineer. He had hinted darkly to Miss Merton that things would have to change. There were plenty of good jobs going for engineers with a steam ticket. Only that very day there'd been at least four jobs advertised in the *Herald*.

'And I bet they don't fill the jobs in a hurry either,' Mayers said. 'Harvison got this bee in his bonnet about the boiler. I'm not saying the idea's bad. I should have been asked about it. As it is, Larcombe just came over and gave the order. I don't like the taste of it.'

279

'Oh, well,' Miss Merton said. 'I suppose it's just not letting the right hand know what the left is doing.'

'Well, they won't want to tempt me too far.'

He looked at Miss Merton and smiled suddenly. She was looking old lately, a bit pinched and weary.

Miss Merton raised the dingy window and trapped a little of the summer sunshine in the corner near the bookcase. Across the way boilers were blowing off steam. Shrill-voiced apprentices called to each other.

'It's far too nice to work,' Miss Merton said.

Mayers walked to the door. He stood jingling his keys in his pocket. He would not be very long away. He began to grin. He came back and stood behind her desk.

'How'd you like to come?' he asked suddenly. 'I don't think Renshaw would mind. How long since you've had a blow in the sunlight?'

'Well—it's a long time.'

'You'd better put on your hat and come.'

It was strictly against the rules, but Miss Merton took down her neat black hat and pinned it carefully onto her head. Then she set the little keyboard. The direct line to ring in Renshaw's office, the outside lines in her own.

'Will you keep an eye on the phone, Patty?' she called through the door to Patty Nicholls, who was working in the office behind her. 'I shouldn't be late.'

It was a fresh summer's day. Outside, the sparrows were lined up on the fence tops, chirping and calling. Little dogs, all a uniform sooty colour, were bounding about the streets. Pigeons were circling, coming around in great sweeps, cutting through the smoke as it eddied up into the sky.

'The city's pushing out,' Mayers said. 'I think the day will come when most of those factories will come down. Especially over towards the bay.'

'Not much sign of it yet.'

As far as the eye could see the chimney-stacks rose, one after the other against the sky.

Mayers turned the car. He headed out of the Parade, leaving Macdonaldtown behind. But instead of going straight to the allotment near the sea he turned in at the gates of the park on the outskirts of the city.

Macdonaldtown lay well behind them. Here were trees, tall and green and dense with leaves. And ahead were flower beds ablaze with colour. They spoke little. Mayers drove slowly. He, too, was taking in the beauty of the scene.

'Bit different from Macdonaldtown.'

He turned the car. Reluctantly, it gathered speed. The pond, the ducklings, the waterlilies, the little purple hedges slid behind. They turned south to that dreary place where the sand sweeps in from the sea onto a medley of discarded machinery and household refuse. The tip. People were walking about, pulling the rubbish over, salvaging a piece here and there.

In a fenced-off allotment, Miss Merton noticed several boilers. There was a large painted sign on a paling fence. It stated plainly, MACHINERY FOR SALE.

Mayers turned off the road. He backed in under the shade of a large-leafed flame-tree. He took out his cigarettes and offered one to Miss Merton. She shook her head, smiling. He opened the glove box and fumbled for matches. Then he sat back sucking the smoke into his lungs.

'Fascinating place, this. Always someone about. Always someone combing through the rubbish. I got a few flower baskets here myself.'

He stubbed out his cigarette and opened the door of the car.

'Well, I suppose I'd better take a look at it. Want to come?'

Miss Merton slid from the seat. She walked, matching her steps as far as possible to Mayers' swinging stride.

'You'd better wait here,' he said. 'I'll cut across and see Mullins.'

Miss Merton watched him absently.

He crossed the paddock and knocked at the door of the weatherboard cottage. The door opened. The man pointed across the paddock to the caretaker's hut in the corner. Miss Merton saw the door close and Mayers turn his back.

'I think I'll just take a peek,' Mayers said.

There was a ladder leaning against a boiler. Mayers climbed to the top and looked in. He was waving his torch about, cutting arcs in the darkness.

'Seems all right,' he said. 'I'll give it a really good going over as soon as I get onto this caretaker johnny.'

He walked towards the hut. 'It might be better if you wait,' he called.

Miss Merton stood leaning against the car, watching Mayers as he strode across to the hut. It seemed very still. Far off she could hear the sea as it thundered onto the rocks. But it was quiet in the paddock. She leaned into the car and picked up the paper, absently scanning the headlines, turning the pages.

Mayers was knocking at the door of the caretaker's hut. There was no other sound. She picked up the paper and began to run. And when she had reached the point of the little bluff she undid the paper slowly and began to read again.

'A man collapsed on a road outside Goulburn last night and was taken to Goulburn Base Hospital, where he was found to be dead. He was identified as Stephen Forrester, aged 60, of unknown address. Police are seeking...'

The paper slipped from Miss Merton's hand. The pages caught in the breeze, fluttering slowly open. Stephen Forrester. The leaves turned. The paper came to rest. It hung, poised for a moment, caught on the edge of the grey rocks. Then it fell gently onto the sand. Gulls resting under the bluff rose in a great cloud. Miss Merton watched them as they hung drifting against the sky.

Then she opened up her handbag.

From a little inner compartment she drew forth a small embroidered silk container. She had stitched it years ago in the late summer sunshine in the days when Stephen was washing on the river. She pulled at the stitches, lifting them with a hairpin. And when she had opened it, she shook it gently.

A small enamelled shield fell out into her palm. It was Stephen's. He had given it to her.

She turned mechanically towards the hut.

From here she had a full view of the garbage dump and the sea. She stood looking towards the horizon, trying to glimpse for a moment the vision that Stephen had seen.

Then she turned and walked slowly towards the car.

To the south of the sandy waste a row of dilapidated houses with broken windows looked out to the sea. In these shambles human beings lived. They went to work. They were known in factory and mill. They helped create the beauty and colour that found no echo in their own lives.

She climbed into the car and Mayers got in beside her. Miss Merton's face was bloodless, grey and drawn in the bright light of the day.

Mayers looked at her sharply as she lay back, her hands clasped over her neat handbag with its useful strap.

CHAPTER FORTY FIVE

After the Staff report had gone across to Head Office, Renshaw began to wish he had noted on it Miss Merton's absence on the morning that the boiler had been inspected.

The efficiency experts were overhauling office procedure in town. There had been some trouble over the declarations and it had come out about Miss Merton taking the morning off. Cuthbert got onto the phone about it to Renshaw. He was annoyed and he let Renshaw know that he was.

'It's hard to believe,' Cuthbert said. 'Miss Merton is a trusted servant of the Company. Not only is she out of the office during a time when she should be working, but she was actually engaged in carrying out a boiler inspection.'

Renshaw, hanging onto the phone, said nothing. It was often a pretty sound principle to let the other fellow do the talking.

'The thing that upsets me,' Cuthbert said, 'is your report. There's nothing here to indicate that Miss Merton was absent that morning. I had a query on the declarations. The efficiency people are working out an analysis; they took the matter up with Mr Harvison. When I turned up this report I was confident they'd made a mistake. But you admit now that she was absent. Away two hours, forty minutes. That's almost half a day.'

'She's never absent,' Renshaw said quickly. 'I didn't think it would matter just for once.'

'*These records* show that she's never absent. But on your own admission they're not very reliable,' Cuthbert said coldly. 'I'm not raising any specific objection to Miss Merton having a few hours off. What I do object to is the way these records are cooked up. The whole thing reflects badly on the office administration. Particularly on the Dyehouse. These fellows don't miss too much, I can tell you. And anyway we're going to look pretty fools if we can't trust our own records. Does Larcombe know anything about it?'

'No,' Renshaw admitted reluctantly.

He had not been particularly worried about Miss Merton taking the time off. But after the ring from Head Office his attitude changed. They were not going to let it drop. The efficiency people would make a mouthful out of it. Cuthbert would get on to Larcombe. And Larcombe would come over, spluttering and expostulating and demanding further explanations. He had enough to do running the place without getting involved in these bouts over paper work.

In Cuthbert's office Time and Motion people were discussing the re-dyes and charges. They had finished with the cards. Mr Jamieson, who was in charge, had the reports neatly filed. The analysis from the declarations was on his desk. The job now was routine. The final balancing and the recommendations. With the work assembled, he was in the process of assessing it all in terms of time.

Precisely at three o'clock the phone rang on Cuthbert's desk. It was Miss Uliffe. Mr Harvison was ready. Would he let Mr Larcombe know—and Mr Jamieson?

'Oh, well,' Larcombe said when Cuthbert looked into his office. He was never really at ease with paperwork men. He distrusted them instinctively. But he had cultivated several useful expressions. These didn't mean very much. In fact he didn't really know what they meant at all. But they sounded impressive and if he was cornered he could use them. But in general he would be glad to stay a little in the background and answer questions if they were flung at him. After all, these were the bright boys, the fellows that knew all the answers. And Harvison was handing them a packet to straighten out the offices.

Larcombe scarcely followed the conversation as it ebbed and flowed, tracking through the office procedure. What happened at Head Office didn't interest him. How the statements got out, and when, were not his pigeon. Whether the work hit the machines for posting at two or four o'clock scarcely aroused his interest. It would be of interest to Miss Graham, of course, who might find herself out of a job. Miss Graham had been a fast girl on the files and the sorting. But by cutting one simple operation they could start the dissection almost two hours earlier and Miss Graham could start reading the Positions Vacant.

Cuthbert listened intently. Once he rose and called through to Mr Dennet in the General Office, and they went all over it again. Right to the point where the re-dyes and the charges came into the picture. Jamieson held them in his hand, flipping the pages.

'Hours of time,' he said, 'wasted. Hours of time spent on repetition.'

He took a pencil and wrote across the bottom of the re-dyes 'at 1s 9d per lb.' He handed them to Harvison.

'Well?' Harvison said.

'The re-dyes will become the charges,' Jamieson said. 'It will save hours of time. What purpose does it serve to have two books? First it's entered by hand into one book and then the process is repeated in another. What for? For the express purpose of writing in "at 1s 9d per lb." It's interoffice work and could have been wiped out years ago.'

Jamieson placed the book before Harvison.

'And that brings us to the question of the Dyehouse office.'

Larcombe stirred uncomfortably. He moved almost imperceptibly closer to Mr Dennet.

'The cutting of the re-dyes will eliminate approximately four days' work a month at the Dyehouse,' Jamieson said. 'Elimination of two entries on the cards will reduce the time significantly.' He placed the figures before Harvison. Cuthbert examined them quickly.

'There's too much telephone work for a small office,'

Jamieson said. 'More than half the calls should be handled from here. And there are far too many personal calls.'

Harvison looked suddenly at Larcombe. He had given a direction about personal calls. Laid down an inflexible ruling. But he let it pass.

'This Miss Merton,' Jamieson said thoughtfully. 'Does she handle all this work on the Dyehouse declarations?'

Larcombe nodded.

'Funny how none of them ever forget their declarations out there.'

'Declarations? Oh, well,' Larcombe said, 'I suppose she reminds them. She knows most of them.'

'She paid to remind them?'

'Well, no,' Larcombe admitted.

'And hours of good time are wasted every month by people walking about reminding other people. The onus is clearly on the employee.'

'I suppose so,' Larcombe said. 'It is.'

'The way I see it,' Jamieson said unemotionally, 'is this. All these things cost you money, after all, she's on the Staff. Paid to look after the Company's interests. There's far too much running about reminding these people.'

'I suppose you're right,' Larcombe said impatiently.

He was feeling uneasy and tired. He wished Jamieson would leave the Dyehouse office alone. Shuffle up his papers and get out. Stop talking about Macdonaldtown. God alone knew when the light might be turned onto himself.

Harvison leaned back in his chair, listening, but ready to act when the time came.

'I've been thinking about those declarations,' Jamieson

said. He took out a bundle of continuity-of-service notices and placed them significantly on top of the declarations. Then he sat back and looked at Larcombe.

Larcombe smiled.

'It won't affect Macdonaldtown very much. Not too many fellows will stay there long enough to worry us about their long service leave.'

Jamieson passed to the recommendations. He had them listed. Cuts could be made on the re-dyes, the card system, the telephone work, the declarations. A good third of the work would go by the board. A good lively junior could handle the job. And maybe better.

'We'll have to think about it,' Cuthbert said. 'We'll go into it later.'

'We'll make it tomorrow,' Harvison said. 'We'll make it early.'

Jamieson was not invited to the meeting next morning in Harvison's office, but the reports and recommendations were ready. There would be a big shake-up all round. Three people would be finishing at Head Office and the question of the Dyehouse office was yet to be resolved.

The Chairman of Directors might have overlooked the position at the Dyehouse office. But Jamieson's reference to the declarations had ruffled him. It had hit right up against the rigid code that he liked to think existed among Staff workers. There was only one side of the fence to be on if you were a Staff worker and that was the Company's. And if you weren't with the Company then you must be with someone else. Harvison brushed aside the question mark.

'This Miss Merton,' he said.

He was leaning well back in his chair. He was holding a bundle of declarations and handwritten reports from the Dyehouse.

Cuthbert opened up a journal. He extracted a small slip of paper.

'Well,' he said, 'it could pay us to keep her on. We'd need a pretty sensible girl there. Twenty-one at least. We pay Miss Merton the minimum. There's not such a lot of difference in money spread over twelve months.'

'Not much difference?' Harvison said. He was suddenly shouting. 'Not much difference? Meddling about with the declarations! On-side with these people all the time! Junketing around the country when she ought to be working! God knows what else is going on.'

Larcombe sat with his face on his hand. He felt he had known Miss Merton for a long time. There were a lot of things he might have said in her defence. But he had himself to look after. Any time, Harvison might lift the lid and look in at him.

'On the basis of economy?' Cuthbert asked finally.

'On the basis of economy,' the Chairman of Directors agreed.

He smiled suddenly, and the General Manager, reprieved, smiled back.

'Get rid of her,' Harvison said. 'Tip her out. Clean the place up. Easy to read between the lines. Old bitch a bit deceptive. Very deceptive, when you come to think of it. Still, tip her out and clean the place up.'

Miss Merton was talking to Mayers when Larcombe

291

walked in. He pushed roughly past into Renshaw's office and closed the door.

Larcombe had steeled himself for this. He had nothing personal against Miss Merton. In the time she had worked at the Dyehouse he had always thought of her as a pale, shrinking figure, reliable and courteous. But Harvison had been adamant.

Now, facing Renshaw, he went over the points that Harvison had made.

'It's not that we want anything for nothing,' Larcombe said. 'It's not even that it's important about the declarations. Or those explanations with regard to continuity of service. It's the principle. Harvison was most upset about the principle. He said it could lead to almost anything.'

Larcombe bent over and placed a sheaf of papers in front of Renshaw. When he looked up a cloud had passed across Renshaw's face. It was expressionless.

They were silent.

'It seems a bit tough,' Larcombe said. He laughed apologetically. 'But you know how Harvison is. Especially about this kind of thing.'

'You have anything to say?' Renshaw asked.

'I've got my problems,' Larcombe said, 'looking after my own neck. And anyway, I don't know that much about her. Could be political.'

Renshaw laughed.

'I'll bet the old duck hasn't a political thought to rub together. I'll bet she always has to ask someone whether she puts crosses or figures.'

Renshaw sat tapping the desk with his pencil.

'Weren't thinking of sticking out your neck?' Larcombe asked.

'No,' Renshaw said slowly. 'Not thinking of sticking out my neck.'

'I'd take the whole thing a step at a time,' Larcombe said. 'Let her know which way the wind's blowing. I can have her money made up and bring it across tomorrow. Nothing unusual about that, you know. Policy of the firm to get rid of Staff people smartly when the time comes. Better to pay them the money than have them hanging around.'

Miss Merton was typing reports when Renshaw's door opened and the General Manager appeared. Miss Merton noticed that his mouth was pursed and tight. He went swiftly across the vestibule and let himself out.

Renshaw waited for a while. After Mayers went through to the boiler-house, he came out and sat on the edge of Miss Merton's desk.

'It's unlucky,' he said. 'Dashed unlucky.'

Miss Merton placed her hands on her lap. She knew suddenly what he was going to say, but she waited quietly for him to say it. She had thought once that big firms were particular about questions of ethics. The thought amused her now, and she smiled.

'It's not that they're unsympathetic,' Renshaw said. 'It's just that they don't believe in that sort of thing. And in any case, Harvison's got this economy drive on.'

Miss Merton suddenly saw it clearly. All these little men sitting up, pulling in their chins and acting the part of God. They were outside of society. Above it.

But we're all part of it, thought Miss Merton. All of us.

Renshaw got up from the desk. He picked up the production figures lying on Miss Merton's table.

I'll tell her the rest tomorrow, he thought. I'll ring Larcombe tonight. And I'll tell her tomorrow before lunch.

But it was no easier in the morning.

The Company had decided…Mr Harvison had given the instruction…Mr Larcombe would bring her money over in the afternoon.

Miss Merton sat quietly. If she were working in the factory she could go to the shop steward. She could talk it over with Barney and Oliver Henery. She had always thought she was above that sort of thing. She could hear Leila singing as she pushed a truck over the concrete floor.

You lift sixteen tons and what do you get?
Another day older and deeper in debt.

But if you were on the Staff, thought Miss Merton, you got a letter from the Company, a fiver or so at Christmas; you got a party at Head Office, a handshake from the Chairman of Directors.

But Barney would not be with you.

She walked slowly across the vestibule to her own office. She was trembling a little. She got up and threw up the window, letting in the summer air heavy with dust.

She could hear Goodwin shouting up the stairs.

'What the hell happened to the twelve-nine-sixes?' She heard him start up the stairs, and then May's answering cry, 'In your bloody date! What do you think we are?'

Miss Merton repeated the words mechanically. It was a defence mechanism.

CHAPTER FORTY SIX

It was four o'clock.

Miss Merton heard the phone click. Larcombe opened the door of Renshaw's office and called to her.

He was sitting back, holding the familiar pay sheet. Miss Merton looked at him steadily. His smile was fleeting. It was all to be handled on a firm, civilized footing.

Nevertheless he watched her face to see how she was taking it.

'I was expecting it,' she said.

Her voice sounded cool, almost impersonal, in her own ears. She put out her hand. It was a small hand. But there was no tremor, although her heart beat fast. She read aloud. One week's pay. One week in lieu of notice. So much holiday pay. It looked right and no doubt it was legal. When Mr Renshaw had put her on the Staff he had said, 'One extra week's holiday a year. That's fine, eh?'

And it had sounded fine then. Miss Merton raised her eyes to Larcombe's. They were smiling but unchallengeable. In them Miss Merton read the meaning of Staff privileges. They weren't for people who got out of step.

'Don't forget,' Larcombe said. 'Anything wrong with your pay, just give Mr Cuthbert a ring.'

He shot out his hand and then let it drop quickly.

'I'll be in to see you before I go.'

He rose and walked to the office door with Miss Merton. He was friendly, suave and smiling.

'I'll be in the warehouse for a while if anyone should ring.'

Miss Merton watched him as he threw open the glass doors and disappeared into the warehouse.

She could hear his voice raised a little, telling Renshaw about the interview.

'I said to her...I told her...'

She turned away and bent her head over her desk. There was no dignity left in labour.

She took papers from a folder and read them mechanically. So much glauber salts. So much soda ash. So much peracetic acid.

Then for some reason she thought of something else. The Son of Man could find no place to rest his head. Why had she thought of that?

She thought of Barney chained to the hydro, of his child and his ageing wife. She thought of Mary in the sweat-box pulling down the blue, green and scarlet folds of the cloth with a stick; of Hughie lying crumpled under the loading dock; of Charlie vomiting into the drain under the dye vats, clutching at the hernia for which both the Company and the Compensation officers denied responsibility.

There was not long to go; it was after four. She put her head down on the window-sill. The soot left a bar, dark and smudgy, across her forehead.

And for the first time she thought of Mary and Jane and Margaret, not as them, but as us.

'All the same,' thought Miss Merton. 'All thrown into the same cauldron.'

The telephone rang, imperiously, demandingly.

'Mr Larcombe,' said the operator. 'Mr Windon of Western Worsteds on the line.'

She walked to the door, precisely, because she knew no other way of walking.

'Mr Windon on the line,' she said.

She pulled down the key and for a moment she heard Larcombe's voice, thin and effusive.

She looked around the office. The familiar keyboard with its six extensions, the typewriter, the little adding machine, the files that she had made because for some reason it had seemed important at the time. Across the vestibule she could see into Renshaw's office, littered now with his soiled shirts and socks. She could hear Larcombe still on the line with Western Worsteds. He sounded suddenly vain, pompous, important.

When he came out of the office he shook her hand. The best of luck wherever you go. He was still smiling when he opened the door. He just had time to reach Head Office. It had gone off very well and Harvison should be pleased.

It was almost time to go. The drawers were tidy. The Daily Attendance Sheets, the Dye Reports, the Chemical Reports, the Returnable Miscellaneous Reports, the Price Lists all in their appointed folios. There was a shrill wail.

The bundy whirred. The girls filed past. They looked at her incuriously. As yet, no word of her dismissal had reached the Dyehouse floor.

'Good night,' they called.

'Good night,' said Miss Merton.

It was the last time she would stand at the window and smile at them as they filed past. It was goodbye now. Goodbye, Mary. Goodbye, John.

The men filed past. Barney and Oliver were talking over the shop committee they hoped to get started, Goodwin and John Avery about the best horse going on Saturday. Collins and Sims drifted out. Collins had a copy of the *Herald* protruding from his pocket; he had been combing through the Wanted ads.

'Goodbye,' Miss Merton said.

She went swiftly to her desk. She gathered up her handbag.

It was time for her, too, to go.

It was quiet now, as she bent her head and combed up her hair. Soon it would be over, this interminable day.

Suddenly she turned around.

Renshaw had come up silently and was standing behind her.

His head hung down a little and his familiar fair hair, usually so neatly combed, was brushed up and dishevelled. He put his hand against the door.

He wants something from me, Miss Merton thought. Some little thing to present to his conscience.

'You're not outside it,' Miss Merton said suddenly. 'You, too, are just a tool. Caught up and used like the rest of us. You're not outside it at all. The trap's set for us all.'

He did not seem to hear.

'You'll come back and see us some time?'

Miss Merton shook her head. 'No,' she said.

She placed the cover over the typewriter. She patted her hair and got out her gloves.

The trains were speeding past. Getting on to the peak. And as she listened she heard the familiar blast.

Cock-a-doodle-doo.

No victory. No. But defeat? Miss Merton fastened her glove. Not defeat. There were lessons to be learned. Tomorrow she would learn to fight.

In your date, Johnny, in your date. Cock-a-doodle-doo.

Text Classics

textclassics.com.au